# MISREPRESENTED

# MISREPRESENTED

*A Novel*

*Renée
Morgan-Hampton*

Ken and Dennis,

A life long dream to write this story. Always follow your passions and dreams.

Renée Morgan-Hampton

iUniverse, Inc.
New York Lincoln Shanghai

**MISREPRESENTED**



iUniverse books may be ordered through booksellers or by contacting:

iUniverse
2021 Pine Lake Road, Suite 100
Lincoln, NE 68512
www.iuniverse.com
1-800-Authors (1-800-288-4677)

ISBN-13: 978-0-595-37317-8 (pbk)
ISBN-13: 978-0-595-67484-8 (cloth)
ISBN-13: 978-0-595-81714-6 (ebk)
ISBN-10: 0-595-37317-8 (pbk)
ISBN-10: 0-595-67484-4 (cloth)
ISBN-10: 0-595-81714-9 (ebk)

Printed in the United States of America

*TO MOM FOR HER LOVING SUPPORT AND ENCOURAGEMENT TO FOLLOW MY DREAMS.*

*TO DAD FOR HIS SUPPORT IN BEING THERE FOR ME.*

"In every man's writings,
the character of the writer
must lie recorded."

**—Thomas Carlyle**

# *SPECIAL THANKS*

To George Saunders, my special friend and mentor for encouraging me to continue writing.

# *ACKNOWLEDGMENTS*

My research was key to writing this novel. I learned a great deal about crimes, the role of the homicide detectives and DNA. It made a significant difference in my life and taught me a great many things about the criminal mind. We work in society everyday and have no clue about the lives of one another when they conclude a day's work. I interviewed, homicide detectives, Judges, DNA specialists, drug rehabilitation doctors and other professionals and consultants.

There were many people that made this novel possible. I am eternally grateful for their tireless enthusiasm, patience, and time. These people include: Lieutenant Gil Carrillo, Los Angeles County Sheriff's Homicide Bureau, Geoffrey Moyer, M.D., Ph.D, Laboratory Director of Quest Diagnostics, West Hills, CA, and the California Cyrobank, Los Angeles, CA.

I am grateful and thank Bliss Bowen for being a great editor. Special thanks to Christine Fessenden for the creative and wonderful jacket design and photograph.

A fantastic group of friends: Deborah Feliciano, Dr. Sheila Newton, Georgi Matsunaga, Raphael Lachmiller, Judy Seckler, Liz Altounian, Donnie Grubbs, Joanna Foster and my long time childhood friend Kristie for her legal expertise.

# CHAPTER 1

Shana Bernstein grinned. She had good reason: she had just won a big slander case in favor of a movie director who'd been accused of impregnating his leading actress, and his studio—in which her boss, Matthew Daytona, held a controlling interest—had sent her an enormous bouquet of orchids with a note promising that her hard work would be amply rewarded. It was an important victory for her firm, Daytona, Bernstein & McDunn, and for Shana as well. Forty-five and single, she was a highly successful litigator who'd been building an impressive resume ever since her first award-winning moot-court competitions back at Harvard Law, from which she had graduated *summa cum laude*, fourth in her class.

She hit the latches of her briefcase, grabbed her blazer from the coat rack near her office door and walked briskly toward the lobby. The firm's receptionist caught up with her just as she was stepping into the elevator.

"Excuse me, Ms. Bernstein," she asked, pushing back the elevator's steel doors to prevent them from closing. "Do you have a ten o'clock deposition tomorrow morning?"

"Oh, thanks for checking, Erin—yes, I do. Please do the regular setup of the coffee service in the main conference room."

"Sure, no problem." Erin stepped back and the doors closed quietly as she waved goodbye.

Shana pulled back her sleeve and checked her watch; two-and-a-half hours until dinner. When the elevator car reached the underground parking garage, she hurried out and hopped into her jet-black Beamer.

Out on Wilshire Boulevard, she dialed up *XM Café* on the satellite radio panel while waiting at the traffic signal. When the light flashed green, she turned left and joined the rush-hour parade inching west on Santa Monica Boulevard. Traffic was no better on the freeway, mockingly referred to around the office as the "405 parking lot." When she finally reached the 10 Freeway, she nosed her way through more bumper-to-bumper traffic until she was finally able to exit onto Pacific Coast Highway. Glancing to her left, she saw the sun, low and red, dipping into the Pacific Ocean.

Not far from her Malibu home, she dashed into the Yogi Yogurt Bar to buy a half-gallon of her favorite yogurt then zipped up the hill, making a sharp right turn onto a secluded canyon road before stopping at the huge wrought-iron gates that guarded her driveway. She pressed a remote-control button from within her car and the gates opened slowly, then locked securely behind her as she parked on the circular cobblestone driveway. She unlocked the antique front door and turned off the alarm, then ran upstairs to take a quick shower.

The house was modest, by Malibu standards, but classic: a two-story, 1914 Craftsman with a wooden balcony wrapped around its second floor. Its interior "shabby chic" décor reflected the subtle vibrancy of the surrounding hillsides and its owner's personality. Green-and peach-colored throws were stacked neatly atop a white wicker chest behind the pillow-strewn sofa in the living room; a hand-worked brandy snifter beckoned from the coffee table. An elegant Stickley table and chairs graced the dining room nearby. In the pantry, wooden boxes cradled an assortment of onions, potatoes, garlic, apples, cinnamon sticks and other spices whose fragrance wafted into the kitchen.

Freshly dressed in jeans and a crisp white shirt, Shana stepped lightly down the stairs and uncorked a bottle of cognac on the coffee table. Her thoughtful and diligent maid, Rosie Patelle, made a practice of placing it there on a silver tray before departing each day at four o'clock for her own home in East L.A. Shana looked over at the clock on the fireplace mantle: seven o'clock. She poured the aromatic brandy into a snifter, trying not to spill any as her faithful feline companion, Lilly, wrapped around her ankles. She reached down and gave the fluffy white Himalayan's ears a loving scratch. Lilly responded with a steady purr, then trotted to the kitchen doorway and meowed expectantly. Shana took a few relaxing sips of cognac as she followed Lilly into the kitchen and filled her dinner bowl. As she was taking food out of the refrigerator and rinsing off vegetables, the phone rang. It was Matthew Daytona.

"Hi, Shana! Where have you been? I've been trying to call you on your cell."

"That damn thing! I'm sorry, Matthew. You know how dreadful reception is up here, especially in the house."

"Ah, yes. Cellphone hell. So, what's for dinner?"

"The usual," she replied, cradling the phone between her ear and shoulder while chopping bell peppers. "Vegetarian: pasta primavera, roasted garlic, romaine-and-parsley salad and, of course, my favorite yogurt for dessert."

"Sounds great! I'm starved. See you in ten."

Ten minutes later Matthew pulled up in front of the gate, and Shana buzzed him in. He parked his flashy black Rolls Royce behind Shana's car. He stepped out onto the cobblestone walkway in an Armani double-breasted suit and European leather shoes; like his blended blond-brown hair, they complemented his olive-toned skin. At sixty years of age, Matthew was admired by many women lawyers as the most eloquent, attractive and enterprising entertainment attorney in the Beverly Hills legal community. Shana greeted him with a warm smile as he handed her a bouquet of peach-colored roses.

"They're beautiful, Matthew, thank you." She motioned him toward the living room as she closed the front door.

"No, thank *you*," he replied. "That was a great win today. Congratulations!"

He pulled off his tie and jacket and tossed them over an overstuffed chair near the doorway as Shana took the flowers to the kitchen and placed them in a vase. "Thanks for having me to dinner," he called out.

"It's no bother. I love having you here. Wine?"

"Yes. What kind do you have?"

"Pinot Grigio, Chardonnay, Chianti and Cabernet."

"Chianti."

Lilly hopped up on the arm of the chair and rubbed her head against Matthew's hand, purring.

"Well, hello there, little friend," he said, scratching her ears. He looked up at Shana. "How long have you had her now?"

"Ten years," Shana answered as she stepped back into the kitchen. "She's the perfect roommate!"

Shana uncorked a bottle of San Vincenti Chianti Classico, poured the wine into a pair of Riedel glasses and carried them out to the living room. "So, Matthew, which case did you want to discuss?"

"The Sousushi family case," he replied. "You know I told you earlier how close I am to it." He paused. "Then there is the managing partner position."

"I remember that case," Shana said. "But—wait! What managing partner position?"

"Well, I've sorted through this decision for a few months now and…I've finally made up my mind. I'm offering you the position, Shana. I'm sure Hillary would love to have it, but I strongly feel that you're more qualified and better connected in the legal community."

"That's quite an honor and I must say I'm in good company."

"With respect to the Sousushi family matter," Matthew said, "I'll go over that with you tomorrow at the office." He paused and Shana looked at him, deep in thought.

"OK," she finally said. "Listen, dinner is just about ready. I'm hungry."

"Great! I love Italian," Matthew said, sitting down at the dining table.

"Italian or bleu cheese dressing?" she asked as she emerged from the kitchen bearing a large bowl of freshly prepared salad.

"Italian."

"Roasted garlic?"

"You really want me to smell up the office tomorrow," he chuckled. "Garlic, please, yes!"

Shana brought out a rustic loaf of bread and a small plate holding several foil-wrapped bulbs. "Garlic tastes so good with this bread," she said, peeling the foil away from the garlic. "I just love it!" She placed a heaping platter of pasta in the middle of the table and took her seat across from Matthew.

"Pass the bread, please," he said, chewing.

They ate in silence for a few minutes before Shana resumed the conversation.

"The Sousushi family have been through a lot since the death of Taka Sousushi's wife," she commented, still eating.

"I know. I really miss her. Her death still puzzles me."

"Yeah, I was puzzled by it too. Did they ever find who killed her?"

"No. They're still investigating it."

Matthew looked tense, so Shana tactfully changed the subject.

"Hillary's brought in a considerable amount of business over the past few months," she commented. "Convincing her to come over from Boston & Lynne was a smart move, don't you think?"

"Yes," Matthew agreed. "She has brought the business in. But I'm not totally convinced she is the best person for the job."

"McDunn…Is that Irish?"

"Yes, it is. She's a keeper—daughter of a bus driver in Boston, won a full scholarship to Harvard."

"Impressive," Shana replied. "More bread?"

"Sure, thanks. Say, how's Amanda Weddington?"

"My old roommate?" Shana shot Matthew a look. "She's fine."

"How often do you two get together?"

"Enough." Shana paused. "I love her dearly, but she's, um, a little…"

"Temperamental?" Matthew suggested.

"…needy." Shana finished the last sip of wine in her glass. "More Chianti?"

"Yes, please. Mmm, pasta!" he exclaimed as he spooned another helping onto his plate. Shana smiled as she poured more wine into their glasses.

"More salad or bread?"

"Oh, no, I'm fine."

"You know, Matthew, a managing partner position is a lot of work. It won't leave me much time for getting new business or maintaining what I've brought in."

"I knew you'd say that. Hillary could work with you, I thought."

Shana took a sip of wine and cracked a smile. Then she pushed back her chair and started clearing dishes off of the table. "Are you ready for dessert?"

"I'm pretty stuffed," Matthew answered. "But I'll have a little."

"OK. Why don't you sit in the living room and I'll bring it right out?"

Shana pulled down two green, frosted tulip bowls from the kitchen cupboard and filled them with yogurt, a dollop of fresh whipped cream and a sprinkle of apple crunch. In the living room, Matthew stretched his six-foot-two-inch frame across the white brocade sofa and took in the surroundings.

"Shana," he called out, "why do you have so many pillows? You've got them on the chair, the loveseat, the sofa, stacked in the corner—everywhere!"

"What can I tell you? I'm obsessive-compulsive." She carried the dessert bowls into the living room and set them on the coffee table.

"Ah, yum!" Matthew exclaimed. "You got the usual."

"Of course. You know I can't live without my favorite—I love orange-and-vanilla swirl. It's luscious."

"Let's get serious, Shana. I really want you to be managing partner. Next to me, you're the eldest partner at one of the most prestigious law firms in L.A. County. You've got twenty years of experience as a trial lawyer, ten of them as a successful criminal defense lawyer. Your courtroom track record is beyond excellent. So why not you?"

"I appreciate what you're saying," Shana said. "But I sure love to bring in the money. Taking on the managing partner position would keep me in the administrative arena—running the firm and connecting with the legal community. I'm just not quite sure I want to do that."

"Don't worry," Matthew assured her. "You'll be fine." He finished off the yogurt in his bowl and checked his watch. "Damn, it's eleven o'clock already. I'd better go—I've got an early breakfast meeting tomorrow."

He rose and retrieved his jacket from the chair. "Dinner was wonderful, as usual," he said as Shana walked him to the door. "See you in the morning?"

"You got it. I've got a ten o'clock deposition."

After cleaning up the dinner dishes, she turned the lights off in the living room, climbed upstairs and slipped into her four-poster bed alongside Lilly, who stretched her brown-tipped paws across the white satin pillows. Shana contemplated a newly purchased novel on her nightstand before setting her alarm clock and turning off the light.

A strong wind across the ocean kicked up, and Shana heard windows slamming outside her bedroom. Startled, she moved to close them when she heard a creaking sound on the wood balcony outside and saw a shadow through the white curtains briskly pass by the window—just as a tree branch smacked the roof of the house.

Frightened, she ran to her bed. It's probably just a cat, she told herself.

She snuggled up alongside Lilly, who was sleeping very soundly. She had just started to doze off when she heard a book being knocked from its shelf and other disturbing noises downstairs.

Someone had entered her home.

She crept softly toward the door and peeped out, looking down below the railing toward the darkened living room and foyer. The bright moon reflected enough light for her to see someone moving from the front doorway into the living room. The oriental rugs were yanked aside and the entire room turned upside down in a matter of seconds. Shana saw the intruder pick up keys and a notepad from the coffee table and rip off the top sheet of paper before moving quickly across the living room floor. The front door was still standing wide open.

Her heart thumping like a drum, Shana gently closed her bedroom door and walked softly to her nightstand; she opened the drawer and pulled out a herringbone-and-ivory, 9-millimeter revolver. But when she picked up the box of bullets next to it, she realized it was empty. She heard footsteps hitting the hardwood floor of the foyer, moving closer and closer to the stairwell—then suddenly, they changed direction. The house became silent. Shana heard two forceful plops of liquid hit one of the brandy snifters on the silver tray of her coffee table. In the background she also detected some kind of muffled sound, like pillows being tossed onto the floor.

Soaked with sweat, her adrenaline high and running, Shana quickly moved to the phone and dialed 911. The phone was dead. Frightened and nervous, she pulled her cellphone from her purse nearby and dialed 911; she heard a beeping tone and read the dreaded "Call Ended" message on the screen. No reception. She tried to turn on the low-wattage, white porcelain lamp on the nightstand, only to find the electricity had been cut off. Below her, she could hear jars being scraped against tiled counters and dishes crashing in the kitchen.

Then she heard footsteps moving up the stairs. Shana carefully clicked the bedroom door's brass deadbolt lock immediately to the right, grabbed the empty gun and hurried into the adjacent bathroom. It had a small window, but she knew she wouldn't be able to get through it and climb down from the second floor. She glanced around. The only potential weapon in sight was a razor blade. With one quick flick of the hand, she closed the shower curtains. She clutched the gun, hoping it would be enough to fool whoever it was approaching from the hall.

She heard the bedroom door's hinges creaking, and Lilly screeching in startled response. The bedroom door slowly opened and the footsteps abruptly stopped, then proceeded toward the closed bathroom door. The lock twisted first to the right and then to the left. It would not budge. The doorknob abruptly turned to the left and then to the right. Whoever was on the other side was yanking the knob back and forth, harder and harder, without stopping; Shana burst into tears when she heard a sharp click. The lock had broken. The door swung open and a cold breeze swept through the bathroom. The intruder walked over to the wash basin, pulling towels down from the racks along the way.

Tears rolled down Shana's face. This was no time to think of an alternative plan. There wasn't one. There was no hope—just the cruel knowledge that this was happening, and it could happen to anyone.

In less than a second, the intruder approached the bathtub. The footsteps stopped. Immediately, the shower curtains opened with one strong pull of the drawstring. Shana rolled her eyes up to the intruder as the gun was knocked from her hand and thrown aside. In her last moments she remembered Lilly and that evening's meal with Matthew.

A sharp, heavy instrument slammed against Shana's head and her body hit the cold tile floor hard. The intruder ripped off her nightgown with one tear and shredded it, scattering pieces of white satin around the bathroom floor.

Shana's naked body was moved around the bathroom floor and then thrown upon the oak toilet seat. Her body was pale white with sporadic pink spots on the skin. Her tired and panting killer grabbed both of her legs and spread them apart as far as they would go. A sharp jolt to the body shook the pewter perfume bottles on top of the porcelain tank lid adjacent to the toilet. Then another jolt of the body shook her breasts and her entire body. A long, red silk scarf was wrapped loosely around her neck two times.

Complete and total silence overcame the house as Lilly looked out from underneath the bed with a somber meow. The sight of Shana Bernstein was a fading memory as the intruder quietly left the residence.

Rosie arrived early for work that morning. She parked her car in the usual spot and walked up the steps to the front door. When she placed her hand on the doorknob, it was unlocked.

# CHAPTER 2

The sound of frogs emerged from the thick gray fog still enveloping the Malibu hills; leaves rolled across the luscious green lawn and cobblestone walkway of Shana Bernstein's home. In the distance, ocean waves could be heard pounding the sandy shore below.

The first police officers on the scene approached cautiously. Their flashing red lights illuminated the balconies and a figure standing in the front doorway: Rosie Patelle, a Mexican woman of small build who was visibly nervous and shaking from the gruesome discovery she had just made. Not wanting to scare her, they moved forward slowly.

"Ma'am! We're from the Sheriff's Department. Are you the one who phoned?"

"Miss Shana!"

"What's your name?"

"Rosie Patelle. Miss Shana!"

"Who?"

"Miss Shana *es muerte*!"

"Ms. Patelle, do you speak English?"

"*Si, si.* I so upset—Miss Shana, she like my daughter!"

"Ms. Patelle, please calm down. Let's move outside, over here near the driveway, please. Where did you find her?

"Upstairs, in the bathroom."

"OK, ma'am. Please stay outside. The detectives will be here shortly. We're going inside. OK?"

They left her and proceeded toward the front door. They walked through the foyer and headed upstairs. Bracing themselves for what they suspected they would find on the other side, they carefully opened the master bedroom door.

A messy room testified to the struggle that had taken place there. Then, there it was: the closed bathroom door off of the bedroom, the dead naked woman slightly perched up against the toilet in a sitting position on the floor with her head leaning back, facing the ceiling. One of the officers walked over to the body; there was no pulse. They went back downstairs and left the house, returning to the front yard. The wind started to blow harder.

Rosie Patelle watched tearfully from a distance as the officers wrapped fluttering yellow tape around the property, securing all entries. Fifteen minutes later, another dark, four-door sedan parked below the circular drive. Two men emerged wearing dark suits. Both looked serious. Detective Tracey Sanders was forty, tall and thin, with sandy brown hair that highlighted his mixed Caucasian/African-American heritage. His much shorter, graying, fiftysomething partner was Detective Zack Grimes, whose olive-toned skin reflected his Italian ancestry. Zack's stomach bulged slightly over the black belt of all of his suits; floors and windows shook when he walked past.

Tracey didn't mind his partner's visible shortcomings; he was the best partner Tracey had ever had. After twenty years on the force, ten of them spent working homicide, Zack Grimes commanded the respect of the other officers on the force. He possessed a keen detective's mind and knew how to ace a murder case.

Tracey, on the other hand, was the new kid on the block, relatively speaking. Five years before, he'd been just another rookie in the NYPD, married to a beautiful African-American officer on the force, Marina. Life had been good—until Marina was brutally raped and murdered while on duty. Bereft, wanting a change of scenery and a new life, Tracey had moved to Los Angeles. L.A. had given him his life back, at least for the time being. But it couldn't erase the pain of her memory.

Tracey needed Zack, and Zack needed Tracey. Call it a give-and-take relationship or a love-hate relationship—and they called it both—but either way, they were best friends and very close.

The detectives met the officers halfway up the walk, inquiring about the details. Zack was chewing his favorite gum, Juicy Fruit. He refused to part with it. The idea of chewing and talking at the same time embellished his tenacious self-image.

"How long has she been dead?" Zack asked.

"Oh, about eight to nine hours or a little longer," replied the first officer.

"Who found her?" Tracey asked.

"The maid, Rosie Patelle. Apparently, she set her up for a dinner party last night before going home around four, maybe a little earlier. She says she discovered the body in the upstairs bathroom when she returned this morning."

"What's her name?" Zack asked.

"Shana Bernstein."

Tracey and Zack entered the foyer of the home as they cautiously looked in the adjoining rooms and proceeded toward the stairwell leading upstairs.

Items of clothing, artifacts and furniture were tossed about the house in complete disarray. They entered the master bedroom, walked into the adjoining bathroom and found the dead, naked woman up against the toilet.

While very much aware of the gruesome scene before his eyes, Tracey's mind went into rewind mode as he thought of Marina. When he tried to jot down notes, his hands became hot and sticky as he tightly clenched his pen. He could not write. Frozen in thought and despair, he flashed back to the news reports about Marina's death: *"Cop used as decoy to catch possible suspect in grisly murder-rape case, becomes latest victim"...*

He remembered the medical examiner's findings ("She fought him off hard, Tracey"), and the profuse apologies from his fellow police officers for not reaching Marina in time. And the sight of her gruesomely mutilated body stretched atop the cold metal table in the coroner's office. *Marina...*

The aroma of vanilla oil tugged Tracey back into the present moment; it was wafting up from a pool of bath oil and blood on the floor.

"Tracey?"

Tracey looked up to see Zack staring at him hard.

"Yeah, I'm here."

The bathroom was completely ransacked. Floral-patterned towels were sopping up the bloody puddle on the floor. Pieces of clothing, torn into fine strips, were scattered about the bedroom and bathroom. Tracey and Zack examined the murder scene intently as the wind continued to blow vigorously outside, rattling the windows of the house.

"A possible rape victim?" Tracey looked over at Zack.

"Could be," Zack replied. "It looks like someone tried to eat the flesh on her body. He sure hit her hard." He shook his head. "What's with the toilet?"

"No idea," Tracey answered. "Nice-looking lady." He pulled out his notebook. "Five-six, medium build, strawberry-red curly hair...maybe forty?"

"What an animal!" Zack exclaimed, his dark blue eyes flashing. "Who would do something like this?"

The detectives returned downstairs and approached the first officers.

"Any witnesses?" Tracey inquired.

"Man, no! Not a one. It's such a secluded area. You're dead in the water on this one."

After briefly canvassing the neighborhood, Tracey and Zack returned to Shana Bernstein's house, where they found Rosie Patelle sitting on a wooden bench on the front porch.

"Hello again, Ms. Patelle," Zack greeted her. "Are you all right?"

"*Si*, I'm…fine. *Gracias*."

"Is there anyone you want us to phone?" Tracey asked.

"Oh, no! I just sit here. Gives me time to think."

"Think?"

"Yes. I like working for Miss Shana. I like Miss Shana's house. My house is dirty."

"Dirty?" Tracey echoed.

"Dirty sons of mine."

"So you do have family here?"

"Yes. I like it here. My sons dirty and no good. Always in jail, on drugs, lots of *guilas*."

"Where do you live?"

"East L.A."

"How long?" Zack inquired.

"Long enough. I don't like that place."

As she spoke, Tracey felt her pain and saw her eyes filled up with water.

Turning back toward the house, Tracey and Zack spotted Randy Yew, a thirtysomething Asian with black, trendily spiked hair, climbing out of his car. The crime scene technician wore a dark suit and carried a silver case resembling a tackle box in one hand and a cellphone in the other. Zack and Tracey greeted him with instructions at the front door.

Yew worked the entire upstairs bathroom and bedroom for two hours, combing surfaces for fibers and taking swabs of blood from the bathroom walls, toilet seat and floor. He was joined by another crime tech who covered all of the residence's tabletops, white porcelain ginger jar lamps and decorative crystal artifacts with a light film of dust, looking for latent fingerprints. He dusted myriad objects throughout the downstairs rooms but an hour later still hadn't even started upstairs; it was looking like it was going to be a long day.

A bright light suddenly flashed on the Malibu shore, while other flashes went off continuously throughout various areas of Shana Bernstein's home as photographs were taken. A blue van pulled up outside and two investigators from the county coroner's office hopped out. One wore dark pants and a white shirt with rolled-up sleeves; the driver wore a dark blue jumpsuit. They walked into the foyer and addressed Tracey and Zack.

"The victim is Shana Bernstein," Zack told them. "The maid found her. This is what you've got to watch out for: it looks like a sexual assault."

Just as they started upstairs, a small meow was heard from beyond the porch.

"Did you hear that, Tracey?"

"Yeah, Zack. It sounds like a cat."

"It is. Look over there—underneath the stairwell. Hey, kitty! Kitty-kitty!"

Zack walked slowly toward the animal. Leaning down to pick up the cat, Zack said, "Tracey, isn't he cute?"

"That's enough, Zack. We've got a serious problem and you don't need another animal. You've taken in enough animals since your wife left you, and you're hardly home to feed the ones you have."

"Look, Tracey, he's got a tag on him."

"What does it say?"

"Lilly. I guess he's really a she. She's a pretty cat."

"OK. Don't go gettin' soft on me. We're not driving around with a cat."

"Did I say anything about that?"

"No. But I can hear it in your voice."

Turning to the police officers still standing outside, Tracey said, "Officer, please contact the animal shelter representative. We'll be upstairs."

"No, Tracey! You're cruel! Maybe we can locate a family member. I'll take her."

"Zack…" Tracey hesitated.

"Eh!" Zack stood up and glared at him. "I said I'll take her, *capish*?"

"Oh, all right, take her!"

Tracey, Zack and the county coroner investigators walked upstairs and entered the bathroom, where the crime scene technician was still diligently working.

"Are we doing the rape kit or you?" Tracey asked. "The body has not been touched. We wanted the house worked up first for fibers."

"Let's have your people do it right now," the coroner replied. "She's all yours."

Tracey yelled to Randy Yew in the next room. "Could you stop what you're doing and come do this?"

Yew locked his box up and asked if the coroner could move the body downstairs, so he would have more room to work.

"The wind is blowing pretty hard up here," he said with concern, motioning toward the bathroom windows.

"I know," Tracey acknowledged. "Is that a problem with the fibers?"

"No, not if your guys close all the windows and doors. Normally, we usually move the body downtown, but it's just too windy to even do that. I don't think you should take any chances."

"Sure. No problem. I'll notify my guys to seal this baby off before they do the rape kit."

The coroner investigators wrapped the body in plastic and then a white sheet and carried it downstairs to the living room. The crime scene technician shined the black light over the body searching for evidence of semen. Two Q-tips were dabbed in a small bottle of distilled water before doing a vaginal swab. Three empty vials were placed on a plastic sheet for the blood. A fingernail clipping was conducted, looking for any pieces of skin underneath the nails that would evidence a struggle. Pubic hairs were clipped from the victim as well.

"Check her entire body—be real thorough," Tracey advised.

After Yew finished the vaginal swab, they returned upstairs and scanned the black light over the entire toilet seat for any signs of semen. A toxicological exam was done at the same time.

A half-hour later, crime scene technicians built a plastic tent and placed the body on a cot. Then they opened a packet of colorless chemicals, creating fumes throughout the tent—a chemical process they hoped would aid their search for prints on the body.

Meanwhile, Tracey and Zack did another inspection of the house. "Did you see those bruises on her head and legs and in her vaginal area?" Tracey asked. "She was ripped to shreds. The entire vaginal wall was like tissue paper, as if some type of heinous animal chewed it up. I don't like this one at all."

"Yeah. This is a bad one, Tracey."

"What's with the red silk scarf?"

"I don't know," Zack said. He pulled his glasses down below his eyes and looked at his partner. "Are you thinking what I'm thinking?"

"Another Hillside Strangler? I hope not. God! I hope not."

"What if it is, Tracey?"

They continued their investigation down at the end of the hall on the second floor, and entered the office overlooking the ocean. They could hear the crashing noise of white foam breakers splashing against the rocks. They stood there with their eyes focused on a lighthouse in the distance.

"Shit, man!" Tracey exclaimed. "Who would do something like this?"

Zack shook his head. "I've never seen a rape victim like that."

"You know what, Zack? You can't figure out a killer's mind—especially a serial killer, if that is what we're dealing with here. I think the assholes do it to become famous. That's their motive."

"Maybe. Who knows? We're not sure yet. Let's not draw conclusions. This is just a dead woman with a red scarf wrapped around her neck."

"Let's take it one step at a time," Tracey agreed. "We'll need an autopsy."

Yew approached the detectives from behind, clearing his throat for recognition. He held out a small card.

"Shana Bernstein," he said. "She's an attorney. I found her business cards on her desk in the office upstairs. Works for Daytona, Bernstein & McDunn, a prominent Beverly Hills law firm. From the looks of her desk, she was a very busy lawyer.

"And," he added, "here's a gun. I found it underneath the bed. It's empty; it was never fired."

"OK," Tracey answered. "We'll run it."

Tracey and Zack conferred one more time with the forensic team as Yew wrapped up his investigation. They had been working Shana Bernstein's home for six hours. The county coroner examiners tightly wrapped her body in plastic and a white sheet, rolled it into their van and left. Tracey and Zack hopped in their car and headed toward Pacific Coast Highway.

Back at their office at the precinct in downtown Los Angeles, Tracey and Zack closed their office door and blinds; Zack flicked on the brass Stifle lamps located at each end of their desks and switched off the glaring fluorescent lights overhead.

"Coffee and a doughnut, Tracey?"

"Yes. Just the coffee, cream and sugar, please."

"Well, our investigation is underway. Why don't we pay a visit to the law firm of Daytona, Bernstein & McDunn?" Zack suggested.

"No problem. Did they run a match on the gun?"

"Yeah, it belongs to Shana Bernstein," Zack said, pouring the coffee.

"Great!" Tracey rubbed his forehead. Zack placed a coffee cup in front of him.

"You've been on edge lately. What's wrong?"

"A little. It's been five years since Marina died. The house is empty without her and…and I'm trying to move on, and…This murder…"

Zack listened silently.

"I can't really date," Tracey continued. "You know how it is. My job gets in the way. The computer games keep me busy, though. I'm trying not to think about it. But…this brings it all back."

"You know, if you're still mourning your wife, maybe I can put—"

"Someone else on the case? No way! I want this guy."

Matthew Daytona was known for being eloquent—and shrewd. On the street he had a reputation as the "alley cat lawyer." Elegant and somewhat eccentric, he kept his own counsel and hired only women as partners and associates. He regularly attended celebrity-studded dinner parties and other gatherings with investors for various entertainment ventures, all of which generated steady business for his firm. He was a real partygoer and loved lavish surroundings.

His law firm was headquartered on the thirty-eighth floor of a large, beige stucco building of Italian Renaissance design in the heart of Beverly Hills, and commanded an imposing view of the tree-lined celebrity magnet otherwise known as Rodeo Drive. The handsomely appointed offices were distinguished by Art Deco flourishes, abstract paintings and childhood drawings displayed as fine art.

The firm itself was comprised of fifty lawyers who specialized in civil, transactional, tax, real estate, healthcare, probate and information-technology law. But its primary focus was entertainment law.

When Zack and Tracey stepped off the brass-and-glass elevator, they were greeted by white marble letters spelling out "DAYTONA, BERNSTEIN & MCDUNN" on black lacquered walls. They briefly took in the artwork adorning the lobby, as well as the long stares from employees, as they walked toward the receptionist, Erin Peters, who glanced up at them as she concluded a phone call.

"Mom, you won't believe this, but there are two men standing in front of me in dark suits. They look like the FBI—no, more like *Men in Black.* I'll call you back." She hung up the phone and faced the detectives.

"We're here to see the manager of the law firm," Zack informed her.

"Mr. Daytona is the person in charge, but I'm not sure if he's in yet. I'll check. What is this regarding?"

"Shana Bernstein," Tracey replied.

Erin's eyes widened. "Please have a seat," she said. "I'll see if he's available."

Tracey walked toward the large window that looked out over the city, while Zack anxiously paced the floor behind him. Legal magazines and newspapers were arrayed across the coffee table next to a bouquet of red and white roses in a Waterford crystal bowl accented by lemons at the bottom.

Tracey turned away from the window just in time to spot a man exiting the elevators and walking through a side door off of the elevator bay. He wore a red silk scarf.

"Hey, Tracey!" Zack exclaimed, holding up a magazine. "You ever read *California Lawyer*? Look at this cover: 'Ernst & Adams Dissolving Partnership.' This lady on the cover's one of the partners, canyabelieveit? She's a real knockout! Ooh-lala! You really oughtta take a look, Tracey. She's beautiful!"

"Zack, we've got a lot to do. Put down the magazine!"

"Says here she's a civil litigation and criminal defense lawyer…Harianne DeCanter. That's her name. She's what they call a 'rainmaker.' Wow! And gorgeous!"

"All right, let me see that." Zack handed him the magazine. "Whoa, you're right. She's a keeper. What's her name?"

"Harianne DeCanter." Zack smiled. "See, I knew you'd like that."

"Look at those eyes!" Tracey marveled.

"Yeah, but what a bunch of barracudas," Zack snarled. "Can you believe the fees these guys charge? Some are well over $500,000 just for one invoice—usually they're divorce lawyers. Just like my divorce. You know that son of a—"

"Zack! You're pushing it."

"How so? Lawyers! They're all alike. Did you know ninety percent of them just cover anything and everything up?"

"Some of them are fair, Zack. And right now we're surrounded by those so-called sharks. Be professional."

"You know ever since Eve left, I've been drowning in attorney's fees over this divorce and have consulted some divorce lawyers. Most of them are high, but you gotta do what you gotta do."

"Zack, you're so naive sometimes!"

Zack angrily threw the magazine on the table and started toward the elevators for an immediate exit.

Tracey hurried after him and placed his hand on his shoulder.

"Hey, hey, I didn't mean that. I'm sorry for yelling at you. This is a tough time for you. I'm really sorry."

"Ah, it's OK," Zack replied. "No hard feelings."

Zack sat back down on the sofa as Tracey checked his watch. "We've been waiting for quite a while," he commented.

As if on cue, Matthew Daytona entered the lobby and greeted them.

"Hello, detectives. I'm Matthew Daytona. We can go into the main conference room down the hall."

He turned toward his receptionist.

"Erin, please call Maggie and ask her to come to the conference room."

"Who's Maggie?" Zack asked.

"Maggie is Shana's secretary/assistant."

"That's good," Tracey said. "We'll eventually have to speak with her anyway."

As they followed Matthew down the long hallway leading to the conference room, Tracey could feel the office staff looking at them, their noses pressed up against the frosted glass cubicle dividers. Matthew opened the double glass doors and walked over toward the cherrywood conference table, big enough to seat forty. He turned and greeted them coolly as they entered the room.

"Please have a seat," he said. "Coffee or water?"

"No, we're fine," Tracey replied, as he pulled his pad and pen out of his coat pocket. "We'd like to learn as much as possible about Shana Bernstein, your connections and business dealings with her. OK, Mr. Daytona?"

"Sure. No problem. Please understand I'm still in shock over her death. We all are."

"I'm sure it was a shock. I understand that you were with her last night. Were you not?"

"I went to her home for dinner after working at the office late, yes. We were very good friends outside of the office."

"Just answer the questions as they are given to you, Mr. Daytona. Do you understand?"

"Yes. I was only trying—"

"I said just answer the questions, OK?"

"Tracey, take it easy! We're only questioning him." Zack stood up, ready to approach him.

Tracey motioned him back into his seat and turned back to Matthew. "After dinner what did you do?"

"That all depends. You know what I think? I think I need a lawyer. You're asking entirely too many personal questions."

"You've got that right! Get yourself a real good one, too. Answer the question."

"I went home because I had an early breakfast meeting this morning."

"Nice red scarf," Tracey said.

"What do you mean? I'm not wearing a red scarf."

"It was you that got off the elevator about fifteen minutes ago."

"I don't know what you're talking about."

"I saw you wearing a red silk scarf over your trench coat. Is it imported or did you purchase it here?"

"It's imported!" Matthew replied angrily.

"From where?" Zack asked.

"Japan. My previous partner ordered them. She ordered them for herself and I liked them, too."

"Ordered? Is that what you said?"

"By whom?"

"MacKenzie McShay. She's no longer with the firm."

"What was her position at the firm?"

"Partner. She left to pursue other interests."

"Like what?"

"She had a hard life. It's a long story."

"Well, we've got time, but we'll get to that later. What time did you leave Shana Bernstein's house?"

"It was late—around 11:15 p.m., to the best of my recollection."

"Did you have Shana's calendar for today?"

"No. Why would I have her calendar? She keeps her own. Even Maggie doesn't know."

Suddenly, there was a knock at the door. A woman with curly red hair and freckles covering her entire face, wearing a black tailored suit beyond anyone's expectation of "professional," cautiously walked into the room and sat down next to Matthew.

"Well, I'm glad you could join us," Tracey said.

"I was on a rush. I'm sorry I was late."

"It's fine. We're just getting started. What is your full name?"

"Maggie Weiner."

"Did you maintain Ms. Bernstein's calendar?"

"No. Actually, she keeps her own calendar."

"When was the last time you saw her, Maggie?"

"The day before yesterday."

"Where are you from Maggie? I detect a bit of an accent."

"New York."

"Ah. How long have you been living here?"

"Not long. My husband just died of cancer; I'm a widow."

"Oh, ma'am. I'm sorry I had to ask you. Fine. You can leave now. No more questions. Thank you."

She looked at Matthew with great concern before leaving the room. The doors quietly shut behind her.

An hour passed as the detectives continued to grill Matthew with questions about Shana. There were so many questions that he couldn't keep up.

"Did you know that there was a red silk scarf found at the crime scene?" Tracey asked.

"No, I didn't," Matthew insisted. "That's odd. I always wear red silk scarves. They're so chic and rare, don't you think?"

"Listen, you bastard!" Zack growled. "It's chic to beat an asshole to death like you. You damn bastard! I know you killed her."

"Easy, Zack," Tracey cautioned. He turned back to Matthew. "Since the scarf was found at the crime scene, I think it would be a good idea if you could tell me how it got there."

"Are you referring to the scarf I wore today? I've got several. Obviously, it's not the same one, but the same kind. Shana used them herself to complement her black suits. It's sort of a trademark—my logo for the firm."

"Can you give us a good reason why we should believe you?" Tracey asked in a firm voice.

"I don't expect you to believe me," Matthew retorted. "I've got no problem with that. I didn't ask for your approval and I didn't kill her!"

"Tracey, that's enough," Zack interceded. "Let's wrap it up!"

"Fine." Tracey leaned in toward Matthew as Zack looked on, chewing his gum in slow motion. "I'm finished questioning you for now. I'll tell you one thing: if you try to go anywhere or go under, I'll be your worse nightmare. Remember you wanted a lawyer. Now find one, fucker! We'll be watching and returning. I'll contact you later with the time."

Not satisfied with Matthew's responses about the murder, Tracey and Zack exchanged grim smiles with the receptionist as they headed for the exit sign. They stopped to take in the surroundings one more time before stepping onto the elevator.

An attractive woman came running up behind them, threw her briefcase between the steel doors just as they were closing and entered, out of breath. Zack tried not to notice her, but she was a beautiful vision to the male eye: blonde, in her thirties, attired in staunch executive fashion. Her flirtatious actions were focused on Tracey as she turned and slightly smiled. A mutual smile was returned.

"Hello, Miss…"

"Smith—Lara Smith," she said, arranging her suit.

"Are you an attorney or a client of the firm?"

"An attorney. I'm an associate."

"I see. How long have you worked with the firm?"

"Not too long, why?"

"Just curious. I'm Detective Tracey Sanders, Homicide Bureau, Sheriff's Department."

"Oh, I see. You're here regarding Shana Bernstein's murder?"

"Yeah. Sorry I didn't come right out with it."

"It wasn't hard to figure out," she said with a slight grin.

"Tell me, how well do you know Matthew Daytona?"

"Who doesn't know of his reputation in the legal community—that's why I chose to work here. We have a great entertainment clientele—several movie stars, studios, some Oscar-winning directors. Matthew was once a Hollywood agent, so he's got great connections.

"You know, he built this firm from scratch," she continued. "Hard work has been a part of his whole life. I don't know what's going on, but your suspicions are wrong. He's a good man. Really! I think I've told you enough." The elevators doors opened and she stepped out into the ground-floor lobby. She turned around and faced them.

"Did you actually think I'd badmouth him?"

"Just doing my job, lady," Tracey called after her. "Have a nice day. It was nice meeting you."

He and Zack rode down to the parking garage, got in their car and headed out onto Wilshire Boulevard.

Up on the thirty-eighth floor, Matthew returned to his office. The clock read noon. He sat in his chair and faced the window in despair, then rang for Maggie.

"Maggie! Please bring me my attorney reference file."

She brought him the file within minutes. "Is this the right file? Are you OK? What did they say?"

"Yeah. I'm fine. What cruel detectives! They just asked a barrel load of questions. Everything is going to be fine, though. I'll call you if I need anything else."

Maggie shut the door gently and returned to her office.

Matthew immersed himself in memories of his family.

Turning back toward his desk, he flipped through a copy of *California Lawyer* until he came across a particular article. He picked up the phone and punched in a number.

"Ernst & Adams, may I help you, please?"

"Harianne DeCanter." Matthew stared out the window while the receptionist put his call through.

"Hello, this is Harianne."

"Ms. DeCanter, I'm Matthew Daytona. How are you?"

"Fine." There was a long pause.

"Ms. DeCanter?"

"Yes, Mr. Daytona. How can I help you?"

"Well..." He cleared his throat. "This is very awkward."

"Try me."

"I think I will be arrested very soon for a murder."

"Mr. Daytona, I am a civil litigation lawyer. I quit criminal law ten years ago. I got tired of never knowing what secrets my clients were keeping."

"I'm aware of that. I'm a lawyer also. We met once at a Los Angeles County Bar Association ethics seminar, and again at the Los Angeles Trial Lawyers Association convention. Please hear me out."

"How could I ever forget you, Mr. Daytona? I'm listening."

"I'd rather not talk about it on the phone. Can I meet with you tonight over dinner? Please say yes."

"It had better be worth my time."

"Six o'clock at Prego?"

"All right. Please bring me any pertinent papers and a calendar with your daily schedule. My time is money, just like yours."

At her office at Ernst & Adams in downtown Los Angeles, Harianne DeCanter completed a brief, turned off the lights and walked toward the elevator. Her thoughts regressed to1986, when she had just completed her LSATs and wanted desperately to enter law school at UCLA. She contemplated Matthew Daytona with a bit of anger.

She slammed the door to her Mercedes and headed up Third Street toward Beverly Hills. The drive was not too bad since it was on her way home. Tree-lined, quaint streets gradually gave way to brightly lit stores. She pulled up in front of Prego, handed her keys to the valet and approached the maitre'd inside the front door of the restaurant.

"Matthew Daytona?" she inquired.

"Yes, ma'am. Right this way."

Moving with uncommon grace, Harianne followed him to a table near the window. Matthew rose to greet her.

"Harianne? Matthew Daytona. Thanks for meeting me."

"Yes, of course. It's hard to believe you're in any trouble like this. I'm shocked."

"Well, it's a long story. I could not tell you everything over the phone."

A waiter placed two glasses of ice water in front of them, and pulled out a pad to take their order. "What will you have to drink?"

"Perrier on the rocks," Harianne replied.

"I'll have the same."

The waiter departed, and Harianne looked at Matthew intently.

"You don't remember me, do you?"

"Of course I do. I told you on the phone we were at a convention together and I heard you give a speech."

"I don't mean that. Think back to 1986 at UCLA."

"UCLA…1986…no special memory. I don't know what you're talking about."

"I had just passed the LSAT and submitted numerous applications for law school at UCLA. You were the dean of admissions at the time and very staunch in your thinking and ways."

Matthew scrutinized Harianne closely for a few moments. "Oh, my God…you're the girl who was—"

"Black, but with very fair skin."

"Ms. DeCanter, I'm so sorry—"

"For what? For denying me entry into law school based upon my race? Or for sweeping it under the carpet?"

Matthew took a measured breath before responding. "Forgive me, Ms. DeCanter. Why don't you refresh my memory so we can clear the air and get down to business?"

"You claimed that my cultural background made a difference because I applied as Caucasian," Harianne fumed. "Somehow you found out that I had some black—or, as they call it now, African-American—blood in me. You accused me of 'misrepresenting' myself. I was so hurt by your comments. I kept asking myself, 'How do I have control over my family history, or my ancestors' skin color?' I know that I could have passed as a white woman to get in, but you persisted with your investigation into my family background. You just kept digging the hole until you reached my adoption. My adoptive parents are Caucasian. I know the adoption had a lot to do with it."

"I admit it," Matthew said candidly. "I wasn't very fond of blacks—excuse me, African Americans—at that time. The school system, in actuality, was supposed to admit anyone with high LSAT scores to law school. It was personal for me."

"How did you find out this information?"

"Through the archives in a research center over on Santa Monica Boulevard in West L.A. and records in New York."

"Why?"

"What can I say?" He shrugged. "Really, I'm truly sorry. I've grown."

"And now you want me to represent and defend you. What a switch!"

"Listen, it was a mistake," Matthew apologized. "I had forgotten about that entire episode."

"Easy for you," Harianne said heatedly. "I ended up going to law school back East because of you, Mr. Daytona. My anger is coming back just thinking of your actions."

"I'm truly sorry, Ms. DeCanter," Matthew said apologetically.

"Now you want a half-and-half woman to defend you?"

"Yes. Yes, I do. Please accept my apology."

Trying to calm down, Harianne took a sip of water, wiped her mouth, and sat back in her chair very gently.

"I'll try to forgive you," she agreed. "You know it will take some time, though."

"I can understand that," Matthew said. "But you see, I think I might be arrested for the murder of Shana Bernstein."

"Shana Bernstein? Wasn't she a partner in your law firm?"

"Yes. Did you know her?"

"No. I heard some scuttlebutt around the office this afternoon."

Matthew groaned. "The gossip's started already?"

"What do you expect?" Harianne asked. "You're a big shot in legal and entertainment circles. So what happened?"

"The police think that I killed her."

"Why would they think that? Did you have motive?"

"I was with her the evening she was murdered. She was murdered after I left."

"What condition was she in when you left her?"

"She was fine. I left around 11:15, 11:30."

"You're sure of the time?"

"Yes."

The waiter arrived with their drinks, took their order and discreetly departed.

"Mr. Daytona," Harianne continued, "I told you on the phone that I don't practice criminal law anymore."

"I'm well aware of that. I've done my research." He gave her an appraising look. "You're a Stanford graduate. You speak four different languages. You hold a Columbia University J.D. They call you 'the Velvet Voice.'

"There are plenty of other attorneys in this city, but none that I trust. I don't want them. I want you. You were the best in criminal law, and you're an outstanding trial lawyer. The case that impressed me the most was the district attorney's case."

"The district attorney's case? I don't remember…"

"Think," Matthew urged her. "The Cassidy family murder?"

"Oh, yes! The father was out of town at the time on business. If it hadn't been for the message he left on the answering machine after the murder occurred, he would have been on death row." She shook her head. "That was ten years ago, Mr. Daytona. You certainly have done your homework."

"So…what do you think I should do?"

"Well, you haven't been arrested yet. Why don't we wait until something breaks?"

"I didn't kill her."

"Mr. Daytona, I'll see what I can do, but—"

"That's fine, really fine."

"I'm not making any promises," Harianne emphasized. "My firm is dissolving."

"Yes, so I've read. Why is that, exactly?"

"Fast-paced restructuring, downsizing, high overhead expenses, low billables and high salaries. They're broke."

"So where does that leave you?"

"Well, I'm not quite sure yet," Harianne admitted. "I'm thinking of quitting law and moving to Europe. Who knows? Maybe I'll be a chef at Le Cordon Bleu."

"Why don't you go into practice for yourself?" Matthew suggested. "I could help you get started."

Taken aback by his offer, Harianne paused before answering. "I have to admit I have been thinking of that."

"I have a lot of powerful friends. Let me make it up to you for…"

Harianne stared at him hard. Matthew shifted.

"Please, Ms. DeCanter. I need you."

"Honestly, for your own sake, I'm not the best candidate for you right now."

"I'll take my chances. I want you."

Harianne took a couple of sips of her Perrier, placed her hand on the side of her head and contemplated the fear on Matthew's face.

"I'll let you know of my decision in a few days, if not next week," she finally said. "Let's just wait this out. Be patient."

Matthew gazed out the window and spotted a black car, possibly a Ford, parked in front. With a start he realized it was Zack and Tracey sitting in the car, looking straight at him through the window.

# CHAPTER 3

It was evening and a light mist draped the sky in Los Angeles—"the City of Angels," the place where dreams supposedly come true. Not far below Harianne's house lay Hollywood, also known as Tinseltown, just one of L.A.'s many exotic suburbs. Harianne remembered that Matthew Daytona had once been a well-connected Hollywood agent, before he became a celebrity in the field of law.

Harianne's cream stucco house, much like an English cottage, was surrounded by a gorgeous garden filled with peonies, tulips, daisies, roses and green ferns; moss-covered flowerboxes were connected to very window. Redwood bark and white rocks were scattered throughout the flowerbeds and rosebushes. Nestled in the hills of Coldwater Canyon, adjacent to Beverly Hills, it was a quiet retreat. Ivy topiaries in round and square clay planters sat on either side of the front door, and green moss outlined the cement walkway. An identical guest house in the rear was occupied by her childhood nanny, an Englishwoman named Austria Fairden. Harianne could see by the darkened windows that she had already turned in for the night.

Upstairs in her own bedroom, Harianne turned on one light, creating a seductive and subtle mood. She looked at her bed. It was covered in fine linens sent by her Aunt Michelle in Nice, France: beige satin pillows, a cotton down comforter—350 thread count, no less—and lots of big, white and beige goose-down pillows covered with the best white-thread linen. They covered her bed, on which her white Maltese dog, Melissa, was curled up sleeping. Harianne leaned over and picked her up, as Melissa returned the affection with lots of licks.

It was a feminine, elegant room. The Queen Anne cherrywood dressing table was decorated with lace, on top of which rested a wide selection of perfumes and a very rich-looking, fourteen-karat gold mirror-comb-and-brush set. The closet was the size of a horse stall, holding enough sweaters and stirrup pants for a polo match. There were only a few hand-carved shelves, which had prompted the purchase of an antique mahogany armoire. It contained her remaining wardrobe: tailored suits in black, navy, burgundy and white, plus a huge assortment of white cotton and linen blouses that had been crisply ironed by the nearby French Laundry. Harianne's signature style had a glowing effect when she entered a room. She selected her business attire for the next day and draped it across the peach-chintz chaise lounge that snuggled under the beveled-glass bay window.

Harianne tried to unwind, but even after getting into bed she couldn't close her eyes. For quite some time, she had trouble falling asleep. She looked at the clock: eleven, exactly. She retrieved her brush from the dressing table and ran it through her long, light brown, wavy hair as she walked down to the kitchen.

Her stress level was high, which necessitated comfort food. Normally she leaned toward healthier foods: whole grains, fish, soymilk, green salads and fresh fruit. Most of the cooking was done on the weekend when she could relish her favorite gourmet delights, with leftovers for dinner during the week. But right now what she needed was a late-night snack. Brandy and warm milk? That worked just fine some nights, but left the lingering effects of a little hangover, which she couldn't afford in her profession; her early-morning court appearances required several cups of hot, strong coffee and a little cream. She settled for warm milk, a dab of chocolate syrup and biscotti.

But they didn't do the trick. She thought about Matthew's case. She'd somehow felt he was telling the truth, but deep in her mind, something continued to eat away at her. It just didn't add up.

She thought of law school and contemplated the legal definition of murder: *The unlawful killing of a human being, with malice aforethought.* In her earlier days as a criminal lawyer, Harianne had dealt with malice on a daily basis. Had Matthew Daytona cruelly murdered a successful and powerful lawyer, a colleague, with malice aforethought?

It had been a while since she had wrestled with such concepts. Murders occur in every major city, all the time. One never knows when a murder will occur, she mused, or how. Will it be the strangling of a throat, or a bullet to the head? Only the murderer knows because the malice lies within. The destiny of life is unknown. The mind of a murderer is strong, willing and determined. It creates a flurry of havoc within itself, much like society—a constant flow of negative and destructive energy.

The next morning, Harianne followed the scent of fresh coffee to the kitchen, where it was percolating in the coffeemaker. She found Austria busily making French toast.

Austria Fairden had been Harianne's live-in nanny when she was a child, and had remained in the DeCanter family fold even after Harianne had moved out on her own. She had only one relative remaining in England, a brother, and she loved Harianne as much as if she were her own daughter. When Harianne's parents relocated to Hawaii, Harianne had offered Austria the guest house; the arrangement offered just the right balance of privacy and family togetherness for two strongly independent women. Austria was now in her late fifties, with her graying hair cut short and styled like Audrey Hepburn's in *Paris When It Sizzles.* She loved rising early in the morning, taking Melissa for a walk, and then returning to the main house to fix Harianne her favorite breakfast.

Harianne rubbed her head as she poured herself a cup of coffee and turned on the TV inside the kitchen armoire to see the local morning news. Her stomach made funny sounds as she dug into the thick slices of toast smothered in butter and sweet syrup.

"I might take on a murder case," she told Austria.

"Murder? That's not like you. It's been years—"

"Since I've practiced criminal law? I know what you're trying to say."

Austria poured herself a cup of coffee and sat down at the table beside Harianne.

"Who's the client?"

"Matthew Daytona."

"I remember him." She paused. "What did he do?"

"He's suspected of murdering his partner, an attorney in his law firm. I'm still getting all the facts."

"Harianne! That's awful."

"There's a part of me that thinks he's innocent."

"Be careful."

Harianne continued to drink the coffee and popped two aspirin for her growing headache, but it only intensified as she ate. Her body was tired, and the prospect of yet another sleepless night was disheartening. A co-worker had recently given her the name of a doctor who specialized in migraines. Walking slowly back upstairs to her office, she grabbed the business-card organizer in her briefcase and looked up Dr. Zenfried and dialed his number.

"Hello, Dr. Zenfried's office."

"I'd like to make an appointment with Dr. Zenfried. I'm a referral. Can you fit me in today?"

"Are you experiencing headache pain?"

"Yes. Constantly."

"All right. Let's see…Not until three o'clock this afternoon. Is that OK?"

"That's fine."

Harianne finished the last drop of coffee in her cup, then slipped into the black suit and cream-colored, slightly sheer blouse she'd selected the night before, topped with a black-and-cream scarf. She had a keen eye for her business attire. Not too conservative, she had a sophisticated flair that fit her perfectly. She rummaged through the dresser's hosiery-filled bottom drawer for a pair of off-black stockings and pulled black suede pumps from a shoebox inside the closet. On her way to the front door, she retrieved her leather briefcase from her office.

The day was warm and mild, but still left a bit of a chill. Harianne's headaches persisted to the point where her vision blurred. The dark sunglasses tucked conveniently inside her briefcase came in handy. The drive from Coldwater Canyon to downtown Los Angeles was not far, but far enough as the traffic grew heavy on the local streets. It seemed as though she would never reach her office. A sea of red lights flooded the southbound 101 freeway.

Half an hour later, Harianne pulled her Mercedes CL 500 into the parking lot, swiped her parking card and headed for Lower Level C Parking, two floors down. En route to the escalator, she stopped for a cafe latte at the Mocha Bar to help alleviate the headache.

Stepping off of the elevator into the main lobby of the thirty-year law firm of Ernst & Adams, she overheard conversations regarding its dissolution. In one corner a huddle of secretaries whispered and giggled, while others had their faces fixed with somber looks. In the main conference room, an executive committee meeting had just begun. Associates in great numbers were standing inside each other's offices, immersed in serious discussion. Harianne heard muffled voices from nearby cubicles as she hurried down the hall corridor. She caught only bits and pieces of conversation until she heard one of the labor law partners speak candidly from his office doorway: "closing the firm at the end of the month." Finally, there was clarity.

Nothing was actually final yet, as Harianne shortly learned in a management meeting; the executive committee and the management committee were still ironing out the particulars. The next few months would tell the story: who would take certain clients, who would team up for a spinoff law firm and who would retire from law altogether. Harianne knew she had to decide which direction she would take.

Everyone exited the main conference room when the meeting concluded. Staff watched the partners' faces for their reactions. Some smiled, others had drooping heads, and some wore stern looks of concern.

Back in her own office, Harianne threw her blazer over the chair in front of her desk and began checking her voicemail. Her legal assistant, China Rowan, an exotic mixture of African-American and Irish ancestry, poked her head through the door.

"Is the firm really dissolving?" she asked.

"It seems that way, but don't worry," Harianne replied, comforting her. "Everything will be all right."

She continued to plow through the papers on her desk, dictating letters and memos to the files on all of her cases for an hour until China once again knocked on her door.

"Harianne, the management committee would like all the partners to come to the main conference room this afternoon at four-thirty."

"I've got a three o'clock appointment, so I might be a little late. Please let the partners know."

Harianne's stomach quivered inside at the thought of the firm's decision. She continued working diligently until two-thirty, knowing she only had to travel up the street. She arrived at the doctor's office promptly at three o'clock.

"Please come in, Ms. DeCanter. Right this way."

Dr. Zenfried greeted her at the door of the examination room. Tall, with black hair and a reserved, almost grim personality, he looked to be in his fifties, but according to her referral was only in his late forties.

"Hello, Harianne. How are you?"

"OK. Just a lot of bad headaches."

"Well, let's see if we can do something about them. What's bothering you? Tell me what's been going on lately."

"A lot. My firm is dissolving, I've got a potential client and I can't make up my mind if I want to return to being a sole practitioner or venture out to another law firm. I've got to make a lot of decisions. It's difficult, but I know I can do it."

"That's a good start. What about your personal life?"

"Um, well, I'm having trouble sleeping because I constantly think about the firm."

"I'm sure you do. You've got to stop."

Dr. Zenfried picked up his medical instruments, looked deep into Harianne's eyes and flashed a light into them. He held up two fingers, then one, then five, and asked her how many fingers she saw each time. He followed with a full examination.

"I want you to take some Xanax to help you sleep," he said. "Then I want you to take the Fiorinal for the severe headaches."

"OK."

"What else? There is something else bothering you, isn't there?"

"Yes, but it's a long story and I'll need more time," Harianne replied, looking down toward her feet as she twirled her hair with one finger.

"Let's give it a shot," Dr. Zenfried said, leaning back in his chair.

"Well, my sleepless nights are filled with visions of different faces and confusion. It's upsetting."

"It's going to be all right. But I want you to come back in one week. We need to run some tests."

"What do you mean?"

"We'll work it out. Make an appointment with my nurse on your way out," he said, closing the door.

Ravenous, Harianne stopped at the local coffee shop and ordered a chicken-salad sandwich on wheat bread. She had twenty minutes until the start of the meeting. She hurried back to the office and joined the other partners in the large conference room, where they were officially informed that Ernst & Adams would be closing its doors at the end of the month. A staff meeting was scheduled for ten o'clock the following morning.

Harianne looked up a number in her contacts list on her computer and phoned Jasmine Thomas, her best friend.

"Hey, girl!"

"Hi, Harianne! What's up?"

"It's Friday night. Remember our late-night-ice-cream-sundaes-and-old-love-stories movie night?"

"Yes..."

"Can you meet me at the house around seven o'clock?"

"Sure. What's up?"

"I have to talk to you. I need a favor. Don't forget your pajamas!"

Jasmine Thomas, a tall African-American woman with long black hair and gray eyes, arrived at seven o'clock with her pink leather tote bag and two bottles of red wine in a wicker basket. Harianne greeted her at the door wearing white flannel pajamas and white bunny-face house shoes—a scene reminiscent of their childhood together.

"Hey, Jasmine, come in!"

"Where's my girl?"

"In the kitchen. Where else?"

Jasmine walked into the quaint white country kitchen adorned with modern appliances; the fragrant smell of garlic and basil filled the room. Austria, dressed in black pants and a white T-shirt, stood over the stove stirring a large pot of spaghetti sauce.

"Austria!"

"Oh, my! My sweet Jasmine!"

"How are you?" Jasmine asked, giving Austria a big hug.

"I'm doing well, dear."

Harianne and Jasmine set the table, while Austria put the finishing touches on the Italian dinner: spaghetti and meatballs, green salad, hot garlic bread and a dessert of pound cake with vanilla ice cream. They all sat down at the table, which was decorated with floating white candles and gardenias, one of Jasmine's favorite flowers.

"What movie are we going to watch tonight?" Jasmine asked.

"I vote for *An Affair to Remember*," Harianne said. "It's my favorite."

"Austria?"

"*The Sandpiper*."

They enjoyed their meal and then flipped a coin for the movie. *The Sandpiper* won.

Jasmine, with her bluish-black complexion and hailing from the "other" side of the tracks, had not been as lucky as Harianne at landing great parents. She had lived in poor foster homes in the ghetto most of her life, with families plagued by alcoholism. Beans and rice had been her standard breakfast, lunch and dinner for many years. She had struck out on her own at age eighteen, and gradually established herself as a very intelligent private investigator with a knack for digging up the most accurate information. She and Harianne had remained close ever since becoming fast friends in grade school.

"You know, I could never watch movies at the foster homes," Jasmine said somberly.

"You're kidding!" Harianne replied.

"I was bounced around so much…there was always a new set of rules to learn."

"How many foster homes did you live in?" Austria asked.

"About ten," Jasmine answered. "My parents were alcoholics. They died when they were still teenagers."

"That angers me so much," Harianne said. "I never could understand why the county couldn't find a family to adopt you."

"No one wants a child as dark as me," Jasmine said. "Don't forget, African Americans have their own racial issues within their own race. The differences between light and dark skin are very real; they're like two breeds apart. And back then few people felt they could afford to be colorblind. Didn't matter if they were black or white—everyone was concerned about it."

"So many celebrities adopt children of all different colors and different hues now," Austria mused.

"Now they do, yeah," Jasmine agreed. "But when we were kids, that wasn't the case. Besides, African-American families very rarely adopt."

"Really? Why is that?" Harianne asked.

"The African-American family feels a disconnect, while the Caucasian family feels different. Caucasian families are more willing now because there are very few Caucasian babies. Any race will do, although most folks prefer Caucasian."

"When we were in grade school, I didn't see any racial problems," Harianne said.

Jasmine looked over at her and made a face. "There were racial tensions. You just didn't have to deal with them. You're so light, you can pass for white, if need be. And you did."

Harianne was silent.

"I mean, your parents did," Jasmine added. "Look, I'm not trying to be mean, it's just a fact. I love your parents—you know that. They did right by you. Just look at the life they gave you: rich family with all the right society connections, big house on the Westside, fabulous vacations every year, the best boarding schools, the best foreign-exchange programs in Europe—hell, I would have loved to have moved in some of those circles. Best of all, you had Austria. And you turned out great, Muffins."

Harianne smiled. "So did you."

"Speaking of your parents," Jasmine said, briskly changing the subject, "have you heard from them lately?"

"They're living in a condo in Kona, Hawaii. They keep an apartment building here in L.A. as income property, but they're busy down there with volunteer work. We talk once a week."

"That's good. Tell them hello for me next time."

"You got it."

Harianne and Jasmine cleared the table while Austria fixed their dessert plates, then the three hurried into the living room to watch the movie. Austria remained focused on the screen while Harianne and Jasmine continued their discussion.

"You know, sometimes I wonder about my childhood and background," Harianne said.

"Why?" Jasmine asked.

Austria looked away from *The Sandpiper* and turned to Harianne. "What? I told you about your parents' plane accident in Tahiti; it happened when you were three years old."

"Yes, but what about their backgrounds?" Harianne asked. "I don't know anything about their heritage."

Austria took a deep breath. "Harianne, you have the strength and character of your father, Andres Volkbacher Duet, and the good graces of your mother, Marissa Belvedere."

"I know, you've told me that before, but—"

"Which one was part African American?" Jasmine broke in.

"Marissa," Austria answered. "She was a beautiful woman—of mixed Irish, Cherokee Indian and African-American ancestry. Many of her friends said that Harianne looked just like her. Harianne's father, on the other hand, was a successful lawyer. Very witty man." She looked at Harianne warmly. "I guess you could say you followed in your father's footsteps. Except he practiced in France as well as the United States. He and your mother made a lovely couple."

"OK, now wait," Jasmine interrupted. "I'm confused, Austria. How do you know so much about Harianne's birth parents?"

Austria smiled. "They hired me to be Harianne's nanny when she was still a baby."

"But then how did you wind up with the DeCanters?" Jasmine asked.

"They were all friends," Austria explained. "After Marissa and Andres were killed, the DeCanters stepped in and adopted Harianne, and asked me to stay on as her nanny. There were no other relatives to take her. They were a godsend, really."

"No shit," Jasmine said. "I mean—sorry, Austria."

Austria reached over and gave Jasmine's arm a loving squeeze. Harianne did the same.

"Did my parents have brothers or sisters?" Harianne asked.

"No, they were both only children."

Harianne shook her head. "Austria, I need to ask you this. I vaguely remember seeing my mother—and seeing a needle going in her arm. I've had dreams about it. But I can't tell who's giving her the shot. It's all a blur."

Austria hesitated. "Your mother was…sick sometimes, Harianne. Sometimes she was bedridden for a week."

"She always had another person in her room, didn't she?"

Austria looked at Harianne thoughtfully. "You were pretty young at the time."

"I know; that's why I'm having such difficulty remembering. I just can't make out—"

"It's been a very long time," Austria said abruptly, and turned back to watch the movie.

Harianne grabbed a wool blanket from the back of the sofa and spread it over Austria, who had drifted off to sleep. She tiptoed into the kitchen to join Jasmine, who was talking on her cellphone.

"Who are you talking to?" Harianne whispered.

"Rikko!" Jasmine responded cheerily. "He says hello."

"Rikko Paracelli?"

"In the flesh, or should I say 'in the smoke.'" She held out her cellphone so Harianne could hear coughs emanating from the tiny speaker. "Rikko, you suck on those cancer sticks so much you'd make a good fire for smoking meats on a smoker."

"Tell him to call me," Harianne said. "I might have something for him."

"Hear that, Rikko? Give Harianne a shout. Listen, I've gotta jump. Talk to you later." She snapped her cellphone shut and turned to Harianne. "What's up?"

"Do you remember I told you about Matthew Daytona?" Harianne asked.

"The rich, bigot lawyer?"

"Jasmine! Contain yourself. Truth. He might be indicted for murder."

"Murder?"

"An attorney in his law firm was found dead. I don't know all the details. He wants me to represent him."

"You haven't practiced criminal law in a while."

Harianne shrugged. "There's a possibility I might return to it; after all, that is where I started out. But he's involved in something shady and I can't put my finger on it."

"How can I help?"

"Find out anything and everything you can about Matthew Daytona."

"You bet. What's your time frame?"

"One week."

"I'll start first thing in the morning."

"Thanks, Jasmine. I don't know what I'd do without you."

Jasmine smiled, and hugged her friend. "Love ya, Muffins! You and Austria are all the family I've got."

# CHAPTER 4

The following Monday morning, Harianne's head was pounding. Even with the Fiorinal medication, the headaches persisted with sharp shooting pains on one side of her head. Concerned and worried, she returned to Dr. Zenfried's office that afternoon. He carefully examined her, and ran several blood tests. He leaned forward in his chair and spoke frankly.

"Harianne, your prolactin levels are very high."

"Prolactin?"

"A protein hormone related to a growth hormone. It is secreted by a broad range of other cells in the body: various immune cells, the brain, the decidua of the pregnant uterus. Its primary target organ is the mammary gland. The stimulating mammary gland and milk production define the functions of this hormone."

"But I have headaches."

"We have to do an MRI. I think there might be a tumor on your pituitary gland."

"A tumor?" she replied, raising her eyebrows in surprise and concern.

"Now, don't get overexcited," he cautioned her. "These tumors are usually benign and are considered to be micro-adenomas, but cause severe headaches until the prolactin level is controlled."

"I have a major case. I have to be—"

"You have to have an MRI, Harianne. It will take all of thirty minutes. I'll schedule it for next week."

Harianne left with an empty feeling in her stomach. She phoned Austria on her cell, but there was no answer. She needed the comfort of a familiar voice.

She tried Jasmine, but there was no answer there either. She headed toward the office.

The firm was bustling with people boxing files and moving furniture; phones rang constantly. China greeted Harianne.

"How's everything?" she asked.

"I'm doing OK," Harianne said. "What's going on?"

"Everyone is packing up files and getting organized. Have you made a decision yet?"

"I think I'm going to start my own firm."

"What about—"

"I sincerely hope you'll come with me, China. I really depend on you. It's a lateral move, but I can't offer any more for a while."

"That's fine."

"First, let me formally tell the partners."

"Sure."

Harianne walked into the managing partner's office and offered her resignation. He told her that she didn't have to attend the final meeting with the partners; it could all be handled on paper. She informed him that she would be taking some clients with her. They agreed to discuss the money allocations later.

When Harianne returned to her office, she found Matthew Daytona waiting for her.

"Matthew! What's wrong?"

"Nothing. I need to talk to you about something that is very private."

"Come in, please." She closed the door behind them. "Water, coffee?"

"No, thank you. Look, I need to level with you."

"About what?"

"Drugs and prostitution."

"What?"

"In the past, I was involved in a drug-and-prostitution ring in Japan."

"You're kidding me."

"I lived in Japan for a while with my uncle, Taka Sousushi. He dealt cocaine and hash, and laundered it through a prostitution ring in Tokyo."

"Well, you just look better and better with time," Harianne said. "I cannot believe you."

"I'm leveling with you before this gets any worse."

"You'd better," Harianne retorted. "What else do I need to know?"

"After my father's death, Uncle Taka raised me in Japan. He's part Japanese. My father and Uncle Taka were half-brothers—same mother, different fathers."

"Do you still deal?"

"Not really. OK, every now and then, but in Japan, not here."

"Anything else?"

"I also practiced law over there for a while."

"This will have to come out in court," Harianne warned. "Do you swear that that is all?"

"The prostitution was controlled by my uncle," Matthew said. "I only dealt with the drugs."

"Crime is crime, Matthew."

Matthew left and Harianne continued to work until dark: closing out files, writing letters, preparing Substitutions of Attorney and Notices of Change of Firm Name and Address to be filed with the court.

When she was finally ready to leave, she took the elevator to the underground parking structure. Her Mercedes was parked in the corner at the north end of the parking lot. The rims were off and all four tires were slashed. Harianne hurried back upstairs and phoned Rikko.

When Harianne returned to her office the next morning, China met her at the door with a concerned look and an urgent message from Detective Tracey Sanders.

# CHAPTER 5

Harianne opened her office door and turned off the fluorescent ceiling lights before turning on the distinctive Craftsman-era Tiffany lamp on her desk. She sat in her chair for a few minutes, taking in the silence of the room, before returning Detective Sanders' call. The headache was getting somewhat better, but it was starting to hurt her eyes. She opened the bottom drawer of her desk, removed a pair of sunglasses, put them on and picked up the telephone.

"Detective Tracey Sanders, please," she said to the voice on the other end.

"One minute, please."

"Detective Sanders."

"It's Harianne DeCanter."

"Uh, uh, uh—"

"I'm returning your call. You called me earlier today? I really don't have a lot of time. I've got a meeting in fifteen minutes."

"Oh, Ms. DeCanter! Yes. I'm sorry, I get so many calls during the day—I was trying to remember who you were. Thanks for calling me back."

"What's going on?" she inquired in a hurried and anxious voice.

"We were at Jasmine Thomas' office earlier this morning. The building manager phoned us. Apparently a person from the cleaning crew found her. She has an assistant, Raquel Nash, but she wasn't available."

"Found her how? What do you mean?"

"I'm sorry, Ms. DeCanter, but Jasmine Thomas was found dead this morning. She was murdered."

"Is this some kind of a joke? Are you sure?"

"Yes, we're sure," he responded in a firm voice.

"Dead? Jasmine? No, that can't be true!"

"I'm sorry, Ms. DeCanter, really, but I need to ask you some questions. Can I, please?"

"I just can't believe what I'm hearing," Harianne sobbed.

"We tried to locate her family, but found no one. How well did you know her? Do you know if she has any family?"

Harianne paused for several seconds before answering him. Clearing her throat, she responded, "Actually, no. I'm her family." She continued sobbing and sniffling.

"We found a tablet of paper with your name on it. Are you related to her?"

"No. We're like sisters, you might say. Jasmine and I were orphans. We've known each other since grade school."

"I see."

"She's working for me. We help each other out from time to time. I'm a lawyer."

"What kind of practice?"

"Civil and some criminal."

"Did Jasmine have any enemies? Anyone that hated her? Did she owe anyone a bad debt? Did she get along with Raquel Nash?"

"No one comes to mind. Not that I know of. Yes, they got along well, as far as I know."

"I'm not trying to pry. I just want answers. There's no coroner's report yet. An autopsy will be performed. Estimated time of death, we think, is between nine and eleven o'clock yesterday evening. It looked like she's a pretty busy private investigator."

"I'm sorry, Detective—"

"Sanders, Tracey Sanders."

"I'm sorry, Detective Sanders, but I'm upset and tired," Harianne replied. "I can't answer any more questions right now, but I need to ask a few. How did she die? Was she shot?"

"No, ma'am. She was raped and suffered blunt-force trauma to the head—she was bludgeoned to death and had a multitude of gashes on her body. There's more, but I can't go into detail at this time. What made you think she was shot?"

"I just assumed."

"No. It was a completely different kind of murder. We're not sure of all the details and particulars. I'd like to meet with you after you've had a chance to take all this in. Do you mind?"

"No. Anything. Just…I'm shocked; it's unbelievable!"

"I'll call you later this evening or tomorrow morning."

Leaning back in her swivel chair, sniffling with tissue close to her nose, Harianne thought about Jasmine. What kind of beast would do something like this? Did it have anything to do with Matthew's case?

"Jasmine!" Harianne moaned. "Who did this to you?"

Lost in thought, Harianne's headache returned before she could get her prescriptions filled. She heard a knock on the door, and lifted her head to see China entering.

"So I guess this means you're leaving?"

"We're both leaving the firm, I hope," Harianne said. "You're coming with me, if you want."

"I'd love to. Hey, what's wrong?"

"Jasmine was murdered yesterday."

"Murdered! She's your best—"

"I don't want to talk about it," Harianne replied firmly. "I've got to find out who did this to her."

"How can I help? Do you want me to start packing up the files and do memos on—"

"Yes!"

Three hours had passed. Dark gray clouds layered the sky and covered the entire Los Angeles basin. Tired, eyes puffed and red, Harianne desperately tried to work; a large pile of files and law books stared her in the face, requesting her undivided attention. But she kept catching herself staring off into space. All brain waves connected to Jasmine. Just as she turned to pick up the phone, it rang.

"Ms. DeCanter, please?"

"This is she."

"Detective Sanders."

"I'm on my way out the door. Can I call you back later?"

"Sure. I'd like to talk to you tomorrow morning."

"Eleven o'clock?"

"That works."

"I don't know how I'll be, Detective Sanders," she said, pulling her jacket from the chair. "I hope I'll be able to help you."

"See you tomorrow at eleven."

Putting her necessary papers, a yellow legal tablet and her Day-Timer in her briefcase, she exited her office and briskly walked to her car, drove out of the building and emerged onto the 10 Freeway headed west. It started to sprinkle, so she slowed her speed to fifty-five miles per hour until traffic congestion brought her to a halt. She sat, waiting, and remembered Jasmine in silent thought.

She came to mind as a little girl with dark chocolate skin, thick hair almost too short to make two ponytails, large gray eyes and—her most memorable feature—a bright smile. Harianne remembered them sitting in the kitchen during Jasmine's frequent overnight stays at the DeCanter home, huddled over large hot-fudge sundaes with bananas that Austria would fix for them. On rainy nights when huge claps of thunder shook the bedroom window, the two little girls would sleep together in one twin bed, pulling the blankets over their heads until they peeked out the next morning, trading socks and walking arm in arm.

It was hard to believe Jasmine was gone forever—her family, her friend and her sister. There had been no time to say goodbye. Harianne cried aloud and promised, "I'll be there with you some day. Love ya, Muffins."

"Love ya, Muffins" had been their secret code. It was the last statement Harianne made to Jasmine the day she left their school to live in another, more upscale area of Los Angeles. Harianne had always considered that the saddest day of her life, but this day was far sadder. The scar in her heart would remain there forever.

Harianne wiped away her last few smears of makeup as she pulled into the driveway of her quiet cottage. She entered the dark foyer and turned off the bright green alarm pad next to the door. Melissa greeted her with wet licks of affection, which she welcomed after this dreadful day.

Thirsty for something to drink, Harianne walked into the kitchen and saw a note on the kitchen center island: *"Off to my knitting class—home around 11. Grilled chicken in the fridge. Love, Austria."*

Glancing into her study down the long hallway, she saw the non-flashing red light on her answering machine; no messages. She continued on to her bedroom and kicked off her shoes, letting them fly in opposite directions, to ease the annoying pain in her toes. She wanted to rest her eyes, so she pulled back the white down comforter on her pine sleigh bed and climbed in. A half-hour later, the 1920s clock on the nightstand read nine o'clock. She noticed a stale taste in her mouth as she awakened from her nap. She lay there for a few minutes, thinking. Suddenly, she remembered Rikko.

Harianne had met Rikko Paracelli six years earlier through Jasmine. Son of an Italian restaurant owner, he was an excellent chef but had chosen to drive limousines rather than cook in the family restaurant. Harianne loved him because he made her laugh; he allowed her to relax. She reached for the white antique phone on her nightstand and dialed his number in Hollywood.

"Hello, Rikko? Are you there?"

There was no response. Harianne heard sporadic sounds of heavy breathing and moaning in the background. Then there was a horrible and very loud cough.

"Rikko?"

"Yuh, yuh," Rikko coughed into the phone. "Yes, I'm here. What's up, darling? You sweet baby!"

"Rikko, do you still have that horrible cough? It sounds awful. Why don't you stop smoking?"

"Don't worry about it, OK?"

"I do worry. You've been smoking for the last ten years, at least as long as I've known you."

"It's not contagious, darling. God forbid!"

"This is ridiculous. You might get cancer."

"Everyone has to die from something. Whaddya need? I'm busy."

"Like what kind of busy? I need a favor."

"Anything for you."

"Are you busy tonight? Can you drive me downtown to Sixth and Olive in the next twenty minutes?"

"Well, uh…uh…uh-huh…Oh, baby! Yeah, baby! Aw, shit!"

"Rikko, I'm serious. I really need your help."

"That feels good! C'mon, baby, more! Right there! Go down!"

"Rikko, what are you doing?"

"Well, I was right in the middle of—"

"Screwing! Rikko, you dog! What's this one's name?"

"Monique. Tonight?"

"Yes. Tonight!"

"It's Monica and I'm leavin'," said a female voice in the background. "Forget it, babe! If you can't remember my name, I'm out of here! Fuck you!"

"Just a minute, Harianne—Hey, Monica! I'm sorry! Please come—"

Harianne listened to footsteps slowly fade away in the background. Out of breath, Rikko returned to the phone.

"I'm not busy now," he said. "What time? You name it."

"Half an hour."

Harianne unscrewed a jar filled with bath crystals on the table next to the tub. The bath felt good after a long, stressful day. She removed her clothes, dropped them on the floor, and carefully sat in the lukewarm water for ten minutes. Then she changed into a pair of designer jeans, a black knit sweater and white leather tie-up shoes. A black comb clamp embraced her light brown curly hair, pulling it back from her face. Melissa looked curiously at the quick change of clothes.

When she heard the sound of a car door closing in the driveway, Harianne grabbed her black leather jacket and headed downstairs. In the foyer, she peeped out the side windows.

"Rikko, is that you?"

"Yeah! It's me."

She opened the door slowly as the smell of cigarette smoke wafted through the door. At age forty-five, Rikko Paracelli was a great friend to her despite his fast lifestyle. He hadn't aged much since she'd last seen him. He was still good-looking: Italian, of medium build, six feet tall, with black curly hair and a wonderfully seductive voice.

"Come in," Harianne said. "I'll explain our mission."

"Mission?" He looked puzzled.

"Rikko, Jasmine was murdered this morning."

"Murdered!" Rikko yelled. "What?"

Harianne briefly relayed what little she knew about the details of Jasmine's death.

"I thought I saw something in the newspaper about two women murdered the same way," Rikko said.

"Really?" Harianne said. "I wonder if that's what the detective wants to discuss tomorrow."

"It sounds like a serial killer," Rikko replied seriously.

Harianne started to cry. "There's more to it and I'm going to find out what it is."

"What do you mean by 'more to it'?"

"I sent Jasmine on a private investigation of an attorney. She never phoned me back, not even one message. That's not like her. We talked every day. I had no idea whether she'd gotten into trouble. We're a family."

"You're really the only thing she had. How can I help?"

Rikko walked toward her, put his arms around her and ran his hands through her hair. Wiping her tears away, she pulled away from him and slipped into her jacket.

"For starters, her office is downtown. That's where we're going."

"No problem. The gas tank is filled, and I'll take you anywhere. But don't you think it's a little dangerous?"

"A little dangerous? A lot! I don't care. I've got to know the truth. It bothers me."

"OK," he said, concerned. "But it could get sticky, Harianne."

They walked down the driveway toward a black Lincoln Town Car with tinted windows; Rikko opened the passenger door for Harianne then took the wheel. They headed downtown and took the Sixth Street exit. At Olive Rikko hung a hard left into an alley next to an early-'50s brick building. He turned off the headlights and slowly coasted down the alley. They stopped in front of the third door, marked "Unit C." Harianne jumped out of the right side of the car closest to the fence, while Rikko grabbed a flashlight and his gun.

"A gun!" Harianne exclaimed.

"Hey, you never know," Rikko said. "It's a jungle out here. I'm drivin' all over L.A. and the streets are rough. Don't worry, it'll be all right."

They walked carefully to the door, making as little noise as possible.

"Look," Rikko said, pointing. "There's yellow tape and it says 'KEEP OUT.'"

"I figured that. It's just crisscross tape across the door jam. We'll tape it back. I don't have to break anything. Jasmine gave me a key a long time ago."

"OK. Go for it! But you'd better wear these." Rikko pulled two pairs of black leather gloves from his coat pocket and handed a pair to Harianne. She looked him in the eye.

"You think of everything. That's why—"

"Just get to work. We don't have much time."

Harianne put the gloves on and put the key in the door. Giving it a wiggle, she turned the key to the left and it finally opened. The office was dark, cold—and ransacked. Chairs were upended, drawers had been pulled out onto the floor and papers were scattered about the room; empty Coke cans rolled across the floor.

"The intruders were looking for something," Harianne said quietly.

She and Rikko moved toward the middle of the room. They kept the lights off. Jasmine's desk was in a corner near the window, facing the inside corridor of the building. Looking behind their backs, they approached the desk and focused Rikko's flashlight on the entire desk as if it was a telescope.

“Where do we start?” Rikko asked.

“I haven’t a clue. Except—”

“What?”

“The pink and blue flowerboxes in the glass cabinet by the desk. She told me that she kept important papers in the pink box and condoms, damning information on people and lawyers in the blue box. Most of the bad lawyers were kept in the blue box. I think; I could be wrong. At least that’s what she told me.”

Harianne tried to open the cabinet, but it was locked.

“Do you see a key anywhere? Look in the desk,” she said, motioning to Rikko.

Rikko looked in all of the drawers but nothing was in sight. Piles of papers were on top of the desk. He moved them away with his hands only to find a Chinese ginger jar. When he lifted the jar, something like loose change or keys could be heard inside. He took the lid off to find the entire jar was filled with keys.

“Well, good luck. This could take us all night. There are enough keys in here for two prisons.”

“Oh, don’t be silly! One of them must fit the cabinet. Give me the jar. I’ll look for it.”

Rikko handed the jar to Harianne and she rummaged through the jar with her delicate fingers. But there were too many keys; she couldn’t find it. She smashed the cabinet lock with a metal paperweight sitting on the desk.

“Yeah, right,” Rikko urged her. “Let’s hurry up. This place gives me the creeps. The smell, the odor, the walls, the rug—all the smells. It reminds me of a morgue.”

“Calm down! We’ve got a lot of paper to muddle through.”

Harianne removed the blue box from the cabinet and placed it on top of the desk. As she glanced through all the papers, she came to an account ledger listing all of the cases Jasmine had been working on. Most of them were lawyers, including Matthew Daytona, and had been clients of Jasmine’s for the last six months. The only distinct difference was that most of the lawyers had the letters “ND” marked by their names, while the others had a “D” marked by their names. Amazed that she was even in Jasmine’s office and reading through her papers, Harianne’s mood turned sour when she spotted Matthew name. It was marked with “JD.”

“What does ‘JD’ mean?” she asked as she studied the names on the ledger.

"Now what?" Rikko asked. "You can't just sit there all night and read. We're not supposed to even be in here. It's a crime scene."

"Rikko, chill!"

"Well then, let me read some. Doesn't she have a computer?"

"Yeah, it's over there, but she always keeps a hard copy of everything she does. Thanks but no thanks for the help. I can do this. If you want to help, just keep looking out the window to the alley in case someone comes."

Two chilly hours later, Rikko peered out through the Venetian blinds; he could hear male voices echoing in the corridor, but he couldn't see anyone yet. He hissed at Harianne.

"Hurry up! Someone's coming!"

"Got it—let's go!"

Putting his fingers to his mouth and tiptoeing toward Harianne, Rikko pointed to the closet across the room. They could hear the voices grow closer.

"I don't know why this can't wait until morning, Tracey."

"I need to find some information on Thomas' death. I could be wrong."

"You're right. I was in the middle of the best pepperoni pizza and a classic movie when you called."

"Ease up, Zack! This information has to be here."

"What kind of information?"

"About Matthew Daytona."

"I'm with you, partner, but it could wait until tomorrow."

"Did you feed your animals earlier?"

"Yeah! Why?"

"Nothing. You just have so many animals and you're never home to take care of them."

"Tracey, don't worry about it. You don't have to be responsible for anything but yourself. You're so bitter."

"Sometimes I just forget what comes out."

The voices stopped. Rikko grabbed Harianne's hand and she grabbed the boxes. But the closet door was locked. Rikko broke the lock with his pocket-knife and they ducked into the closet just as Tracey and Zack entered the office.

"There's got to be more information in her files," Tracey said. "Zack, check the files in her desk drawer. Usually that's a good place. You know, current files she's working on."

"OK," said Zack, shaking his head as he walked to the messy desk.

"That's Detective Sanders," Harianne whispered nervously to Rikko. "Do you think they saw the car in the alley?"

"No," he whispered back to her. "It's pretty dark, and I parked it pretty far away. They came in the front door. We came in the back."

Tracey pulled out the bottom left drawer of Jasmine's desk. With a quick glance, he assessed the alphabetical files in the Pendeflex folders. He pulled out the files from the "A" divider and perused them carefully. Then he pulled "J" and found one labeled "Japanese Drug Cartel." Nothing jogged his memory in connection with the murder.

But one file in the "B" divider did: Matthew Daytona's. There it was. Tracey's mind began racing with every thought imaginable.

"Hey, Zack, look! Our illustrious lawyer of Beverly Hills."

"Matthew Daytona?"

"Who else? Bernstein's partner."

"Really! Whaddya have?"

"There's one name in the file: Harianne DeCanter."

"Well, what else?"

"There's a file labeled 'Japanese Drug Cartel.' Nothing is in it. You see, Zack, Harianne DeCanter's friend is a private investigator who was probably investigating Matthew. Matthew got wind of it."

"Couldn't be! Are you sure? Give me the file. Let me take a look."

Tracey handed the file to Zack with a convincing pat on the shoulder.

"I've got him and her."

"What do you mean? So it says 'Harianne DeCanter.' So what? We still don't know if he murdered Jasmine Thomas or Shana Bernstein."

"True, Zack. But why is her name in Matthew Daytona's file? Remember that night we followed him to Prego's Restaurant?"

"Yeah. He was eating dinner with a young lady. We don't know if it was Harianne DeCanter, though."

"Yeah, that's true. But I think I'm right. Jasmine is black, so it wasn't her."

"Harianne's a civil litigation lawyer, though, not a criminal lawyer. I checked it out." Zack scratched his head.

"She was a criminal defense lawyer and got a heavy-duty murder suspect off," Tracey replied, pacing the floor. "She won. I did some research on her too."

"When?"

"When the first officers found her name on the tablet of paper here the other day. She's the lawyer on the front page of that *California Lawyer* magazine you showed me."

"Yeah, I remember. But what you've got to keep in mind is that they're both lawyers. Maybe he knows her on a personal level."

"No! We've got him. I'll talk to her tomorrow at her office. There's a connection and it will come together soon. I love puzzles. Grab the ledger, Zack, and let's go. I'll have the guys make a photocopy."

Tracey put the files back in the drawer. They walked out the door, locked it and proceeded down the corridor.

"Harianne!" Rikko hissed. "Let's get out of here, now!"

"OK. I'm taking the blue flowerbox with me. Put the pink flowerbox back for me, please. Did you notice that they didn't even check the glass cabinet?"

"Yeah, yeah! C'mon!"

Harianne took the blue flowerbox, locked the back door and left. Loose gravel in the alley crunched beneath their feet as they hurried to the car. Rikko opened the door for Harianne then hurriedly hopped in himself. He carefully backed out the long alley to Olive Street. He found Tracey and Zack standing out on the sidewalk waiting to cross, looking him dead in the eye.

# CHAPTER 6

Harianne awakened the next morning alongside Melissa, who was silently dreaming as her paws fluttered in synchronized motion. It was cold and damp in the canyon, with the usual early morning mist. Concerned and worried about Rikko, Harianne grabbed the cordless phone next to her bed and called him.

"Rikko! It's Harianne. Are you all right?"

"Yeah, I'm tough. But that was a close call last night. Good thing I've got those tinted windows, eh?"

"I know. But it'll be fine. The detectives are coming to the office to question me in about three hours. I'm the one who should be ready to jump over the bridge. I'll stay in touch."

"OK. Bye, Harianne."

Coffee was the first thing on the agenda after making the bed, followed by six miles on the treadmill while making notes on a yellow tablet about Matthew Daytona. The treadmill loudly beeped when it reached six miles. She took towels from the nearby shelf, wrapped one around her head and the other around her neck to keep her body temperature stable. The fresh aroma of coffee enveloped every room. She poured her coffee, sat down at the farmhouse table located conveniently in the middle of the kitchen, and contemplated the blue flowerbox at the other side of the table. Still chewing the last pieces of her toast, she reached across and lifted the lid, curious. Yellow ruled ledgers were perfectly placed in alphabetical order with metal dividers in between. She didn't have far to read to reach the letter "D" for Daytona. The Daytona ledger revealed the Japanese drug exchanges in Japan. Notated by Matthew Daytona's names were the letters "JD" and "C." On another page she found short synopses of other lawyers; the letters "JD" and "C" did not appear anywhere. Nor did they appear on any of the other ledgers, which had no marks on them. Harianne recognized Jasmine's handwriting; she had written in blue pen on all of the ledgers. She knew that the only person who knew anything and everything about Japan would be Matthew, but she wasn't ready to reveal her new discovery.

"Jasmine, what were you into?" Harianne asked herself in silence.

Harianne quickly got ready for work and waved goodbye to Melissa. She had Jasmine's memorial service to plan, and she still needed to find a new office and organize the move. She only had a few days left to prepare for a trial for an AIDS-afflicted doctor, but her mind stayed focused on Jasmine and Matthew.

Very pressed for time at her office, she wrote memos for the files she was leaving behind, dictated notices of appearances, BAJI jury instructions and other necessary trial documents. At eleven o'clock China knocked on the door and opened it slightly.

"Excuse me, Harianne, you've got a Detective Sanders and a Detective Grimes here to see you."

"Fine. Show them in."

China ushered the detectives into Harianne's office and softly closed the door.

"Hello, detectives," Harianne said.

"Ms. DeCanter," Tracey replied.

"Ma'am," Zack said with a nod.

"Please sit down, gentlemen. Coffee?"

"No, thanks, we're fine."

"We'd like to ask you some questions about the murder of Jasmine Thomas, if you don't mind," Zack told her.

"No, I'm OK," Harianne said. "Go ahead." She sat back in her chair in a comfortable position. Zack and Tracey sat directly across from her with piercing looks on their face. Tracey did most of the talking while Zack stared at Harianne like he was seeing right through her.

"Ms. DeCanter, as you know, the body of Jasmine Thomas was discovered in her office," Tracey began. "When we responded to the call from the building manager, we found her dead on the toilet seat in the bathroom. She was completely naked and, from the looks of it, she was raped. Streams of urine were lined across the toilet seat, running down the side of the toilet to the floor. We found a multitude of contusions, deep gashes to the head and eyes with a blunt instrument, and a red silk scarf wrapped around her neck. There were no signs of drugs at the scene."

Harianne began to cry intensely.

"You have no heart," she sobbed.

"Yes, I—"

"No, you don't. I bet you've never lost anyone in your life."

"That's not true." Tracey dropped his head.

"How's that?" Harianne looked up wiping her eyes.

Tracey looked her in the eye. "I'm intuitive and I look for a person with good morals and values." He fished for something in his pocket. "Tissue?"

"I've got some, thanks," Harianne said. "I can't believe what you've told me. That is cruel."

"It's not a very pretty world out there," Zack said. "We think we're dealing with a serial killer. It's still just speculation, but we think we know who's behind it."

"You do? Who is it?"

"I'm sorry, but we can't divulge that information," Tracey said. "You know that."

"Yes," Harianne sighed. "Excuse me for being brazen."

"It's OK. I know all you lawyers love to try us."

"What does that mean?"

"Nothing."

"Detective, I don't like your attitude."

"You don't have to. When was the last time you saw Jasmine Thomas?"

"I didn't. We're both so busy. She works on cases until late at night and I'm usually working late as well. I spoke to her on the phone the other evening. Actually, I was calling for a status report, but she never returned my phone call."

"Really. The status of what? Did she say anything was wrong with one of her cases? Anybody mad at her? Can you remember?'

"No. Nothing! I wish I knew. Jasmine never had any enemies, not even in her line of work. At least no one that I knew about. We're pretty close—like sisters. Neither of us had any siblings."

"I see. Can you tell me one more thing?"

"Sure."

"What is your connection to Matthew Daytona?"

Harianne sharply turned her head in surprise, and her eyes rolled away from Tracey to take a quick glance out the window. Concerned, she hesitated.

"Excuse me," Tracey said. "Did I say anything wrong?"

"No," Harianne replied, looking back at him.

"We found your name in one of her files. Can you explain that?"

"I hired her to work for me. I just told you that."

"Why?"

"That's none of your business."

"Fine. I'll find out anyway. Ms. DeCanter, we're looking at Matthew Daytona as the primary and only suspect in the murder of Shana Bernstein, who was also murdered the same way as Jasmine Thomas."

"You think they're connected? Matthew Daytona is a very prominent attorney in the legal community."

"So you're familiar with him?"

"I didn't say that. He's my client. I'm representing him in this case." She stood and straightened papers on her desk. "Are you finished? I've got to review these letters and finalize the funeral services for Jasmine."

"No more questions," Tracey said, "but we'll be in touch."

Zack and Tracey walked through the lobby toward the elevators.

"What did you think, Tracey?"

"I don't know. I don't know."

Tracey and Zack returned to the station and ran composites of Matthew Daytona against others. Zack phoned one of Shana Bernstein's neighbors, Amy Kanter.

"Hello, Ms. Kanter. This is Detective Zack Grimes. I'd like to ask you a few more questions. Did you see a man with a Rolls Royce at Ms. Bernstein's home in the past?"

"Actually, yes. He was always there in the evenings, mostly."

"Thank you, Ms. Kanter."

The phone rang and Zack picked up.

"Detective Grimes."

"Forensics. We found heavy doses of cocaine, plus traces of saline and seminal fluid in your vic. Ms. Bernstein was definitely raped."

"What about Jasmine Thomas?"

"The same."

"Thanks, Nick. I'll tell Tracey."

Tracey sat at his desk, sipping coffee. Memories of Marina rushed back as he mulled over Harianne's statement regarding the funeral services for Jasmine. Sad and distraught, he sat as if in a trance until Zack interrupted.

"Hey, Tracey! Are you all right?"

"I'm fine. Just thinking about Marina. I just can't stop thinking about her. When I think I've got it licked, it returns."

"Sorry, man. Listen, forensics just phoned. Our ladies had heavy doses of cocaine in their systems. And they're both victims of rape."

"You're kidding! Both of them?"

"Yep!"

"OK. I'll make a note of the findings."

Still in her office, Harianne phoned close friends and told them about Jasmine. "Services are scheduled for Saturday morning at eleven o'clock at Forest Lawn" was her standard statement throughout the day.

Harianne left the office and headed home to Austria. Austria's light was on in her cottage living room. The television was on with the volume turned down low. Harianne knocked and entered. Austria sat knitting at a very rapid pace.

"Hello, Austria."

"Hello, Harianne. How are you?"

"Fine. Are you OK?"

"Yes, dear," Austria replied. "Why?"

"I'm afraid I've got some bad news."

"What?"

"Jasmine died the other evening."

"Oh, my God! What happened?"

"It was a brutal murder. I'd rather not tell you all of the details right now, but I'll tell you soon. She's gone."

Harianne's knees gave way and she fell onto the sofa in front of her. She rested her head in Austria's lap and cried continuously. Austria felt Harianne's pain and cried too.

"She was like a sister to you. I'll miss her terribly. Who would do such a thing?"

"I don't know, but I'll find out," Harianne replied.

Austria hugged Harianne tight, placed her hand in hers and comforted her, pulling the tissues from the Kleenex box on the end table.

Harianne began to rub her temples and hold one side of her head.

"Are you still having those headaches?" Austria asked.

"Yeah. They're really bad. I can't seem to get rid of them, but I'm trying."

"Have you been to see the doctor?"

"Yes. I forgot to tell you—he wants me to have an MRI next week."

"Why?"

"He thinks it might be a tumor. On my pituitary gland."

Harianne began to cry nonstop. Austria stroked her hair and tried to comfort her.

"Ssh, Harianne. Everything will be fine. You're just having a tough time right now. I'm here for you."

# CHAPTER 7

Zack and Tracey simultaneously arrived at the precinct at eight o'clock the following morning, parking beside each other. Sluggish Zack emerged from his car with a loud yawn. Tracey patiently waited for him in the middle of the parking lot.

"Hey, Zack, how ya doing? Do you feel all right?"

"Yeah. I'm fine. Didn't get much sleep, ya know?"

They proceeded down the long cement walkway and through the double glass doors of the precinct.

"And why not? Are your animals keeping you up at night?"

"Very funny, Tracey. No! They sleep through the night. It's me. I'm having a hard time sleeping. I keep thinking about Eve and when she'll come home with those pristine blue eyes. I can just see that wavy dark hair, and smell her peach-almond cologne. Man, that shit drives me crazy."

"She's not coming back, Zack. She's just not. You're going to have to accept that, buddy. I know of a good—"

"Shrink? No shrinks! No way, Tracey! I'll work it out myself."

"I know, but you're still—"

"Trying to work it out myself. *Capish*?"

Zack was trying to show Tracey that he was strong, but deep inside he had a soft spot. Tracey knew he yearned for the happy home life, not one filled with pizza and beer and dead silence.

Their conversation turned to the Bernstein and Thomas murder cases as they climbed the steps to their office on the second floor.

"Well, what do you think?" Zack asked.

"Let's talk to the coroner again," Tracey suggested, "and take one last look at Bernstein's body. I want another look at the vaginal area. I want to make sure we're dealing with identical MOs."

"I need coffee first," Zack said

"OK. Grab me a cup, too."

"Cream?"

"A little."

Zack walked into the kitchen, where three detectives were sitting, two with smirks on their faces. The third, Carter McHale, was short and thin with blond hair and a small scar on the right side of his face. He stared aimlessly at Zack as he entered the room and poured coffee into two tall Styrofoam cups. When Zack reached for a canister of cream, McHale forcefully hit his hand, knocking the cream to the floor.

"Don't reach over me, you fat punk!"

"What the…?" Zack sputtered.

"Looks like you guys will never get your high-class lawyer murderer," McHale taunted him.

Zack didn't respond. He opened the door to the other cabinet nearest him and grabbed another canister of cream. McHale grabbed it from his hands. Zack's entire body started to shake with anger.

"You're a loser," McHale told him. "Even your wife knew that. That's why she left you. Asshole!"

McHale turned back toward his seat. Zack jumped him from behind, kicked his knees in with his heavy feet and knocked him to the floor. McHale was face down on the ground when Tracey entered the room.

"Hey, what the fuck's going on here?"

"Nothing! McHale was being an asshole to me. Weren't you, McHale?" Zack straightened his tie and blazer. "Get your coffee, Tracey, and let's go."

Looking at the detectives in the room, Tracey picked up the coffee cups and followed Zack to their office. He set the cups on the desk and pushed away the massive paper mountain.

"What went on in there?" he asked as Zack slammed the door shut.

"He started making fun of my weight."

"What? C'mon! Fuck him! McHale's been on the force for years and he's about to be moved up."

"I guess he has no shame. He feels he's above me."

"Zack, quit putting yourself down. Stop it!"

"I know I shouldn't, but maybe he's right about some things."

"Oh, you won't listen to me, but all of a sudden you're taking advice from Carter McAsshole with five ex-wives back in Montana? Thanks."

Tracey yanked out his laptop and started making notes.

"We've got our work cut out for us today, Zack. Let's get busy."

Zack took off his jacket, threw it over the back of the chair next to him, rolled up the sleeves to his white shirt and sat down slowly.

"OK, I'm ready," he said, cracking a smile. The old Zack was back, better than ever.

Tracey sipped coffee and paced the floor back and forth, sometimes circling the room. He abruptly turned around and faced Zack.

"How is Harianne DeCanter involved with this case? I didn't want to ask her about that at first since we were investigating the murder of Shana Bernstein. It wasn't relevant at the time, but maybe it is now."

"How do you figure?"

"I don't quite know yet. Why is her name in the file with Matthew Daytona?"

"That's her client. She's Jasmine's best friend. That explains her name."

"Yeah, yeah, but why was Matthew's name in Jasmine's files?"

"They both know him."

"He was the last one seen with Shana Bernstein. Jasmine Thomas is just another innocent victim, as far as we know. Do you see any connection besides Daytona—and Harianne DeCanter?"

"Not yet."

Tracey grabbed a bottle of water from the fridge, walked to his desk, picked up a magazine and started reading. Zack sat at his desk chewing gum and perusing the stacks of paperwork on this desk.

"What's that?" he asked, gesturing toward the magazine.

"*California Lawyer*," Tracey answered. "Harianne DeCanter's specialty is civil litigation and corporate transactional."

"You took it from the law office? When did you start reading *California Lawyer*?"

"It doesn't matter. I'm reading it now."

Zack leaned back in his chair and placed his feet on the desk. "I knew you'd like her. She's a real catch, that one!"

"Oh, please! I'm trying to read up on her specialty. I don't know why she's so interested in criminal law. It's not her specialty."

"Uh-huh."

"OK," Tracey relented with a sheepish look. "I will say this: she's smart."

"And?"

"And…beautiful."

Zack grinned.

"Listen," Tracey said, getting serious. "We need a search warrant for blood, hair follicles and saliva. I want this bastard!"

"Judge Landers," Zack suggested.

"Yeah, he'll grant the warrant."

"I'll have Marnetta prepare the papers. It shouldn't take long."

Tracey remained in the office and phoned Harianne at her office.

"Hello, Ms. DeCanter?"

"Yes. Who's this?"

"Tracey Sanders. Listen, I just wanted to say that I'm sorry about your friend. I know it hurts."

"Thank you. Did you find out who did this?"

"No. But, we're working on it. Don't worry. We'll get the person."

"I'm so upset about this. I feel responsible."

"How's that?"

"I asked her to do some investigative work for me."

"May I ask what it was?"

"It's personal."

"Well, this is personal," Tracey said. He cleared his throat. "I like you. I'd like to take you to dinner some time."

Harianne paused before responding. "Sounds good."

"I'll be in touch."

After Zack submitted the request for a warrant, he and Tracey returned to the coroner's office, just two blocks away from the precinct. They took one more look at Shana Bernstein.

"Doctor, forensics said she had enough cocaine in her body to OD," Tracey said. "Do you agree?"

"Yeah, but I have some reservations. Was she a coke addict?"

"We don't know," Tracey said, pacing the floor. "We're still looking into that."

"Her lifestyle was pretty normal, according to her neighbor," Zack commented. "I would say no, but who am I to say?"

"I'm with you," the medical examiner agreed. "Nice-looking lady. On the surface it seems like the typical high-life lawyer coke addict, L.A. style, but it somehow doesn't add up. Maybe I'm speculating. Either way, her body sustained extensive blunt-force trauma. She had contusions and abrasions on her forehead, nose, neck, back of head and abdomen."

Zack placed his hands on his hips and tilted his head. "To hell with the coke, those are serious injuries. Whaddya think, Tracey?"

"I don't know what to think!" he exclaimed. "About this whole damn case. The mere fact that Daytona was the last and only person with Bernstein the night of the murder and wears the same type of red scarves that were wrapped around her neck concerns me." He placed his hand on Shana's leg, pushing it aside slightly and looking more closely at the vaginal area.

"She fought back with a vengeance even though she was defeated," the ME stated.

"That's for sure," Tracey said. He pulled the sheet back over Shana. "Let me see Jasmine Thomas' body."

"You're in luck. We're just about to call the funeral home."

Tracey and Zack followed the medical examiner to the other room just down the hall. "Zack said the findings were conclusive," Tracey said.

"Yes. It was the same."

The medical examiner pulled out the long drawer, and unveiled the slender, black body of Jasmine Thomas.

"Now you know, guys, because she is so dark in complexion, the scars and abrasions will be harder to see."

"Punk, you're an ass!" Zack swore, shaking his head. "What, you have some problem with dark-skinned people? I've been doing this for twenty-some years—over 100 bodies, more than 500 blood samples, broken necks, yadday-addayadda. I'd say we've got the routine down to a science, wouldn't you?"

"Hey, guys, I'm sorry. I know you know the routine. The vaginal area was completely ripped to shreds; pieces of wilted and wrinkled skin were hanging from the clitoris and the vagina. The inner thighs were scraped thin like paper—the obvious signs of a serious and violent struggle to live. Who knows?"

"Tracey," Zack said, motioning him forward. "She looks even worse than Bernstein."

"That's for sure," Tracey agreed. "That's pretty bad. Damn him! OK, I think we've had enough. Thank you, doctor."

As they walked toward the car, Tracey was quiet. He got in and looked over at a nearby playground where three little girls were playing on a swing set, all different nationalities.

"You know it's amazing how three innocent young girls don't have advance warnings of predators," Tracey said. "Life is real difficult sometimes."

"Especially these days," Zack agreed.

By noon they were back at the precinct, where their secretary, Marnetta Hughes, was diligently working on the papers for the hearing. She didn't even raise her head to glance at the detectives, looking straight ahead at her computer monitor as she typed.

"They're not ready yet, guys."

Tracey and Zack worked on other files in their office while they waited. A half-hour later, Marnetta entered and handed Tracey the documents in a manila folder.

"Well, everything looks in order," Tracey said. "If Daytona doesn't cooperate with the DNA, we're ready." He looked over at Zack. "Somehow he just doesn't seem like the cooperating type."

"Yeah. I think we're ahead of him."

The next morning, a judge granted their request for a search warrant on Matthew Daytona. At noon, they arrived at the law firm of Daytona, Bernstein & McDunn. The receptionist was on the phone when they approached her.

"Yes?"

"Detective Grimes and Detective Sanders," Zack said. "We're here to see Matthew Daytona."

"Have a seat. I'll tell him you're here."

A few minutes later, Matthew Daytona sauntered into the reception area.

"Yes, detectives. How can I help you?"

"Is there some place private we could talk?"

Matthew turned to the receptionist. "Erin, is the main conference room available?"

"Yes," she said. "Do you want a regular setup?"

"No, that's not necessary," he replied. "This visit will be short."

Tracey and Zack followed Matthew down the long hallway to the conference room. Matthew opened the door, allowing them to enter first, and then carefully closed it behind him as the staff looked on.

"What's on your mind, gentlemen?"

Zack and Tracey both looked Matthew straight in the eye. Tracey paused and cleared his throat before speaking first.

"Well, we've got a problem here, Mr. Daytona. Our findings point to you. Apparently, you were the last person with Shana Bernstein. In fact, you were at her house a lot."

"What are you getting at? Of course I was at Shana's house a lot. We're friends—longtime friends."

"I'm sure you were. Murder victims are usually killed by friends or people close to them."

Matthew's expression changed drastically. His eyebrows went higher as surprise then fury crossed his face.

"I'm calling my lawyer now! Don't ask me any more questions!"

"That's not quite possible," Tracey said. "You see, we want you to take a DNA test."

"Why?"

"We want to make sure that no stone is left unturned, you might say."

"No way! I want to speak to my lawyer first."

Tracey reached inside his coat and retrieved a manila envelope from the inside pocket. He carefully pulled out the search warrant and placed it on the table. Matthew, startled, read the contents then raised his head slowly.

"I'll contact my lawyer. Please leave."

Tracey and Zack walked closer and stood directly in front of Matthew.

"You'll comply," Tracey said in a firm voice. "You've got no choice. We're not leaving, and we don't mind waiting while you call your lawyer."

Matthew excused himself and returned to his office, where he quickly phoned Harianne. He broke out in a hot sweat as he was dialing.

"Matthew?"

He reached across his desk, grabbed a tissue and patted his forehead dry.

"Yeah, it's me. Get this shit! These guys are causing me a lot of grief. I've got a law firm to run and a reputation to uphold. They've got their nerve."

"Matthew, you sound positively panicked. Tell me what's going on." Harianne sensed that any soothing words she might try to say right now would not trigger in Mathew's brain.

"The detectives just served me with a search warrant for a DNA test."

"DNA?" she echoed, somewhat shocked.

"Yes!"

"OK. Calm down. Listen to me. You know you've got to comply with the warrant. Otherwise, they'll arrest you outright."

"Yeah, but I wasn't with—"

"It doesn't matter. We're dealing with the real thing now. You were worried about this when we first met; we speculated, and now it's a reality. Come clean with them. It's negative. We know that."

"Damn straight it's negative!" Matthew paced the floor back and forth, rubbing his hands and nails through his hair.

"Then quit worrying," Harianne advised him. "Where is the test?"

"Mortimer Lab. Obviously, it's their lab."

"Fine. I'll call you at the office or you call me when you return."

"This is fucking unbelievable!"

"No, it's not. They're doing their job."

Half an hour later, a Mortimer Lab technician escorted Matthew into a cold, private room and asked him to have a seat. The technician retrieved a white plastic instrument, a blue cap, a collection card, a piece of paper and an envelope from a drawer.

"What type of DNA test are you conducting?" Matthew asked.

"Buccal DNA Collection. I'm going to place the collector in your mouth and press up against your cheek and then firmly drag it toward your lips. I will have to do this several times, so I'll need your cooperation. First I need to complete the Database Collection Card."

Matthew patiently answered the technician's questions for the collection card: Social Security number, date of birth, first, middle and last name. Then he rolled his right thumb on the card and signed it. The technician completed the form with additional information from his records.

"'The process,'" Matthew muttered derisively. "It's a waiting game."

While Matthew took the DNA test, Tracey and Zack decided to search his home, a gray-stone mansion not far from his Beverly Hills office. A petite Mexican woman wearing a white apron greeted them at the front door.

Tracey took the lead and held the search warrant in front of her face. Her fear was apparent as she started to cry and shake. Zack tried to calm her with the little bit of Spanish that he could speak. After blocking their way for several minutes, she opened the door further and allowed them to enter.

Tracey and Zack made a beeline for the master bedroom. Zack opened the door of the closet and saw a dark blue box; inside, he found at least fifty red silk scarves. He raised his hand and motioned for Tracey to come closer. Satisfied with their findings, they continued searching the house, but uncovered no other incriminating evidence. They took the box of scarves and headed for forensics.

# CHAPTER 8

Saturday became the darkest memory of Harianne's life.

In the morning she rose and watched rain fall hard on her brick walkway, creating a little rushing river to the curb. A black linen suit hung outside her bedroom armoire on a gold hook, with black pumps beneath it, marking the official day of Jasmine's funeral.

As usual, Harianne had been unable to sleep, but this time it wasn't because of headaches. Grabbing her robe and a framed picture of herself and Jasmine, she stumbled down the stairs to the kitchen to make a pot of coffee for herself and Austria. In the refrigerator she found a loaf of wheat bread sitting next to a carton of vanilla-flavored cream. It somehow seemed fitting. A strong cup of black coffee with a little cream and lightly buttered wheat toast helped to ease the stomachache that was troubling her. She looked out over her backyard as she ate, clenching the picture frame in her other hand so tightly that she felt the engravings on top imprint her fingers. Thoughts of Jasmine never left Harianne's mind as she and Austria silently readied themselves for Jasmine's funeral service.

They were the first mourners to arrive at Forest Lawn Mortuary, located next to Griffith Park between Hollywood and Burbank. They seated themselves in the first of six rows of chairs situated in front of Jasmine's white casket. Raquel, Jasmine's assistant, arrived shortly afterward; she greeted Harianne with a hug and a gardenia. Harianne clenched the gardenia tightly and cried. Rain dampened the spring assortment of flowers draping Jasmine's casket.

Harianne wept in silence as she surveyed the surrounding expanse of luscious lawns resembling green velvet. Drying the last tear from her eye with a tissue, she bid Jasmine farewell, placing two dozen white and yellow roses on her casket. "I'll miss you, little sister. You'll always be my equal in my life. But most of all, you're my hero. All we had was each other. I'll do this for you. You sleep on, my sweet sister, sleep on."

Three days later, sleek, wet streets in Los Angeles caused an array of car crashes while gusty winds blew rain at a slant; seemingly no one knew how to drive in the rain on the city's crowded roadways. Freeways were flooded with cars and beaming white headlights. The weather was the main topic on every news station, with forecasts predicting fog and rain for the entire day.

Tracey phoned Harianne at home.

"Ms. DeCanter?"

"Yes."

"Detective Sanders here. We've found a box of red silk scarves that possibly might match the scarf wrapped around Jasmine's neck. We're in the preliminary stages of—"

Harianne began to cry.

"Where?"

"I'd rather not say because this case is very involved."

"I'm sorry. It's just that—I just buried her two days ago. I'm still grieving and angry."

Tracey could hear the hurt and sorrow in her crackling voice as she spoke. She was still trying to come to grips with the truth that her best friend did not die from natural causes, but was murdered.

"I know, it's hard," he replied in a low voice. "I've been there."

Harianne decided to stay at home and concentrate on the blue flowerbox. The names in Jasmine's notes were unusual, yielding no faces and no clues. Only Jasmine had the answers she needed.

Matthew woke up and hit the treadmill, running almost four miles in three minutes. His heart beat faster and faster as he worked out; sweat poured down his face and the water beads stood firm on his face. He showered and donned a double-breasted gray suit and a yellow silk tie with gray polka dots. As he looked in the mirror, he wondered if this would be the last time he would be able to wear his favorite suit. The thought of it made him crazy. He started getting hot and almost fainted into a chintz chair nearby.

When he finally staked full control over his fears, he hurried into the kitchen and poured a cup of hot coffee from the automatic coffee maker he had preset the night before. He departed for work in his black Mercedes 500SL, one of six in his collection. He parked in his usual visible place in the office garage and strode confidently through the doors of Daytona, Bernstein & McDunn. He greeted Erin and turned toward his office just as two men in dark suits approached him from behind.

"Mr. Daytona," Tracey began.

"God! You startled me. I didn't see you sitting there."

"We could tell by your reaction. Can we see you in your office?"

Matthew began to sweat again, which prompted him to pull a handkerchief from the inside pocket of his blazer. As they walked down the hall corridor, a small amount of white powder, almost like powdered sugar, fell from Matthew's lapel and sprinkled the hardwood floors. Surprised, Zack and Tracey glanced at each other with eyebrows raised. Zack fell behind Tracey and motioned Tracey to walk ahead.

Squatting carefully—holding his huge stomach and trying not to split his trousers wide open—Zack wiped the powder from the floor with his index finger and tasted it. His suspicions were confirmed: it was cocaine.

He silently caught up with Matthew and Tracey and followed them into Matthew's office.

"Have a seat, anywhere," Matthew offered as he felt the blood rush from his body. The detectives remained standing.

"The news from the lab is not good," Tracey declared. "Looks like you're a direct match."

"What! A direct match? You've got to be kidding."

"We're not kidding," Zack replied with a stern look. "The DNA results were conclusive."

Matthew dropped his head into his hands and shook it slowly back and forth.

"I must be dreaming," he said. "I did not kill her. I'm telling you the truth."

"DNA is not a dream, it is a reality," Tracey said as he approached Matthew. "It can prove you innocent or guilty these days."

Zack moved in close and pulled a leaking Ziploc bag from Matthew's blazer pocket.

"Baby powder?" Zack asked sarcastically.

Matthew shrugged his shoulders but said nothing.

"The best white snow in the country," Zack cracked.

He perused the room carefully and noticed a razor blade on Matthew's desk. When he opened the desk drawer, a shiny wooden cigar box met his eyes. Zack tried to lift the latch but it was locked.

He turned and looked Matthew straight in the eye. "Where's the key, Daytona?"

Matthew pointed to the desk and looked away. "In the white jar on my desk."

Zack unlocked the box and found a Ziploc bag packed with cocaine. He held it in his hand, estimating the weight. "About twenty-five grams?"

Tracey whistled. "Are you sure, Zack?"

"Yep!"

Matthew tried to hide his fears, but his face betrayed his feelings.

"Please," he pleaded. "Please do not handcuff me."

Zack briefly assessed Matthew and then nodded. "All right."

He and Tracey waited patiently at the door while Matthew rose and steeled his nerves for the embarrassing scene that was about to be created in his law firm. A renowned lawyer with an impeccable record was about to be branded a killer in the public eye.

After the detectives read Matthew his rights, they each grabbed an arm and escorted him down the hall as the staff looked on. Shana's assistant Maggie nodded her head and Matthew nodded in return, taking in the warmth of her smile as he was marched out of his own firm like one of the criminals he represented.

An hour later, Matthew was granted permission to use the phone in a small room down the hall from his jail cell.

"Hello, Harianne?"

"Matthew? Is that you?"

"You'll never believe where I am."

"You're not in jail, are you?"

"You got it. I'm here."

"How did you know I was at home?"

"Just a hunch. I've got both numbers."

"I really need to meet with you. They found cocaine in my desk drawer."

"Cocaine!" Harianne exclaimed. "Why on earth would you—"

"Listen, I can explain—"

"Skip it, Matthew," Harianne angrily replied. "Now you're faced with drug charges!"

"I should have told you earlier about the cocaine," Matthew apologized. "Yes. I still…Please forgive me."

"Matthew, I sympathize with you, but I'm having serious doubts here. And I feel honor-bound to remind you, once again, that I haven't practiced criminal law in quite a while."

"Harianne, I have faith in you. Let your resume speak for itself. You're the best at representing top professionals who are up against murder. Please represent me."

Harianne relented. "OK, I'll come at four o'clock. You can tell me the facts from your perspective, but I'm not making any promises. If I feel I can't deal with certain aspects of your case, I'm passing it on to someone else."

"Fair enough," Matthew agreed with a sigh.

Harianne slowly hung up the phone and rested her hand on the receiver for just a minute. She was still uncertain about handling his case. Her experience with him at UCLA remained as vivid in her mind as if it had happened only days, not years ago. She knew her ill feelings toward Matthew must cease if she was going to represent him in court.

A cold, crisp breeze blew through the open living room window, causing goosebumps—or, as she'd called them as a child, chicken-skin bumps—to rise on her arm.

As she continued to ponder the situation, the phone rang.

"Hello, Harianne. It's Logan."

"Hi, Logan. How's everything there at the office?"

"Fine. I'm calling to talk with you about the changes to the firm."

"Sure. How can I help you?"

"Well, I'm taking that job with Derma Research."

"Going with Big Pharma, eh?"

"Hey, I've got four kids, and tuition's expensive. But listen, I've been thinking. I'd be willing to give you my clients if you start your own practice."

"Logan, that's very generous."

"Well, I know they'd be in good hands with you."

"Thank you. There's a strong possibility that that's what I'm going to do. It's funny you should call now because I've been thinking about my future and what I should do next."

"I respect you, Harianne. They're good clients and my receivables are excellent."

"Really! Good timing on my part."

"You might say that. Anyway, it's just an idea. Let me know."

"Thanks, Logan. I'll stay in touch."

Still contemplating her decision, Harianne grabbed her raincoat and umbrella.

When she arrived at the jail, she found Matthew Daytona waiting patiently at a little brown table, dressed in orange cotton digs—a far cry from his usual attire.

"I'm glad you could make it, Harianne."

"OK, let's get down to business. When was the last time you saw Shana Bernstein? At what time? Were you ever involved with her outside of work? I need to know everything."

Harianne took notes on a long yellow legal tablet. The words "murder," "weapon," "victim" and "alibi" slowly hit her memory bank. They all felt familiar as she continued writing, preparing to attack the opposition.

"I had dinner with Shana that evening," Matthew said. "We did what anyone else would as friends."

"Which was…?"

"You know!" He gestured impatiently. "We ate, we talked."

"Were you ever involved with her?"

"No."

"Did Shana have any children?"

"No." Matthew paused. "Do you have children?" he asked.

"No. Let me ask the questions. We're limited on time here."

"I make it a policy never to get involved with my employees."

"Are there any other lawyers in your firm or anyone who would have reason to hate you? Any enemies?"

"Not that I know of. But then again, how can you tell in this profession?"

"I hear you."

"I did not kill Shana Bernstein."

"Matthew. I believe you, but you have to convince that illustrious jury and judge that you didn't kill her. Calm down. We've got a lot of work ahead of us."

Harianne briskly loaded her files and papers into her briefcase and turned to Matthew.

"My fees are high," she informed him.

"I can handle the fees. Just represent me."

"You got it: $800,000 to start. Maybe more."

"More?"

"Yes. Get real! This isn't a car accident."

Harianne swung her coat over her shoulders, leaned over Matthew and put her face up against his.

"I'm your business now. Before this trial is over, I will know anything and everything about you."

Matthew swallowed, then nodded, content. "The price has to be paid for freedom. I'm wealthy."

"I'll phone you tomorrow, Matthew. We'll get through this."

He clenched Harianne's warm hands. She smiled kindly at him.

"Remember, Harianne, you're the best. I wouldn't have anyone else."

# CHAPTER 9

On Monday morning, Harianne called China into her office.

"China, it's official: I'm going to open my own office and practice criminal law. Logan offered his clients to me, which will offer a good startup base."

"Great! And?"

"And you're coming with me! That is, if you want to?"

"Oh, you bet I want to come!" China exclaimed with an exuberant outburst of relief.

Harianne stared into the screen of her laptop, searching the Internet for records of spousal abuse committed by lawyers. She wanted to compare other cases to Matthew's. She found some records online, but they were on a secure site. She grabbed her coat and headed for the L.A.P.D. to review the spousal abuse records of Darci Daytona—Matthew's ex-wife.

When she arrived at the police department, she joined a long line of people waiting to review archived records. She completed the required form, paid a fee and waited patiently until the clerk finally handed her the reports. She seated herself in one of the three chairs left at a back table and perused the records with a fine-toothed comb.

The spousal abuse reports marked "DARCI DAYTONA" with a red-and-white label revealed some poignant information. Harianne's cellphone rang as she was reading; it was Tracey Sanders.

"Hi, Harianne. How are you?"

"Fine."

"What are you doing?"

"Reading spousal abuse records."

"Oh, I see you found out about Darci Daytona. She lives up north now in Monterey."

"Well, I'm going to read this information for myself."

"You should read it. My mission still stands. Matthew is guilty."

"I say he is not guilty. We shouldn't even discuss it."

"Well, it still counts. He appears to be quite unstable."

"Not exactly. That case does not compare to this one. I'm his lawyer now. He's obviously under a lot of pressure. He's not there to run his firm, his reputation is tainted and his clients are confused. Can you understand that?"

"Perhaps."

"Suit yourself. Maybe you don't understand what 'human' and 'remorseful' mean."

"Hey! I do know the difference. I apologize. I like you." He paused before adding, "I'll be in touch, soon."

Harianne returned to a report filed by police officers who had been called to Matthew and Darci Daytona's home on a domestic violence call.

*"Officers received domestic violence complaint at home of Matthew and Darci Daytona. Mrs. Daytona stated that she had had her therapist to the house that evening, and they had been surprised in bed when suspect Matthew Daytona arrived home unexpectedly. Mrs. Daytona further stated her husband had kicked her lover in the groin and knocked him unconscious before punching her in the face and beating her with a fireplace iron. When suspect left the house, Mrs. Daytona called police. Officers arriving observed blood on her face and trace amounts of blood under her fingernails, and contusions across her forehead, arms and chest. Mrs. Daytona claimed this was not the first incident of domestic violence in their home this year. Based on officers' observations and statements from both victims, we determined that Matthew Daytona was the dominant aggressor. Both victims were transported to hospital for immediate medical attention. Matthew Daytona was later located at a bar and placed under arrest for the indicated charges."*

Harianne closed the file and sighed. There was more to Matthew Daytona's story than he was revealing.

Two weeks later, Harianne pulled up in front of a three-story office building in the popular Larchmont Village area. Dressed casually in jeans, a navy sweatshirt and white tennis shoes, she inspected the ivy covering the Italian villa-style facing while a Ryder truck backed into the side alley and movers began unloading boxes into the 1,600-square-foot space she had just leased. It was comprised of three offices, three workstation cubicles, a cozy waiting area with a fireplace, and a wrought-iron balcony adorned with wooden geranium flowerboxes.

She went inside and said hello to China, then gave the movers instructions on where to place her furniture, plants, lamps, computers and other office equipment. Floral arrangements in wicker baskets, Italian vases and boxes of baked goods arrived continuously throughout the day.

China piled copies of *The National Enquirer, Globe, Star, People* and *The Hollywood Reporter* on top of one of the boxes. Matthew's story was plastered across every entertainment newspaper and magazine.

Harianne powered up her laptop, placed it on her cherrywood desk, pulled up the only chair in the room and started searching the Internet. Matthew's story had hit the news in a big way. Every news channel had video of the wealthy, well-known, mega-powerful entertainment lawyer Matthew Daytona, accused of the murder of his colleague, Shana Bernstein. Tabloids openly speculated that he might be a serial killer. Reporters revealed all of his notable clients—producers, movie directors, actresses and actors in Hollywood—and paparazzi gathered outside the jail each day. Huge crowds of people formed to get a glimpse of the celebrity friends who visited Matthew to show their support.

Harianne read an excerpt from *CBS Sunday Morning News* about his arrest, and glanced over at the small television in the corner of her office. Breaking news showed Maggie Weiner, Shana's assistant, fielding questions from the press. Standing in the lobby of Daytona, Bernstein & McDunn, dressed in a dark black suit and crisp white blouse, Maggie was a pro, answering only what was asked of her and sticking to known facts.

Harianne contemplated Maggie's performance; Matthew had prepared her well. Even from his jail cell he was orchestrating and managing his image.

In a flash Harianne recalled Tracey's dinner invitation, and realized that they would have to be careful not to be seen in public by any paparazzi. It was crucial not only to Matthew's case, but to their careers.

She dove back into preparations for Matthew's court arraignment, which was scheduled for the next day. As she reviewed her notes, she caught sight of the multitude of boxes across the room. There was still a lot of unpacking left to do.

In one corner sat the blue flowerbox she had retrieved from Jasmine's office; Harianne stepped over to it and removed the lid. Inside she discovered newspaper and *Newsweek* clippings relating to a Japanese drug-and-prostitution ring—articles she vaguely recalled reading when they'd been published the previous year. Continuing to read further, she came across the name Taka Sousushi. Pressed for time, Harianne placed the lid back on the box and returned to preparing for Matthew's arraignment.

Across town at the precinct, Tracey and Zack read through dozens of police reports and viewed bloody, horrifying photos of abused women of all ethnicities and backgrounds until they found the name Darci Daytona. Tracey pulled the blinds closed against the afternoon sun and heat.

"Found her," Zack said. "Let's work it."

The pictures dated back to 1977. At the time Darci Daytona was petite, twenty-three years old and helpless. According to the police report, friends and neighbors had described her as kind-hearted with a strong character, but shy.

The next morning, Tracey and Zack followed their suspicions to Goleta, a small town outside of Santa Barbara. Seduced by the ocean air and scenic vineyards along the highway, they were tempted to stop and forget about the investigation, but they continued on until they reached a vintage Mediterranean-style house on a hill facing the ocean. A young Hispanic woman was standing in the doorway when they pulled into the circular driveway. The detectives approached her with a smile.

"Darci Daytona?" Tracey inquired.

"Oh, no," she replied. "I'm not Darci."

"May we speak with Darci Daytona?"

"She doesn't live here anymore."

"Where did she move?"

"France, but recently I was told she moved to Carmel."

"When was that?"

"In the last six months."

"What is your name, please?"

"Josalyn Gonzalez."

Surprised at the response, the detectives asked Mrs. Gonzalez a few more questions, then left. As they drove along the highway, they spotted a quaint Mexican restaurant and stopped for lunch. Zack loved Mexican food. Sipping lemon water from their glasses, they contemplated the whereabouts of Darci Daytona.

"Man, another mystery," Zack said.

"It shouldn't be too hard to find her," Tracey surmised. "She was his ex-wife, and she's in California. That's a plus."

"I think we should go to Carmel."

"I'm with you, partner. We'll subpoena her medical records later."

"Yeah! I like that."

A light mist was settling over the streets of Los Angeles when they returned to the precinct. Zack took a Danish from the familiar pink bakery box in the kitchen, grabbed a cup of hot coffee, took one sip and made a fresh pot. No coffee filters were left, so he used paper towels from a spindle nearby. Walking in his usual side-to-side way to Tracey's office, he immediately began to fill out the request form for more extensive pictures of Darci Daytona, while Tracey, sitting across from him, wrote out the information for the subpoena.

"Any and all medical records and treating physicians, etc., of Darci Daytona," Tracey said. "That ought to do it."

He handed the subpoena to Marnetta, whose desk sat directly outside their office door. She looked at the clock, which pointed to five.

"I was going home…"

"Yeah, I know," Tracey pleaded, "but could you please type it for me? I've got to move on this and want it out the door tomorrow morning."

"OK, but you'll have to sign for my O.T."

"Don't I always?"

Back at his desk, Tracey sat down and started beating his pencil on a legal pad in front of him.

"Hey, Zack. Got any gum?"

"No. But I got LifeSavers."

"Toss 'em over."

Marnetta stepped in and placed a large black book full of pictures on Tracey's desk. He and Zack hesitated a moment before they started flipping through the pages.

After a while, Tracey slowly turned away and leaned against the window, feeling its cold moisture penetrate his nostrils. His silence took over the room. Zack stood nearby, not saying a word. The phone rang.

"Tracey? Zack? Are you there?"

Zack reached over the desk and hit the intercom.

"Yeah, Marnetta. What's up?"

"We're ordering out. Deli."

"Tuna, onion and tomato on rye for me," Zack replied. He turned to his partner. "Tracey?"

"Nothing," Tracey said.

"Anything to drink?"

"No."

Zack leaned back with a loud sigh and focused on Tracey.

"Hey, man, what's wrong? Talk to me!"

"You wouldn't believe me," Tracey said, wiping his nose in an upward motion.

"Try me."

"Let's just forget it."

"Man, what is your problem? You're miserable! Look at you!"

"No, you look at yourself! You're miserable!"

"Hey, hey! Lighten up, Tracey."

Tracey abruptly turned and with one sweep of his hand knocked all the books and papers off the desk to the floor. Zack continued to sip his coffee and said nothing.

"It still rests on my mind," Tracey said evenly.

"Marina's death?"

"The brutal mutilation of her arms, legs and breasts. Sometimes seeing pictures of victims brings back memories of that whole ordeal. I don't know if I can take looking at them." He stopped and looked at Zack. "I hate cops. The whole damn trashy lifestyle of a cop is fucked. Why am I here? She's gone now."

"I know it's hard. I'll look at them, but you should, too," Zack said, chomping down on a leftover Danish.

Tracey went to the kitchen and poured a cup of hot black coffee. He grabbed some gingersnap cookies and ate a few as he walked back to his desk. Turning his chair around, he stared out the window, lost in thought.

"Tracey, man!" Zack sputtered. "What the fuck's wrong with you? Come on!"

"Shut the fuck up!"

"Bullshit! You shut the fuck up! I've had it with your feel-sorry-for-me-everybody attitude. Marina is dead. No one or any thing can bring her back."

"Oh, really? Shut up!"

"Yeah? Level with me, man."

"No way. I'm not ready yet."

"You've got to cut this shit loose!"

Tracey wanted to respond but remained silent and sat in his chair. Dinner arrived shortly thereafter and Zack showed no qualms about digging into the food right away.

"Hey, Tracey! Want half a sandwich?"

"No thanks, Zack."

"Ah, yum! I just love deli. All right. Let's do it up! I've got to go home at a reasonable hour tonight."

Zack pulled his chair next to Tracey's and opened the book to the first section, which was filled with headshots. Darci Daytona stared up at them, with black and blue marks on one side of her face. The marks were typical of a beating. Tracey immediately turned his head and got up and walked toward the window. Zack shook his head in disbelief.

"Tracey, she's fucked up! This man is deadly."

"Daytona's a destroyer. The man will destroy all women. What's the date on that one, Zack?"

"January 2, 1977. You should really look at these."

"I don't want to look at them."

As Zack continued to look at the pictures, a pattern began to emerge. The dates were the same for the entire year: February 2, March 2, April 2…

Tracey suddenly slammed down his cup and grabbed the book from Zack. "Damn him!" he bellowed.

"Whoa," Zack said. "Look at December 2."

The two men peered at the photo, which showed the number two carved on one of Darci Daytona's cheeks.

"He's a real whacko," Zack remarked.

"Afraid so, Zack. I want a piece of his damn ass!"

Zack turned to the next section, which was filled with full-body shots. The pictures revealed deep gashes to Darci Daytona's leg.

"Well," Zack said. "This is obvious."

The two men stared at each other for a moment in silence, then headed out the door.

# CHAPTER 10

Tracey awakened at six o'clock the next morning and headed to the kitchen for his daily java ritual. As he opened the blinds in the living room, he saw that the lawn and patio were completely soaked from heavy rains the night before. He returned to the kitchen and turned on the TV to catch the morning news while he made his espresso di roma. Matthew's name was plastered all over the news as a possible serial killer. Tracey hit the remote; every channel was carrying the story. The most renowned attorney in the entertainment community was a fallen hero—but he still looked good. Tracey shook his head in disgust and turned the TV off.

He couldn't stop thinking about the pictures taken at his wife's murder scene: her caramel-colored body immersed in a pool of blood, her once beautiful legs vertically cut, her ears hanging from each side of her head. The police had handled the entire situation carelessly, with no sense of compassion for a fellow officer. They had underestimated this killer. Tracey remembered their continuous apologies: "I'm sorry, Tracey, I'm really sorry." Somehow, "sorry" meant absolutely nothing.

The phone rang. It was Zack.

"Hey, Tracey! What time is our meeting?"

"Ten o'clock. I just got up."

"Get moving, buddy. I'll see you down there."

In their office at the precinct, Tracey and Zack sat side by side in their hard cherrywood chairs, sifting through pile after pile of papers.

"All of this pertains to Darci Daytona?" Zack asked.

"Yep," Tracey answered. "It's a bitch, isn't it?"

"To say the least. When do you want to leave for Carmel?"

"Late tonight."

Zack hesitated. "It'll be foggy…"

"We can handle it."

Later that afternoon, a young blond-haired man arrived at the station wearing a blue-and-white Izod shirt with "Legal Breed Document Support" stenciled across the pocket. He pushed a dolly holding five cartons of boxes into Tracey and Zack's office.

"Hello, I have documents for a subpoena," he said.

"Drop them right here and I'll sign your messenger slip," Zack replied.

It took hours for Tracey and Zack to sort through them all. Medical records detailed several visits for bruises and contusions, but there was no real evidence of broken limbs or serious injuries. Darci Daytona's doctor had relocated to Monterey from Santa Monica in 1981.

Tracey and Zack got on the road at one o'clock. The sun wouldn't rise for another five hours.

"Tracey, I'm hungry," Zack said. "Do you think we could stop in San Luis Obispo?"

"Yeah, man. My stomach is growling. It's talking louder than us."

"Hey, what do you think we'll find out in Carmel?"

"Who knows? I just hope we find something. It seems like we're being pulled in all kinds of directions."

"Matthew Daytona is a weird character. A real killer."

"I know, Zack. We have to cover all bases on this one."

In San Luis Obispo, they drove about a mile into town and saw a cafe just turning its sign to "OPEN." Zack ordered his usual: two eggs scrambled, bacon, sausage and toast. Tracey contented himself with oatmeal and fruit. Coffee did the trick for both.

Two hours later they arrived in Carmel. Thick fog blanketed the Monterey Bay in the distance.

"Better call her first," Tracey said.

Zack reached for his cellphone.

"Hello, Mrs. Daytona?"

"Yes."

"I'm Detective Grimes, from the Los Angeles Police Department. I'm in the area with my partner, Detective Tracey Sanders, and we'd like to meet with you for a while, if you don't mind, ma'am."

"How long will this take?" she inquired nervously.

"Not long."

"OK. My address is 2356 Pelican Bay Road."

"We'll be there in twenty minutes."

They followed Seventeen Mile Drive to Darci Daytona's home: a two-story, blue-and-white Cape Cod-style house nestled in a forest of cypress trees, with a cobblestone driveway and a winding brick walkway leading to the front door. Tracey and Zack inhaled the fresh scent of the trees and ocean air as they stepped out of the car.

A thin white woman with ivory skin and dark glasses greeted them. She wore a long, black velvet skirt and white buttoned-up shirt.

"Please come in, won't you? We can sit in the living room."

Tracey and Zack each took a chair in front of the coffee table. They looked around the room, taking in the array of traditional antiques and a large display of Waterford and Baccarat crystal. Everything was immaculate and tasteful. Darci Daytona sat on the sofa. She kept her oversized sunglasses on.

"I've heard all of these awful things about Matt," she said. "What is going on down there? The press is making him out to be a real serial killer."

"Ma'am," Tracey began. "There are a lot of things going on and we're covering all of our bases. Please be patient with us. We need to ask you some questions, if we may."

"Sure. Will it take long?"

"No, ma'am. How long were you married to Matthew Daytona?"

"Six years. We met in law school."

"Are you a practicing lawyer?"

"No. I passed the bar, but I chose to work with nonprofits trying to preserve the environment instead; I research environmental laws and regulations pertaining to water contamination."

"During your marriage to him, did he ever raise his voice at you?"

"Well, all married couples have arguments at one time or another."

"Did he ever hit you?"

"Why?"

"It's just a general question, ma'am."

Mrs. Daytona slowly pulled down her glasses and took them off. With only one eye to see out of, she started unbuttoning her shirt to her waistline. Her chest had one long cut from the collar to her waist with a very visible keloid in place. Teardrops fell out of the corner of her eye.

"This really wasn't necessary, ma'am. Oh, Mrs. Daytona! We're sorry, ma'am."

"He didn't mean to do this," she said. "Really he didn't."

Zack and Tracey were appalled; her scars were worse than the pictures they had seen. She buttoned her shirt and put her glasses back on.

"Is that all, detectives?"

"Yes. We'll be in touch."

They walked back to the car faster and faster, as if they were speed walking. Tracey's stomach started churning and sweat ran down his forehead. He pulled a handkerchief from his inside coat pocket and wiped vigorously. Zack struggled for words.

"That—that was—"

"Never mind, Zack."

# CHAPTER 11

Harianne arrived at the Men's Central Jail at ten o'clock the next morning. The very thought of entering the imposing building made her stomach churn. Shaking from the cold, she stayed in the car for a brief period making last-minute notes. A beige trench coat, dark glasses and a few black and gold accessories complemented her black suit and curly dark hair.

An officer greeted her as she approached the jail check-in and with no hesitation commenced with the usual procedure of checking her driver's license for any warrants, arrests or unpaid parking tickets. A metal detector did the rest, and she proceeded down the long hallway toward the meeting room. She entered through a stainless-steel door and beheld Matthew Daytona. Clean, freshly shaved, he sat up straight with his hands folded, ready to be prepped.

She walked over and extended her hand to the glass window divider; Matthew sat on the other side. Harianne spotted her reflection in the glass and shifted uncomfortably in her worn, gray-leather chair. She had forgotten, until now, how confining the space was for court preparation. She called to the guard on duty and requested a conference table where she could spread out her papers. She caught the concerned look on Matthew's face and picked up the phone on the counter.

"How are you, Matthew?" she asked.

"I'm fine," he said firmly. "I want to get this over with and get back to business. That's the bottom line. I've got a law firm to run. I'm humiliated."

"It'll be OK," Harianne assured him. "The most important thing is your arraignment."

"Yes, I know. I can't stop thinking about how the whole thing happened. Listen, we've got to talk."

"I know, we need to review arraignment procedures—"

"No. I need to talk to you about the media."

"I've seen and heard everything about the media."

"No, you haven't," Matthew said with a dismissive wave. "What you need to remember is that there's a special finesse in dealing with the media. They'll get all over you. Do you understand what I mean? You have to handle them with kid gloves."

"Matthew! C'mon. Are you telling me what to do?"

"Harianne, you're a criminal lawyer—that's why I hired you. You're not a public relations director or press secretary."

"Of course not," Harianne swore heatedly. "You know, I thought I had gotten over your smart remarks, but how could I forget? Once a jack ass, always a jackass!"

"Listen to me!" Matthew hissed. "I have more experience with those jackals than you do. I'm an entertainment lawyer and I do this for a living."

"And I do *this* for a living," Harianne replied. "That's why you're paying me dearly to get you out of this mess."

"Yes, but—"

"Matthew, don't you ever tell me what to do, whether it's about the media, your case, or your law firm. I'm the attorney and you're the client."

"But you don't—"

"Understand? You can't talk to me like that. I will not be controlled by you or anybody. Got it?"

"I'm paying the bill."

"I set you free."

"What the hell do you think is wrong? Look at my reputation!"

"Which one? As a lawyer or a criminal? They're one and the same to me."

"That's cold. I'm trying to—"

"Act out! Yeah! Look, I'm here to help you. We've been over this numerous times, Matthew. I need concrete evidence regarding your relationship with Shana Bernstein. It's key to our case. In fact, it's the whole thrust of this case."

"I'm going to plead not guilty."

"Yes, you will—because that's what I want you to do. I told you that earlier. Now, what's up with the red silk scarves?"

"Nothing. Why?"

"Why? Need I say more?" She sighed sarcastically.

"I order them all of the time from a tailor in Japan," Matthew sniffed.

"Well, those scarves are real evidence—against you, not for you. It's known among homicide detectives as a 'signature killing.'"

"I hear you, but I didn't kill her. I don't even know how the scarves got there. I'm confused."

"Well, it's a visual piece of evidence that makes you look really bad."

Harianne noticed that discussion of the trial was starting to rattle Matthew. She wondered how much longer he would last.

When they finished Harianne departed for Matthew's arraignment at the Criminal Courts Building. She hated the gray, midcentury modern building on the corner of Temple and Broadway. People packed the dingy beige and brown hallways. The aromatic stench of old tennis shoes and body odor infiltrated Harianne's nostrils and unsettled her stomach as she made her way through a field of television and radio news cameras. She spotted the prosecutor, Gaston Reeves, giving an interview to a reporter for KCAL-TV.

Today was a media event. It could prove to be the most embarrassing moment in the career of one of L.A.'s most famous attorneys.

Harianne knew Matthew was being judged, and harshly, for past behavior. But regardless of his previous ostentatious displays of wealth and power—not to mention his arrogant treatment of her in college—for her the day wasn't about spectacle or revenge. She believed in the law, and under that law, Matthew was an innocent man until proven guilty. He deserved a fair trial like Joe Q. Public on the street.

Harianne entered the courtroom, took the table to the left and placed her briefcase on it. The Daytona file was placed on the table. The first example of the new coding system in her office, it was labeled with big, black letters: "DAYTONA, MATTHEW—CRIMINAL C-1." Behind her the courtroom filled quickly with people, creating a very busy and noisy atmosphere. A sudden adrenaline rush reminded Harianne that her life was different now. No more corporate breach-of-contract cases; she was dealing with real lives now, and deciding their fate.

Waiting anxiously in her seat, Harianne knocked her knees together and suddenly struck the hard oak leg of the table, bruising her funny bone. It caused such aggravating pain that she immediately leaned over and grabbed it. Feeling paranoid about the people studying her from a distance, she stopped, and picked up the tooth-bitten pencil that rolled down the table near her hand. The continuous drumming of the pencil on the table was only noticeable to Harianne as she waited for the judge to arrive. She poured herself a glass of water from a stainless-steel pitcher in front of her. Taking a small swallow, she glanced around the room at the various faces until she saw Tracey and Zack. They nodded and she did the same.

Matthew was led into the courtroom wearing a black, double-breasted suit and black loafers. He lifted his head and made full eye contact with Harianne. She could feel his embarrassment and humiliation as the bailiff seated him next to her.

"All rise!" the bailiff shouted.

"The Honorable Jack Stein, presiding," the court clerk called out.

Judge Jack Stein entered the courtroom with a deliberate gait and ascended to his seat. Forty-nine, Caucasian, he had served on the bench for six years and was known to be thorough, methodical and liberal.

The clerk continued his recitation. "Case Docket No. 55-555-66. People vs. Matthew Daytona."

"Very well," the judge declared. "The clerk will proceed."

"Would the defendant please stand, and state and spell your name?"

Matthew stood tall at the long, mahogany table. "Matthew Daytona. M-A-T-T-H-E-W D-A-Y-T-O-N-A."

"You have the right to a court-appointed attorney if you choose." Judge Stein stated.

"I have counsel, Your Honor." Matthew replied.

"Counsel, state appearances."

"Harianne DeCanter representing defendant Matthew Daytona."

"Gaston Reeves representing the people of the state of California."

Judge Stein proceeded to read the charges.

"On December 2, Gaston Reeves, Los Angeles County District Attorney's Office, complains and alleges, upon information and belief, that said Defendant did commit the following crimes in the County of Los Angeles, State of California.

"COUNT I: On or about and between September 30 and November 30, Defendant did commit a felony, MURDER, violation of Section 187 of the California Penal code, in that the Defendant did willfully, unlawfully, and feloniously and with malice aforethought murder Shana Bernstein, a human being.

"SPECIAL ALLEGATION: It is further alleged as to Count I, MURDER, that the Defendant acted intentionally, deliberately and with premeditation.

"COUNT II: POSSESSION OF CONTROLLED SUBSTANCES (NARCOTIC/COCAINE): On or about and between September 30 and November 30, Defendant did knowingly or intentionally possess more than twenty-five grams of a mixture containing the controlled substance cocaine and administered the cocaine to Shana Bernstein, in violation of Health and Safety Code Sections 11350, 11351, 11351.5 and 11352.

"SPECIAL ALLEGATION: It is further alleged as to Count II, the Defendant acted intentionally, deliberately and with premeditation."

"How do you plead to the criminal charges?" Judge Stein asked.

"Not guilty," Matthew replied.

"Counsel, do you waive further arraignment?"

"Counsel waives further arraignment," Harianne and Reeves answered simultaneously.

"Defendant to remain in custody," Judge Stein decreed. "Due to the nature of this case, and its circumstances, Defendant poses a potential flight risk. No bail set. Preliminary hearing is set for December 10."

Harianne shook Matthew's hand, pulled him to her and whispered in his ear. "Everything will be all right. Hang in there."

Harianne slid her dark glasses over her face, bracing for the media huddle just outside. She clutched the leather handles of her gold-studded briefcase and departed for Matthew's law firm.

The atmosphere was very solemn when Harianne arrived at the Daytona, Bernstein & McDunn offices. Some employees acknowledged her with a slight smile, but without a trusting eye. They were obviously deeply affected by Matthew's trial. Harianne greeted Erin at the front desk.

"I'm here to meet with Hillary McDunn."

"Yes, have a seat," Erin said. "I'll tell her you're here."

Harianne picked up a newspaper lying on the sofa in the lobby. The story of Matthew Daytona was trumpeted on the front page: "Fallen Lawyer! An Entertainment Industry Blow!" She continued reading: "Criminal lawyer Harianne DeCanter is counsel to Mr. Daytona…"

"Harianne?"

"Yes." Harianne looked up to see a fortysomething woman with bleached blonde hair standing over her.

"I'm Hillary McDunn. Nice to meet you."

Just over forty years old, Hillary McDunn was well known in L.A. legal circles as a top criminal trial lawyer specializing in white-collar crime. She had been the first woman lawyer to land a million-dollar settlement against a major medical insurance company for embezzlement of monies by the president and chief financial officer. She ushered Harianne into a small conference room.

"Sit down, please. Can I get you some coffee, water?"

"Coffee, please," Harianne said. "Cream and a little sugar."

"Here you are. I'm drinking lemon water. I've got a stomachache over this whole ordeal with Matthew."

"I know," Harianne said. "It's a horrible scandal for the legal and entertainment communities. He's doing fine, though. I believe in him."

"You do?"

"Yes. Don't you?"

"Oh, I'm sorry. I didn't mean to sound like I disbelieve him. I'm still trying to—"

"Convince yourself?"

"—figure out how this whole thing happened. They're close friends and partners."

"I see. What kind of person was Shana?"

"Shana was an excellent lawyer: a fast thinker, heavy negotiator, and just a little bit of a task master. Nothing got by her. Her personal lifestyle was a mystery to me and most everyone in the firm, except Matthew."

Harianne was taken in by her candidness. She paused before replying.

"So you're saying she was really tough."

Hillary leaned back in the chair, positioning her lips for a sip of water.

"No. Just a no-nonsense person. I miss her." She swallowed.

"Were they getting along? Did they have any problems that you know of?"

"What are you searching for? I don't know if I can answer that."

"I'm searching for the truth. This will only help Matthew and you, too. What time did you leave work?"

Distracted by the window washer, Hillary paid little attention to the questions. At times, she picked up items in front of her—paperclips, stickies—and indiscreetly played with them. Harianne knew she was getting nowhere.

Hillary rose from the table, finished off the glass of water, and buttoned her long black blazer, which almost met her skirt hemline. "I'm sorry to be so rude, but I've got additional work since all this stuff happened with Matthew. I left early that evening. Are we finished? Because I've got to prepare for a meeting in an hour."

"Well, yes," Harianne said, "but I'd like to get a list of all the lawyers who worked late that night. I also need to speak with Lara Smith. Is she here?"

"I'll buzz reception for you. I don't mean to be short. I guess I'm still adjusting to the changes in the firm. It's going to take some time."

Harianne waited until Hillary returned with a response. She stood in front of the window, pondering the agonizing background checks of her clients, their buried secrets and extramarital affairs, and her search for the truth. Somehow it all worked out, but sometimes the results were devastating.

"Harianne?" Hillary had rejoined her. "Lara is available. She'll be right in. I'll be happy to answer any more questions later, if you want."

"Thanks."

While waiting for Lara Smith she made notes about her meeting with Hillary on a yellow legal tablet with a stylish Mont Blanc pen. She wondered if Hillary was telling the truth. Would anyone tell the truth?

"Hi, Harianne DeCanter?"

"Yes. Lara Smith, is it?"

"Yes. I'm sorry I'm a little late. I was on a conference call."

"Have a seat. So how long have you been with the firm?"

"Three, approaching four years."

"Third year?"

"Yes."

"Just getting your feet wet, huh? Good for you. Did you get along with Shana?"

"Oh, yes. She's the greatest."

"Matthew?"

"Oh, my God, yes. He's taught me so much."

Harianne stood up from her chair and walked toward the window, carrying her stained coffee cup.

"Where were you the night Shana was murdered?"

"Working."

"Where? At home or the office?"

"At the office. I use the library late at night. My work requires that I research cases—you know, *California Appellate, California Reports, West Law, C.C.P.*, and so on. It's a lot of work."

"I remember those days," Harianne remarked. "What time did you leave that night?"

"Around eleven."

"Anyone else?"

"Matthew was here for a while, but I remember him telling me he was going to have dinner with Shana. It was a late dinner, I think."

"You're right. It was late. OK, I'll be in touch. Please let me know if you think of anything else that might help me," Harianne said, reaching for her briefcase.

"Do you think he'll get off? I would just hate to think the worst."

"Only the jury will tell us the answer."

Harianne gathered her things and walked down the hall to the reception area. She turned when she heard Hillary calling her name.

"Harianne! Harianne!"

"Did you get the list?"

"Here. I had my assistant get it from the security office."

They exchanged genuine smiles and shook hands.

Driving back to her office, Harianne heard the continuous double ring of her cellphone. She reached into her black Coach purse and pulled it out of the inside pocket. It was Matthew.

"Harianne, I've been thinking about my case."

"Glad to hear it. I have too. I need to speak with you."

"Really? OK. Well, the thing is, I'd like to bring in a second lawyer."

"What?"

"I—"

"Just wait, Matthew. I'll be right there."

Harianne changed direction and headed toward the downtown jail. Forty minutes later, she was facing Matthew in the dingy meeting room.

"What the hell is going on, Matthew?" she demanded.

"I told you on the phone: I want to bring in a second lawyer."

"Who?"

"MacKenzie McShay. Do you know her?"

"MacKenzie McShay?"

"She's tough. She studied at New York University School of Law and received her medical degree too, although she hasn't practiced medicine for some time."

"So why do you want to bring her onboard? Have you worked with her before?"

"I met MacKenzie years ago, while doing business in Tokyo. She left the United States and got a law degree in Japan. She's well versed in drug-and-prostitution rings there. The drug cartel is always watching, and they don't know you."

"The drug cartel?" Harianne repeated.

"My father did business with prostitution rings, nightclubs, drug rings."

"You told me before that it was your uncle who dealt cocaine."

"He did. But my father—Uncle Taka's half-brother—was also involved. He was a pilot who became a kingpin in the French mafia. We moved from place to place, country to country, which made for a very unsettled life when I was growing up. But it was the only life I really knew. And we had a very lavish lifestyle to which I've grown quite accustomed. I've no desire to lose it."

"But you swore to me that you aren't dealing anymore. Why should this drug cartel care? Have you been lying to me?"

"No! But because of my uncle, they're watching. I just want…some insurance."

"I see," Harianne said. "You think they won't like the way I handle my cases."

"No, it's not that—don't worry."

"I'm not worried, Matthew. I'm pissed! You should have divulged this information to me from the beginning."

"You wouldn't have taken me on."

"Damn straight!"

"Please, I need you, Harianne," Matthew pleaded. "I *need* you. This isn't about your ability. It's just that I think MacKenzie has experience that can help us."

"How so?"

"She defended my father and Uncle Taka several times."

"Really?" Harianne regarded Matthew with a steely gaze. "When did she defend your uncle against murder charges?"

Matthew looked startled. "How did you know?"

Harianne tried to hide her surprise with a stern expression. "Never mind that, Matthew. You need to level with me. Again. When was your uncle charged with murder?"

"A year ago. It was a drug-related case. MacKenzie got him off."

Harianne eyed her client closely; he looked nervous.

"Matthew, what else are you hiding from me?"

"Nothing!"

"I don't believe you."

"Harianne…" Matthew held up his hands and turned on his patented Hollywood charm. "Come on, I can't afford to lie to you, you know that."

"Ha!" Harianne shook her head. "Matthew, it's up to you, but I can handle this by myself. I thought you had faith in me."

"You are handling it yourself. You're still the lead lawyer and the greatest criminal lawyer of all time, but—"

"Don't patronize me! Be careful, Matthew."

"Hey, I'm sorry, but this isn't an insult or a put-down."

Harianne sighed. "It means a lot to you, doesn't it?"

"Yes. I'm not going to lie about it."

"Well, you're in charge. It's your money."

"Thanks, Harianne," he replied with obvious relief. "You're the best."

"Skip it," Harianne cut him off as she made a swift exit. "Have this woman contact me."

Outside in her car, she pulled out her cellphone and dialed her office.

"China? I need you to drop everything and do some research for me, fast. Listen carefully…"

That afternoon, Tracey and Zack paid a visit to Daytona, Bernstein & McDunn. They stepped off the elevator into the main lobby and greeted Erin, the receptionist.

"Hi, how are you today?" Tracey asked.

"Fine," she answered curtly. She stared at them, not bothering to disguise her ill feelings.

Zack remained aloof. Tracey paused before speaking.

"Is the manager or managing partner here?"

"You should speak with Ms. McDunn. I'll buzz her. Please have a seat."

Erin rang Hillary's office and whispered into the phone, making it virtually impossible for the detectives to hear anything.

"She'll be here in a few minutes," she informed them after hanging up the phone.

Zack made himself comfortable on the posh black leather sofa and checked out the reading material on the coffee table. Law-related magazines were in a neat stack on one side and a copy of *Variety* topped a pile on the other side of the table. He engrossed himself in a *National Geographic* article.

The sound of clicking heels approached the detectives from behind. Tracey rose and extended a firm handshake to Hillary McDunn.

"What can I help you with today, Detective Sanders?"

By this time Zack had stood up and was straightening his tie and adjusting his belt around his plump belly.

"We've got some questions for you and anyone who worked closely with Matthew Daytona," Tracey said.

She flinched, shaking her head in disgust.

"I thought we covered everything when you were here last time," she said sternly.

"Is there a place we can talk privately?"

"The conference room at the end of the hall. Follow me."

"Why did I have a feeling you would say that?"

They walked single file down the long hall. The curious staff looked on, trying not to be obvious. Hillary opened the door and pointed to the seats around the large conference table.

"Listen, we're here to investigate a murder," Tracey said. "Everyone has a story to tell."

"Information, more likely than a story."

"That's fine. I just want the truth."

"I'll give you an hour. Let's get started."

"When was the last time you saw Matthew?"

As Tracey continued with a battery of questions, Hillary's answers grew shorter. She seemed preoccupied with her own thoughts, almost withdrawn.

"Ms. McDunn! Are you with me?"

"Yes. But you might want to question Lara Smith. She works late."

"You seem like you're far away."

"I wish I was far away. Are you done?"

"No. I'll check with Lara Smith later."

Tracey finished up half an hour later. Hillary returned to her office and shut the door.

It was the peak of rush hour as Tracey and Zack nosed their way through traffic on Sunset Boulevard on their way back to the precinct. Zack admired the diverse array of girls on the sidewalks as they passed: African American, Asian, Caucasian, long hair, short hair, short skirts, tight pants.

"A guy could really get used to this," he declared. "Yeah, man. I could get used to it. Count me in!"

"Zack!" Tracey exclaimed. "I'm shocked. I thought you were still mourning your wife."

"I am, but it's OK to dream, isn't it?"

Tracey focused on driving while Zack looked around for somewhere to eat.

"I'm hungry. Hey, there—let's get something over there."

They pulled into the parking lot of small diner on La Cienega; an orange cloth awning hung from the white stucco building. Neither of them had eaten there before. They walked in and took a back booth in a dark corner. The waiter handed them plastic menus and two glasses of water. Zack pulled out his pocket flashlight and turned his menu over and immediately came in contact with a sticky film on his fingers.

"What is that?"

"Jam?" Tracey suggested. "Or syrup?"

"Jam. That's it." Zack dipped his white paper napkin in his glass of water and wiped it clean.

"How's yours, Tracey?"

"Yeah. I got one, too."

"Here, let me do the honors."

They quickly scanned the menu and each ordered a cheeseburger, fries and a Coke.

"So…Hillary McDunn," Zack said. "She's been around a while. It's obvious she was left in charge. Matthew has a lot of allies."

"Yeah," Tracey agreed. "We knew that, though. The office is loyal to him. They should be."

"We've got nothing else on that bastard, except a DNA match, the toxicology report and his prints all over the damn house. It should be a done deal."

"The case is tight, but I want more witnesses. Subpoena! Subpoena!"

"You got it," Zack said, taking a sip of water. "The prosecutor will breathe down our asses. The story's gotta fit. What's the relationship with Shana? They had dinner and he just killed her in cold blood? C'mon, get real!"

"That's the story, Zack."

The cellphone rang on Tracey's belt. He pulled it out and saw a number he didn't recognize on the phone screen.

"Who's this? Goddamn—"

The waiter returned with their food.

"Mustard, mayo?"

"Mustard," Tracey said.

He leaned forward for the mustard with his ear pressed tightly to the phone and tipped his head to his shoulder. He smothered the burger with mustard, and a little mayo.

"Hello?"

"It's Harianne DeCanter."

"Harianne? Sorry, but I didn't recognize your number."

"It's OK," she sighed. "Listen, we've got to meet somewhere private."

"What's this about? You were mad at me the last time I spoke with you."

"It's private."

"Well, give me a minute. I was eating."

"Meet me in Malibu, in front of the Charthouse Restaurant."

"I hope it's worth it."

"Trust me. It is."

"All right. We'll see you at seven-thirty." He flipped his cellphone shut.

"We're going to see her?" Zack asked.

"Yeah. Eat up."

"What has she done now?"

"Who knows!"

Zack and Tracey scarfed down the burgers and salty fries and demolished their watered-down Cokes. Zack's belly stuck out further as the hunger left his entire body. Tracey paid and they left. He wondered why Harianne wanted to meet, but said nothing to Zack.

They took the 10 Freeway to Pacific Coast Highway. Tracey dodged in and out of lanes, driving as fast as he could in the gridlocked traffic. He spotted the Charthouse in the distance and parked on the roadside nearby. A Mercedes was parked in front of the restaurant. It was hard to see the color of the car but Tracey thought it was Harianne's. He and Zack stepped carefully out of the car and looked around; a woman in dark clothing and a hat was standing halfway down the street. She turned and called out their names in the cold night air.

"Sanders! Grimes!" Harianne shouted.

"Yeah!"

They approached her with hands in pockets, looking over their shoulders.

"Couldn't you think of another place, Harianne?" Tracey asked. "It's freezing out here."

"This was the only place that seemed private and out of the way. No interruptions."

"I see. Remind me to pick the location next time."

"How about some coffee inside?" Zack suggested, moving from side to side to keep warm.

"No, thanks. This won't take long."

Harianne, with a despairing look on her face, sighed and started pacing. Then she got up close in Tracey's face.

"Do you know about drug-and-prostitution rings in Japan?"

"What are you getting at, Harianne? Even if I did, I wouldn't tell you." He shook his head, irritated. "We shouldn't be working together at all."

"We're not, detective. But I need to trade some information to prove my client's innocence. I've done my homework. I've got a dead friend, I'm representing a famous lawyer, and I've returned to criminal law practice. And the criminal justice system in the state of California sucks. Do you read me?"

"Copy. Skip the drama and give me the facts."

"You didn't even hear me. Let's sit over there."

They seated themselves on a wood bench nearby. Harianne shoved her hands in her pockets to keep them warm, sat back and began her story.

"Matthew's father, Tyler Harrison Daytona, was high up in the French mafia. He was half-brother to a man named Taka Sousushi, who was involved in the Japanese drug cartel and a huge prostitution-drug ring. He's a powerful businessman in Tokyo. They made millions and millions of dollars. The two of them pulled Matthew into the drug business in Japan when he was a young man, and Matthew worked with Taka on a number of cases. Matthew left Japan and the crime ring years ago but Sousushi stayed in the drug cartel.

"About eighteen months ago, five women employed by the prostitution-drug ring were found murdered with yellow silk scarves wrapped around their necks in bathrooms. Taka had been with each of them the night before they were killed; you might say he indulges with his employees. He was found guilty of the murders because his prints and DNA were everywhere, but he was mysteriously released due to a technicality. Later the DNA evidence was found to be inconclusive."

"Who told you about all of this?" Zack asked. "Daytona?"

"Not exactly," Harianne hedged. "My assistant dug it up for me this afternoon after I asked her to do some research. And here's the thing: I want to have Taka Sousushi extradited here for testimony. I am convinced that he was here and committed these murders. He set Matthew up."

"I remember that case," Tracey said. "We have newspaper clippings on file. No weapon was ever found. There was no evidence, except DNA."

Tracey cleared his throat. "But that means nothing. It's coincidental and may or may not be connected. Ours could be a copycat killer, but that's not likely. Daytona is powerful and could have other people committing the murders under him while he's in jail. We need evidence of Sousushi and Daytona's relationship. There are two different countries involved here."

"Let's get real," Harianne said. "What do you have? My client is innocent. That's the point I'm trying to make."

"Oh, yeah? So Daytona likes red scarves and Sousushi likes yellow. If Daytona didn't do it, who did? And where was he last month?"

Harianne regarded Tracey intently.

"He did make a quick trip to Japan to see Taka prior to the murders," she said. "But he wasn't there when they happened."

"Are you sure?"

He grabbed a white handkerchief buried deep in his pocket pants, sneezed into it and moved forward to the edge of the bench.

"Does your client know you want to get Sousushi over here?"

"Not yet," Harianne admitted. "It's his uncle, and he seems…nervous."

"Here's another question for you," Tracey said. "MacKenzie McShay: ever heard of her?"

Surprised, Harianne turned and frowned. Zack watched as they talked, knowing not to interrupt.

"Actually, yes. I just found out about her today."

"What do you mean, 'just found out about her'?"

"She's my new partner on Matthew's case. He hired her to work with me."

"Interesting."

"Why?" Harianne asked.

"Tracey, tell her," Zack urged. "Come on! It's getting late."

"All right, all right!" Tracey chuckled. He turned to Harianne, watching closely for her response. "She's his ex-girlfriend."

"What!" she yelled.

"Yeah. Didn't you know? Doesn't your big-shot lawyer have the decency to tell you anything?"

"Go to hell! I don't believe you. I just asked you and you said you didn't know a whole lot about her."

"I don't know a whole lot about her. I can't reveal my source, but I received it from his office."

"Funny. He never told me that. What a—"

"Bastard!" Zack interjected, frustrated.

"Zack, please. Stop it."

"It could be a conflict of interest, don't you think?" Zack said, smacking his gum.

"Not necessarily," Harianne replied. "She doesn't work for him anymore."

"Sources say she goes to the bathroom a lot. Maybe she's a customer?"

"You're an ass—"

"—hole!" Tracey interjected. "C'mon, Zack, cool off." He turned to Harianne. "I'm sorry. We're sorry and I apologize for Zack's behavior. We can't compare notes anymore or discuss this case."

"MacKenzie McShay, huh? I'll be in touch, detectives."

# CHAPTER 12

MacKenzie McShay was regarded as an iron woman by fellow attorneys: tough, exact and charismatic. Handsomely dressed and in her fifties, she possessed the wicked demeanor of an angry Joan Crawford and the vivid lawyering skills of Gloria Allred. She held bar licenses in California and New York but mostly practiced on the East Coast. At present, however, she sat across from Matthew Daytona in a gray leather chair at the downtown Los Angeles jail.

"Hi, Matthew. It's been a long time."

"Yeah, it has, MacKenzie. You look good."

"I only get better with time." She gave him a look. "I thought I might discuss your case with Harianne. When will I meet her?"

"I'll call her office. I didn't know you were coming."

"Surprises are my specialty."

Matthew looked at her strangely, while motioning for the guard.

"I need to use the phone."

"What's the number?"

Harianne picked up on the fifth ring; Matthew heard computer keys tapping in the background. MacKenzie sat patiently, listening.

"Harianne? Matthew."

"Well, about damn time!"

Matthew was caught off-guard. "What do you mean? What's on your mind?"

"Aren't you forgetting to tell me something?"

"What?"

"MacKenzie is your ex-girlfriend!"

"Yeah, she was."

"Why didn't you tell me earlier?"

"I didn't want you to quit."

"I won't, but I feel betrayed. You're supposed to tell me everything."

Matthew sighed impatiently, turned his head toward the guard and looked away.

"Harianne, I don't have much time. Can you come over and meet with MacKenzie?"

There was silence on the line for several seconds.

"Harianne?" Matthew asked nervously.

"Yes," she finally replied. "But it will be at least twenty minutes until I can get out of here."

"OK, thanks."

"And Matthew?"

"Yes?"

"If I find out you're keeping any other information from me, I'm dropping your case." She hung up.

Matthew slammed the phone down, dropped his head and slowly shook it back and forth.

"What was that all about?" MacKenzie asked.

"Nothing," Matthew replied quickly. "She's on her way over here. She's a little…anxious. Nothing is wrong."

Harianne drove downtown, pulled into the parking lot and entered the prison building. A guard directed her to MacKenzie, who was sitting at a table in a small conference room off the main hall, perusing a pile of papers.

"MacKenzie McShay?"

"Yes."

"Harianne DeCanter."

"Pleased to meet you, Harianne. I've read a lot about you. Your track record is very impressive."

"Thank you. Shall we get started?"

The women sat in the small conference room for two hours, sifting through police reports, medical examiner reports and DNA records. Harianne took the lead, as usual. Never having worked with MacKenzie before, she wasn't sure of her tactics or style. MacKenzie was cognizant of Harianne's actions and listened in lieu of talking. Eventually, they asked that Matthew be brought back to the conference room.

The next morning a man wearing blue jeans and a black jacket marked "Forensics" in large white letters walked into Zack's office. Zack was having a conversation with the fax machine, which was beeping continuously. Long rolls of thin paper spiraled from the table to the floor.

"What the heck's the matter with this thing. You damn—"

"Excuse me, Detective Grimes? Excuse me!"

"Yes! Yes! What is it?" he answered, turning his chair around.

"I'm Parker Benjamin from Forensics. We found a balancing scale pin called the 'Pin of Excellence' with Daytona's prints all over it."

"Where?"

"The bathroom floor of the Bernstein residence."

"Anything else?"

"Uh, yeah. There's an inscription on the back: 'To MD. Congratulations, GDMS.'"

"Thanks. That's quite interesting. Exactly where was it?"

"Bathroom floor near the toilet, immersed in a pool of blood. It took us a while."

"Yeah, I see that. It doesn't matter. I'll tell Tracey."

Zack turned his chair back around. Sighing and moaning with every movement, he pulled long rolls of paper out of the fax machine until it was empty. Frustrated, he slammed his fist on an adjacent table and pushed everything to the floor, causing a great disturbance throughout the office. Tracey rushed in.

"What the hell's wrong with you now, Zack?"

"Shut up! Nothing! It's this stupid fax machine!"

"Man, you sound like you're making love to it with all that grunting and groaning. Just order some new paper."

"It's a waste."

"Since when did you start paying for things around here?"

"I need it right now."

"It's a fax machine, Zack. A *fax.*"

"You're right. I'm cool. Hey, forensics stopped by—they found a pin on the bathroom floor at the Bernstein residence."

"Really. Whose is it?"

"They say that it's Matthew's."

"More evidence. I like it."

Tracey and Zack paid another visit to the medical examiner, Nick Carlyle, a DNA expert who specialized in forensic pathology and trading insults with

Tracey and Zack. He was detail-oriented and professional, and hated having his work questioned.

"What's up, doc?" Tracey cracked with a smirk.

"Very funny, Sanders," Carlyle said sourly.

"Did you run that stuff through again like we asked?" Zack asked.

"Yeah," Carlyle said. "I've got the results over here in the pending stack. There was something I thought you'd find interesting."

Zack looked at Carlyle. "Yeah? What's that?"

"Your victim was beaten up badly but not fatally. There are a number of contusions involving the soft tissues of the abdomen and chest. She had some evidence of trauma in the head resulting in some subarachnoid bleeding—essentially, a bruise on the brain, but no subdural or epidural hemorrhage, or skull fractures. There were no lacerations or ruptures involving the liver or spleen that could result in exsanguination or fatal hemorrhage."

"Well, what the hell did she die from then? Tracey asked.

"Patience, Sanders, patience," Carlyle taunted him. "I don't know exactly. The presence of cocaine was noted in the blood and a very small amount in the urine at the time of autopsy."

Zack interrupted. "Was it very recently injected or administered? Cocaine has a very short interval in the blood, as you know—what is it, six hours or less? Was it in the metabolized or in the original state?"

"By far the greatest amount was present as the parent cocaine compound. It had to be administered shortly before death."

"Any mainline or nasal insufflations?" Zack inquired.

"None," Carlyle replied. "No suggested crack use or intranasal use."

Tracey scratched his head. "Any smoking paraphernalia?"

Carlyle shook his head. "No evidence of mainline use, and no needle tracks in the skin."

"About how much of a dose are we talkin' about?" Tracey asked.

Carlyle turned back a couple of pages in his notes and whisked out his pencil, using it as a marker as he read: "The level of cocaine in the blood stream that is reached is 200 micrograms per liter in the average recreational use. To reach this level, only five to ten milligrams need to be injected…if the actual needle track was missed at autopsy and mainlining was the route of administration. Didn't you say the suspect had twenty-five grams of cocaine on him when he was arrested? That's roughly equal to about 2,500 doses, uncut. An amount as small as ten milligrams would never be missed."

"Is it possible our vic suffered from an allergic reaction to the cocaine?" Tracey inquired hesitantly.

"Yes, she could have. People have been known to die with very low blood levels. Using xylocaine as an example, people are known to have anaphylactic reactions to xylocaine, which is like cocaine.

Tracey gave Zack a look. "The MO's the same."

Carlyle paused for a second and sat on a nearby stool. "Let me repeat something. The amount that was actually found in the body was about sixty micrograms. This is far less than routine recreational use, let alone a lethal level. Let me also remind you that the lethal level is about 6,000 micrograms per liter or greater in the blood—about 100 times greater than the amount that was actually found in the victim. Cocaine is not the cause of death, excluding sudden death due to anaphylaxis, or just cardiac arrest. Usually, in the latter cases, the needle and syringe may still be in the victim's arm or nearby on the floor. But that was not the case here."

Harianne arrived at home tired. Her migraine had returned with a vengeance, so she stretched out on the bed. Austria brought her a hot cup of herbal tea and her Fiorinal medication before leaving for her weekly book-club meeting. Harianne had been resting for only a few minutes when the phone rang. The answering machine kicked in and she heard Tracey's voice.

"Harianne, it's Tracey Sanders. I need to meet with you in person."

Harianne couldn't even imagine leaving the house for a meeting, but she sensed from the sound of his voice that it was important. She answered just as he was about to finish.

"Detective Sanders, I'm here."

"Oh, you are. How about eight o'clock for dinner?"

"Oh, is this the dinner you wanted to take me out to?"

"It's important."

"OK. I'll see you at eight-The Peninsula."

Harianne showered, changed into some simple black straight-leg pants, a black mohair sweater and animal-print, closed-toe slides. Knowing she'd be at dinner soon she snacked on a green apple topped with thinly sliced Gruyere cheese while checking her messages. Dr. Zenfried had left instructions regarding the administration of her Dostinex medication and her appointment: the day after tomorrow at eight in the morning. Her heart pounded hard at the thought of it. She struggled to control her mounting anxiety.

She found Tracey standing by the door when she arrived at the Peninsula Hotel in Beverly Hills. A meeting haven for business executives, its unique atmosphere invited intimate discussions and small talk. Harianne and Tracey were seated at a table toward the back.

"This seems awkward," Tracey said. "You're the defense lawyer. You wanted to work together and I'm not sure that is a good idea, let alone normal in the judicial process."

"Normal, no," Harianne agreed. "But I think we could work together. I'm telling you he didn't do it."

"You keep saying that. Why do you think he didn't do it? Give me a reason."

"I'm telling you the truth."

"Convince me."

Just as Harianne was about to respond, the waiter arrived and they turned their eyes to their menus. They ordered dinner and coffee.

"So. Where were we, Harianne?"

She looked at him like a bull ready to charge in a ring. He countered with a smile.

"You know, you're not so bad, Harianne. We should stop fighting each other. Let's put this puzzle together. Maybe we can work together. My case, as you know, is for the prosecution. It's tight and it's right until you can convince me otherwise."

"I'll do it. Believe me, I will."

She pulled out a small notepad and pen. Tracey did the same. He knew that the meeting was wrong, but he wanted the information and she was willing to give it up.

"The Japan deal," he started. "What do you know about it?"

"I told you at the Chart House."

"I know you did, and it was great information."

She paused, took a bite of her salad and sat back in her chair. The expression on Tracey's face indicated he had the answers—but not all of them.

"The Japanese drug-prostitution ring—what's the deal?" he asked. "Who started it?"

"Taka Sousushi. He's the front-runner. Matthew was involved in the drug cartel years ago but he's not involved anymore."

"Wanna make a bet? He's in it. Our last toxicology report showed the cocaine was extremely fresh in both Jasmine Thomas and Shana Bernstein. This means that it was shipped recently—a day before the murder.

"And Daytona," he added pointedly, chewing, "had high-grade cocaine in his possession when we arrested him."

Harianne leaned forward. "Matthew called me right away about the drug charges. But just because he had cocaine on him doesn't make him a murderer. C'mon. He's a Beverly Hills lawyer."

Tracey shook his head. "The tests were conclusive. It was a cocaine compound. I'm afraid your client is guilty as hell."

"Oh, really? I don't think so."

"Suit yourself. I can't blame you. I mean, you're his lawyer."

"What else have you got?"

"It's my secret. You'll find out."

"No secrets, I thought."

"I didn't make any promises."

"Well, one thing is certain. Neither Jasmine nor Shana were cocaine addicts. How do you explain that?"

"Jasmine is another victim."

"And she's my best friend. I want to know what happened to her. I don't know how the cocaine got there."

"Was she ever on drugs?"

"No!"

"Don't yell, Harianne. I like you. Listen, let's not discuss this case; let's just have dinner." He placed Harianne's hand in his and smiled. "I really would like to get to know you. Let's just put work behind us for an hour. Is that possible?"

"Maybe," Harianne responded hesitantly. "Sure."

Tracey let go of her hand and leaned back in his seat.

"Were you ever married, Harianne?"

Surprised, she paused before answering. "No. Why?"

"You're a nice, intelligent and beautiful woman. Any man should be proud of you."

"That's very nice of you. I bet you say that to everyone."

"No, I don't. I meant what I said."

Harianne put down her salad fork and eased back in her seat. "How about you?" she asked.

"I was married; I'm a widow."

Harianne's eyes widened. "Tracey—"

He took her hand again in assurance and comforted her.

"It's OK. It surprises everyone. Sometimes even me, but it's the truth. Her name was Marina."

"How did she—"

"It's a long story. She was a police officer, like me, back in New York. She died in a stakeout. It shouldn't have happened, but the circumstances were confusing to the police force."

"I'm so sorry," Harianne said sincerely.

"It's all right. Relax. I meant what I said."

"What's that?"

"I'd like to see you again and really get to know you." He smiled.

Harianne returned the smile and perked up.

"That would be nice."

Dinner arrived: baked potato, mixed vegetables and fish. Tracey picked up his fork immediately, making it known that he was starved. He ate quickly and returned to his notes, while Harianne enjoyed every small bite.

"Where's your partner?" she asked.

"Zack? At home, I guess. I wanted to meet with you privately. For some strange reason, I believe you. But I believe in myself too. It's hard to put my finger on why all these women had drugs in their blood."

"It gets a little confusing," Harianne acknowledged, chewing her food. "There isn't much to tell about the cartel. It's my understanding that Matthew's no longer involved, but there must be some truth to your findings. I don't know the link."

A dessert tray was placed in front of them, but neither partook of the pastries offered. They continued talking over coffee. Twenty minutes later Harianne insisted on splitting the check with Tracey. They bid each other goodnight outside the restaurant and went their separate ways.

Harianne started the drive home. She knew that it was unethical to represent a client and at the same time interact with the detective who'd placed him in jail. But she was puzzled, and didn't know who to believe. Was Matthew telling the truth? It seemed like a dream. The stakes were high for him; he was already facing the loss of his bar license, and the abolishment of his popular rating as an entertainment lawyer.

As she pulled into her driveway, she noticed the side porch light was on. She had turned it off when she left…or had she? She wasn't sure. Something wasn't right. She opened the automatic garage door, parked the car, stepped out and headed for the house. Suddenly, a loud noise erupted and the garage door started closing as the overhead lights went out. Trembling and scared, Harianne pushed the garage door back up as she hit the alarm to the car and tried to open the doors. But in a fit of nervousness, she locked them, causing red lights to flash on the tip of the door locks. She punched the alarm button again. The doors unlocked and she threw herself into the car and pushed the panic button to the house alarm. With sweaty fingers she tried to simultaneously dial 911 on her cellphone and start the car. The ignition wouldn't turn on; the engine was flooded. She looked to the left and the right. There was no one in sight.

In her rearview mirror, Harianne could clearly see a black-clad figure of medium height approaching her car from behind. Her nervousness intensified and she turned the key in the ignition again. It kicked in immediately. She shoved the gears in reverse and slammed her foot on the accelerator. The mysterious figure sprinted down the driveway, Harianne close behind.

At the bottom of the driveway, Harianne cautiously exited the car and surveyed her surroundings. She heard Melissa barking in the house and sirens off in the distance, but otherwise everything was still.

Soon three police cars with flashing red lights and loud sirens pulled up in front of her house. A couple of officers questioned her for half an hour, while others surveyed the property with flashlights.

"Sergeant! An old wood window," an officer yelled.

"What about it?" Harianne asked.

"Forced entry. The bathroom window to the rear of the house was cracked with a crowbar at the bottom. A piece of gum was stuck on the transmitter to evade the alarm sound. Apparently they also blocked out the infrared with a device and evaded the infrared."

Harianne looked around but couldn't tell if anything was missing. The intruder was out of sight, but not out of mind.

# CHAPTER 13

❁

Two days later, Harianne was scheduled for her MRI. She'd hardly been able to sleep the night before for worrying about the mysterious intruder. What had they wanted?

She dragged her tired body out of bed and phoned China, who was retrieving faxes that had arrived in the office the night before.

"Hi, China."

"Harianne! How goes it?"

"Everything is fine, at least I think it is. I won't be in today. I've got a one o'clock doctor's appointment."

"You sound worried."

"No, I'm OK."

"I can tell by the crackling in your voice. Why do you keep swallowing? What's wrong, Harianne?"

"I'll tell you later. I'm just a little anxious and nervous."

"You'll be fine. Stop worrying. I'll handle the office."

"Thanks. That helps. Well, I've got to go. I'm still cleaning up around here. I'll check voice mail. Talk to you later."

Harianne tuned into China's concerns while making the bed. "She's just trying to make me feel better," she said to herself. "If she only knew. I can't tell her right now."

She selected a cream sweater and black wool pants while reflecting upon her life—the sad and the happy times. Her memory clouded with thoughts of the strange woman standing over her mother with a syringe; the face would not materialize in her memory bank.

Harianne recalled a piece of advice her adopted mother had once given her: "Don't waste time. Perfection is imperfection. Either get busy living or get busy dying!" She had never forgotten that.

Nor had she forgotten their special time: tea time, which they had shared every afternoon around three-thirty, surrounded by beautiful teapots from around the world in the DeCanters' elaborate blue-and-white parlor. Even though her mother had been an ambitious attorney, she had always made time for tea with Harianne once they had started the tradition years ago. Now, whenever Harianne spotted a rare teapot, she missed her mother terribly.

Three hours later, Harianne arrived at Cedars-Sinai and was directed to the radiology department. She felt cold air brushing her skin when she entered the clinical room lined with stainless steel and glass cabinets. Rayla, a petite woman with curly short brown hair and a calm voice, was the technician. She handed Harianne a gown and directed her to a dressing room around the corner. After Harianne had changed, she followed Rayla down the hall to the X-ray room, where Rayla asked her to lie down on the long, tubular bed. Five minutes later, Harianne felt heat rush through her body.

"Are you all right?" Rayla asked. She gently placed a hand on Harianne's suddenly sweaty forehead.

"I feel awfully hot," Harianne confessed. "And nervous."

"Don't worry," Rayla reassured her in soothing tones. When Harianne's hot flash subsided a few minutes later, she proceeded with the test.

As Harianne's head passed under the glass bubble dome, she envisioned the *Enterprise* from *Star Trek*; she halfway expected to see Captain Kirk arrive at any minute. But he never showed up. She felt the little razor hairs on her calves bristle when she tried to move her legs closer together. She started to move her legs when she bumped her arm against the railing of the tubular module.

"Harianne, you seem frightened," Rayla called out. "Are you OK?"

"Yes."

"Just lie still. It won't be long."

Harianne closed her eyes and let her mind drift. There was nothing she could do now. Whatever the results said, there was no turning back.

When the test finally ended, Harianne smacked her lips together and complained of a dry mouth. Rayla asked her to wait ten minutes while she checked the X-rays. Fifteen minutes later, she returned with a glass of apple juice.

"Here, drink this," she suggested, handing Harianne the juice. "It'll help with the dry mouth. How do you feel now?"

"Still cold, but fine. Really."

"Just stay there for a minute. Here's another blanket. Your doctor will have the results in one week."

Even though the test had gone well, a cloud of worry fell upon her. What would be the outcome? What was causing her headaches? Would she die? Was there a cure?

She grabbed the cellphone from her purse and called China at the office.

"It's me, China."

"Hi, Me!"

"Anything urgent?"

"No. We're fine."

"Good."

Evening had fallen. The wind wreaked havoc across the city and inland valleys. Temperatures dropped far below their usual level and a heavy mist hung over L.A. Tired and listless, Harianne stopped at a local deli, ordered a chicken Caesar salad to go and returned home.

Later that evening, a creaky door opened to the women's bathroom in an isolated brick building in downtown L.A.

"Anyone there? Who's there?" a lady cried out.

The intruder moved closer to the stall, then turned toward the nearby sink and turned the water on before heading back toward the stall. With a swift maneuver of the lock, the door opened. The lady's mouth dropped in shock and fear. She was silenced by a strong blow to her stomach; her body was flung against the stall siding by her assailant, who proceeded to tear off her clothes.

The victim's legs slumped on either side of the toilet, and blood dripped down from her body into the drain cover in the bathroom stall. The only piece of clothing that remained was a red silk scarf tied around her neck.

# CHAPTER 14

Tracey and Zack were called to the crime scene early the next morning.

"What've we got?" Tracey inquired.

A police officer already on the scene slowly opened the loose-hinged, blood-streaked stall door. Tracey recognized her immediately.

"Hillary McDunn."

Their mouths hung agape with dismay—and consternation: If Matthew Daytona was the killer, and he was in jail, then who had murdered Hillary? A copycat killer?

"Maybe Harianne was onto something with that Japan connection," Zack muttered. "What the hell is going on?"

"Man, I don't fuckin' know anymore!" Tracey fumed.

"On the toilet seat again…"

"…and the legs spread wide apart with the infamous red silk scarf."

Zack paced the floor and tried not to look at Hillary. Shortly thereafter, the forensics team arrived. Tracey instructed them to do the usual rape kit and dusting. The dusting for prints had to be accurate, especially this time. Tracey flashed back to his wife. He had to dismiss his memories quickly in order to proceed with the investigation. He questioned the guard standing nearby.

"Who found her?"

"I think the janitor."

A thin black man shuffled toward Tracey with a broom in hand. Tracey studied him closely. The man's nappy black hair was parted on the side; streaks of gray spoke to his age, which Tracey guessed to be sixtysomething. Hard calluses on his hands suggested a lifetime of hard work. A gold tooth flashed when he spoke. His speech was flavored with a distinct Southern accent.

"What time did you find the body?" Tracey asked.

"Lessee…I cleaned that there bathroom—you know what I mean—the men's room, oh, about nine-thirty or ten o'clock," the janitor replied quietly. "So let's say I got to the women's about, ah, ten-fifteen. You see it's a little ways down the hall from the men's."

"Did you see or hear anything?"

"No, suh. That's the funny thing. Ain't nobody hear as good as me, and I didn't hear a-nothin'."

There were no other eyewitnesses. Tracey and Zack asked a few more questions before taking another look at the body and the murder scene to make sure that no stone had gone unturned. Certainty was key.

They returned to the precinct at three-thirty. The old elevators were moving slowly, so they took the stairs; their arms dangled while they dragged their feet up the cement steps. Finally, they arrived in their office. Zack fell onto the overstuffed sofa.

"Man, let's get some sleep."

"I can't right now, Zack. Neither can you. I thought we had him."

"We do, Tracey. It's a copycat."

"A S ODDI? Maybe. I want Daytona under heavy surveillance just in case there are outside contacts."

"SODDI?" Zack asked quizzically.

"Some Other Dude Did It."

"What about inside the Japanese drug cartel?"

"That, too."

"Maybe he's not the one. Harianne might be right."

"What do you wanna do?"

"Proceed," Zack said. "I still think Daytona killed Bernstein and Thomas. We've got conclusive DNA evidence."

Nick walked in, chewing his usual Tutti-Frutti gum, and handed Tracey a manila folder.

"You've got your work cut out for you this time. A real live one! I wouldn't be in your shoes for anything."

"Hey, what's up with you?" Tracey asked.

"You'll see."

Zack stood by Tracey and leaned over his shoulder as they both read the file.

"No way!" Tracey exclaimed. "I don't believe this! The sequences found in the vaginal fluid and the semen are one in a million. There's a 100 percent correspondence."

"Tracey, that's wrong," Zack said. "Real wrong."

"Who did this work-up?"

"I did," Nick responded in a confident voice.

"Do it over!"

"Won't work. That's the truth. What you see is accurate. I'm not doing it over. Good luck."

Nick left while Tracey and Zack pondered the evidence and stood there as if their feet were stuck in quicksand.

"How the hell could that be?" Zack scratched his head and nodded toward the phone. "You wanna call Harianne?"

"No," Tracey replied. "Not yet."

The next day, Tracey convinced Nick's boss to conduct the test again. It took two days, and came back with the same results. The detectives fueled up on java and brainstormed in their office.

"Did you sleep last night?" Zack asked.

"Not much," Tracey answered. "How about you?"

"Hell, no! I couldn't get her out of my mind."

"Don't I know."

With time running out, they worked all day and into the night.

Arriving at her office, Harianne was greeted by China, who handed her a handful of messages.

"Thanks, China," Harianne said. She gestured toward Jasmine's blue box in the corner of the room. "Would you please put that on the conference table?"

"Sure, no prob," China said as she dutifully picked up the box. "Hey, this thing's heavy—did you put some more files in here?"

"No," Harianne answered distractedly.

China shrugged and carted the box into the conference room, where she placed it on the long cherrywood table. Returning to Harianne's office, she found her standing by the window, silhouetted by the afternoon sun.

"What happened at the doctor's office?" she asked. "Are you OK?"

"Uh, yeah."

"I don't believe you."

"I'll be fine, China."

China sensed the denial in Harianne's speech but held her tongue. She fixed Harianne a cup of hot tea and placed it on her desk. "I'll be right outside here if you need me," she told her.

Harianne turned her head slightly but said nothing. China stared at her for a moment then sighed in disgust. It wasn't like Harianne to be rude. She shut the door and silently forgave her.

Harianne's mind was on her visit to Dr. Zenfried's office. Her life would be changed dramatically if she did, in fact, have a tumor.

After listening to voicemails and completing the paperwork on her desk, her eyes felt tired, but she knew she still had to review the newspaper articles she'd retrieved from Jasmine's office. It was a daunting and time-consuming task; most of the articles were in Japanese, a language that was unfamiliar to her.

Moving into the conference room, she removed the lid from Jasmine's blue box and reached for a rear file labeled "The Family." Just as her fingers gently touched the tip of the file, it wiggled.

Startled, Jasmine jumped back as a red, yellow and orange snake raised its wet-looking head. Its rope-like body was wrapped around the bottom of the files.

Quickly regaining her composure, Harianne scrambled for the lid and carefully used its cardboard edge to push the snake back down, then slammed the lid on top of the box and pushed it toward the middle of the table. Gasping for air, she ran to the kitchen for a glass of water.

"China! Did you know there was a snake in the box?"

"What? No! It was heavy, and I thought I felt something rolling around, but I figured I was imagining things."

"Really!"

"Where is it now?"

"In the conference room. I'm going to call a friend to come get it."

Harianne immediately phoned Rikko; he arrived half an hour later.

"Hello, my darling Harianne!"

"Rikko! The snake is in the conference room down the hall."

"A snake, eh? So much like me, don't you think?"

"Really, Rikko! Please, just get it out of here."

"All right. Take me to the snake pit."

China showed Rikko the conference room, where he removed the lid from Jasmine's blue cardboard box. There at the bottom was the snake, looking straight at Rikko with its red eyes.

"This is an Albino Corn snake," Rikko said. "He's harmless."

"Are you sure?" Harianne asked.

"Yeah. These snakes usually grow to be about three to six feet long, but they're nothing to worry about. They love hair, purses and people." He gave Harianne a teasing glance. "This guy will even love you, if you let him."

"Very funny, Rikko. Take it! But just the snake—I need the box."

"Really, he's related. We're all snakes."

"What are you going to do with him, Rikko?" China asked.

"Ah, that's easy," Rikko said with a wink and a smile. "I know a nice, big field in Griffith Park where he'll feel right at home."

With the snake safely disposed of, Harianne returned to her office, poured herself a glass of Merlot from her bar, settled into the chenille sofa and continued digging through Jasmine's box for information. Her glasses slid halfway down her nose as she studied the "Family" file.

The key players in the "Family" were Matthew Daytona and Taka Sousushi, half-brother to Matthew's father, Tyler Harrison Daytona. Copies of birth certificates for Tyler and Taka were clipped to a packet of letters that had been exchanged between the two men. According to Jasmine's notes, Sousushi was nicknamed "Big Man"—meaning "big mind, little man." He was known for his business acumen, political savvy, and for taking every opportunity presented to him even if it meant risking dangerous situations.

Harianne reviewed several newspaper articles detailing business investments that had gone bad for Sousushi in both the United States and Japan, then unfolded one of the letters. It was from Taka to Matthew—a lengthy apology for bad business investments he had made on behalf of Matthew's father. Harianne grimaced at the enclosed photo: it showed a finger that had been cut off and labeled "Taka Sousushi."

# CHAPTER 15

❦

The next morning, Tracey and Zack returned to Daytona, Bernstein & McDunn. Erin, the receptionist, wiped her eyes with a blue tissue as they approached her desk. Office morale was, predictably, low; frustration, depression, confusion and anxiety were written across the employees' faces as they milled about the hallways, conference rooms and adjacent offices.

"Shit," Zack swore under his breath as he and Tracey moved quickly around the entire office. "Every managing partner in this place is six feet under."

"Except Daytona," Tracey reminded him.

Tracey was stumped and felt cheated. The case was spiraling out of control. Were they dealing with a copycat killer? Or was Matthew Daytona innocent, as Harianne had been insisting all along?

They interviewed every employee in the firm about Hillary Dunn's schedule: how many hours, days and weeks she worked. They asked about ownership of the building, and grilled associates about cases currently being handled by the firm. Nothing yielded any clues.

Toward the completion of their investigation, they arrived at Lara Smith's office. Zack knocked on the door, but there was no response. He was almost ready to knock again when she opened the door.

"It's all right," she sniffed. "Come in."

They awkwardly watched as she curled up in a corner of the sofa. She tossed her hair to one side, gripping a wad of tissues. Tracey and Zack felt uneasy in the presence of her grief.

"Have a seat," she offered.

"We'll stand, thanks," Tracey said. "Do you mind if we ask you some questions?"

"Now?"

"We can come back later, but we should—"

"No, that's all right. Let's just get it over with. I don't know who's next," she cried.

"Did you see anyone strange hanging around here at night?" Tracey asked. "I mean, we know you work late and—"

"How do you know that?"

"Our sources told us."

"No. I left early for once yesterday. The first time since I've been here."

"Why the change?" Zack asked.

"I needed to rest."

"Was Hillary in her office when you left?"

She paused for a long time before responding. "I think so, yes."

"Was it just you and her?"

"Yes. I left at seven o'clock. That's early for me."

"Did you see anyone else?" Tracey asked. "In the elevator, the lobby, etc.? Anyone who might have followed Hillary out of here?"

"No. Just the janitor."

"Any strange phone calls lately?"

"No."

"I see. Well, that gives us something to work with."

"Not much," Zack muttered.

Tracey shot Zack a warning look then handed Lara his business card. "Try to take care of yourself and don't work late if you can help it. In fact, if you're working late at night, call Detective Grimes or me. We'll arrange for surveillance."

Tracey and Zack returned to their car with notepads and pens still in hand.

"Tracey," Zack asked, "do you think we should tell her?"

"Her?"

"Harianne."

"I don't know, Zack. Maybe. She'll find out soon enough if she doesn't know already. It's in the papers. After all, she's representing Daytona, even though we're talking to each other. I kinda got sucked in. I like Harianne."

"Hey, you and Harianne gotta love thing?"

"Zack…"

"Wait, whaddya mean, 'got sucked in'?" Zack asked. "You think Daytona is innocent?"

"We nailed him and he's still guilty as far as I'm concerned," Tracey assured him. "However, it's odd."

"Yeah, I know. We'll have to stay on top of it."

A half-hour later, Tracey's cellphone rang. It was Marnetta.

"Tracey, we've got a fax from the Japanese authorities."

"Why? We haven't spoken with them."

"Hey, I'm just delivering the message."

Tracey tried to remember if he had requested any information. Nothing came to mind.

"All right. We'll be there in ten."

"Oh, no, we won't," Zack corrected him. "Not until we get something to eat first."

"Where?"

"The usual."

It was just before rush hour but there was little traffic on the road. They drove down Wilshire straight to a coffee shop at Wilshire and Westmoreland, where they ordered food to go before heading back to the precinct.

In their office, Tracey found a bright red plastic folder on his chair; inside was a fax from police authorities in Tokyo. He poured himself a cup of coffee and read it over while Zack wolfed down a cheeseburger, fries and a strawberry shake.

According to the fax, Taka Sousushi was a prominent insurance executive whose money was invested in questionable businesses believed to be fronts for a sizable prostitution-drug ring in Japan. He had also profited from numerous investments in the United States. Phone records indicated that he frequently phoned Matthew Daytona at his home and office.

"Looks like Sousushi is Daytona's protector in Japan," Zack said. "Maybe he wanted some favors returned by Matthew over here."

"Sousushi got away with murdering five women in Japan," Tracey mused. "Maybe he thinks he can pull it off again here?"

"We'll see," Zack said. "All the pieces are coming together. The picture will come into focus soon."

"Maybe," Tracey said thoughtfully. "Hey, Zack. Let me run something by you."

Zack listened intently.

# CHAPTER 16

Tracey and Zack worked until the wee hours of the morning, requesting Matthew Daytona's old telephone bills, past airline itineraries, passports, etc. They reviewed the police record from Tokyo for Taka Sousushi. It showed he had been charged and found guilty of the murders and rapes of five women, then released due to inconclusive DNA findings. It also showed that he owned and operated an escort service; although no signs of drugs had ever been found by police on the premises, Japanese authorities suspected the service was a front for a drug-and-prostitution ring that distributed cocaine in Kyoto, Tokyo and Aka. He had been charged with operating the prostitution ring, but had been found not guilty due to lack of evidence.

"I'm totally confused about this damn case!" Tracey exclaimed.

"Me, too," Zack agreed.

Tracey rubbed his hands through his hair and leaned forward with his eyes affixed to Zack's.

"I'm calling Gaston Reeves right now."

"The D.A.? Wait a minute, Tracey. You told Harianne we'd give Matthew the benefit of the doubt first, and *then*, if nothing made sense, we'd go to the D.A."

"We've already got a conflict of interest by exchanging information with Harianne," Tracey replied. "But we really haven't helped her. I'm just not sure if Daytona's the one. There are a lot of players in this game now. Gaston Reeves is the prosecutor who'll try him. He's got the same information we've got, and he'll find out about Sousushi and the drug-and-prostitution ring anyway."

Tracey paced the floor in his soiled white shirt, which was stained underneath the arms.

"I hope Gaston doesn't find out that we worked in tandem with Harianne," Zack muttered, worried.

"We didn't work with her, Zack. I mean, c'mon, we're trying to solve some murders here!"

"Yeah. Right. Any encounters with Harianne DeCanter, lawyer for the defense, are our own business."

Harianne stood on her brick driveway and inhaled the fresh air. Retrieving the morning's newspaper from a pile of leaves, she untied the white string around it and was startled by the headline above the fold: "Lawyer Wrapped in Red Silk."

Slowly walking into her kitchen, she continued reading as she poured a cup of coffee and slid into the bay window seat, letting her back soak in the sun streaming through the panes.

"Who's doing this?" she whispered to herself. "It couldn't be…"

Matthew had been in jail for weeks. The thought of a copycat killer was chilling. Had semen been found on Hillary? What evidence had been found at the scene?

Austria entered the living room, carrying a breakfast tray laden with fresh fruit, Swedish pancakes, a boiled egg, a small porcelain cup of syrup, a crystal dish full of Hollandaise sauce and a small glass of orange juice. She sat down next to Harianne and handed her a white linen napkin.

"Good morning, Harianne! Here's your breakfast. I thought you might need a little something special today, so I added your favorite pancakes as a treat."

Not wasting any time, Harianne grabbed her fork and the syrup and dug in.

"Great! Thanks, Austria. You know how much I love these with lots of syrup. Just like the old days."

"What are you reading?"

"An article on Matthew Daytona. It's not good."

"How so?" Austria inquired, sipping her coffee.

"All the tabloids will eat this story up and ruin his reputation."

"I know he's your client, but I can't say that I feel sorry for him," Austria said. She placed her hand on Harianne's shoulder. "Remember what he did to you and how he ruined your chances at UCLA?"

Harianne pushed her plate aside. "Of course. Those were the worse days of my life. I can never forgive him for what he did to me. I had to leave home, my family, you, Jasmine—everything I knew—and attend school out of state just because of his ignorance. Because of my skin color."

Austria hugged Harianne and reassured her with a pat on the back.

"What goes around eventually comes back around, dear. He's a racist. Now that he's faced with opposition, he'll say anything to get back into everyone's good graces."

Three hours later, Harianne arrived at the office. After listening to her voicemail messages, she phoned Tracey.

"Tracey Sanders?"

"Hello, Harianne. I like when you call me Tracey."

"Never mind. This is business. How long have you known about Hillary McDunn?"

"A day. Why?"

"Why didn't you tell me?"

"I don't have to and wasn't going to. You know now."

"We're supposed to be helping each other. You made me a deal."

"No, I didn't. There's no deal. I just listened. We're actually not supposed to be working together. I'm with you on this, though. It's hard to figure out why people are being murdered and he's in jail."

"Was semen found on her?"

"It's conclusive. Semen was found all over her. It's a rape."

"No way! Where did it come from? I told you he's innocent. I've got to tell MacKenzie."

"Wait a minute, Harianne. It could be a copycat, but he still murdered Shana Bernstein. That's without a doubt."

"Don't be so sure about that."

"I can't figure it out myself. This is a challenging one."

"To say the least. So what next?"

"Wait it out."

"We'll see. I'll call you later."

"I'll look forward to that."

An hour later Harianne was facing her star client at the jail. As a prison guard escorted him to his seat, she noticed that Matthew was starting to look worn. She pressed her hand against the glass divider and he pressed his against the glass from the other side when she picked up the phone to speak.

"Hello, Matthew. Looks like you're in a good mood today."

"Sorry. I hate this dump."

"I'm concerned about you."

"I'm concerned about me too. I want my life back!"

"And you'll have it back," she assured him. "But listen, things have heated up."

"Heated up?"

Harianne reached her hand between the leather dividers of her briefcase for a yellow pad and pen and cleared her throat. "Give me a minute to explain."

"I've only got the rest of my life. You know, it's funny. Remember when I didn't let you into law school?"

"How could I forget," Harianne responded dryly.

"Now I know what it's like to be a minority. Trying to convince people that your character and content are important, not what they see on the outside. It's…difficult."

Harianne leaned forward.

"The world is unpredictable and chaotic. That was then and this is now. Let's move on."

"Well. Talk to me. What's going on?"

"Hillary McDunn was found dead."

"What? No! How?"

"Ultimately, the same MO: rape, drugs and murder."

Matthew dropped his head and wept silently. "Where was she—at the office?"

"No. She was at some building downtown."

"Dear God, I hope she didn't suffer."

Harianne and Matthew conversed for one hour and she took notes on everything. Trial was approaching and she was preparing him for the worst scene of his life: defending himself before a jury.

That evening Harianne resumed her search for valuable information in Jasmine's files. She felt like Nancy Drew, or Jessica Fletcher in some episode of *Murder, She Wrote*, as she retrieved a flashlight from the desk drawer to guard against any snakes or items unknown to her.

In the back of a red file she discovered handwritten notes by Jasmine. She pulled them out and read the first page: "*MacKenzie McShay born 1948. Place of birth, New York. Attended New York University School of Law. Later attended New York School of Medicine. Married shortly thereafter and divorced some time later. Dated Matthew Daytona regularly and worked for Daytona, Bernstein & McDunn. Was once up for managing partner, but departed firm hastily.*"

Something about that bothered Harianne deeply. Why would MacKenzie leave before becoming partner? She pushed her curiosity aside as she reached for a blue file labeled "Office of Professional Medical Conduct/New York." It contained the goriest information of all.

*"In mid-1990s, MacKenzie McShay employed by a New York hospital as a doctor specializing in endocrinology and pathology. Dismissed from post after throwing violent tantrum in operating room; OPMC concluded episode was triggered by anesthesiologist giving patient an injection. It was further determined that Dr. McShay had had numerous problems during previous surgeries. Board of Regents barred her from practicing medicine in the state of New York."*

Harianne shook her head in confusion as she read the details of MacKenzie's outburst in the operating room.

"Who *is* this woman?" she wondered. She thought hard about MacKenzie's professionalism.

As she dug further through Jasmine's files, she found a white ruled telephone log showing several phone calls to a number in Tokyo, Japan. The calls were charged to Daytona, Bernstein & McDunn. Jasmine's notes were made in red ink: *"Five red silk scarves were ordered and a—"*

Jasmine's handwriting abruptly spiraled off the page in a jagged curve. With a chill, Harianne realized it must have been what Jasmine was writing at the moment she was attacked. Harianne pulled a tissue from the box and wiped away her tears.

# CHAPTER 17

Harianne was still perusing Jasmine's files when the phone rang. She gingerly maneuvered through the thicket of boxes and legal pads covering the floor and picked up the receiver; it was Tracey.

"A peace offering: I've got Chinese food. Have you eaten yet?"

She chuckled. "Where are you, Tracey?"

"Look out your window."

Harianne peeked through the sheer curtains covering the bay window. Tracey waved from his dark sedan, which was idling at the curb.

"Are you writing?" he asked.

"Uh, trying. How can you tell?"

"I hear the telltale tap-tap-tapping of computer keys in the background."

Harianne giggled. "You got me. I'm hungry. I'll buzz you in through the gate."

Melissa barked incessantly as Tracey strolled up the brick walkway. Harianne calmed her with a peanut-flavored dog treat.

Tracey greeted them at the door with a smile. He wore a black crewneck shirt with black wool pants.

"Don't you look nice," Harianne said, extending her hand out to his in greeting. "I like your cologne. Smells like…sandalwood, with almond and vanilla."

"It's rated this month's best cologne in GQ."

"Mmm. You wear it well."

Harianne felt butterflies run wild in her stomach. Standing so close to Tracey, she was conscious of a new tension between them, and new feelings.

"Hey, I'm sorry about this afternoon," Tracey apologized.

"You are? It's OK. Apology accepted. We're all under stress on this case. Let's eat in the dining room. I'll get some plates."

Tracey admired his tastefully decorated surroundings while Harianne grabbed burgundy-and-gold plates and ivory-and-gold silverware resembling elephant tusks from a kitchen drawer.

"I like your home," he said. "It speaks to you; it's comfortable."

"Thanks," Harianne said. "I like it here a lot." She placed the dishes on the sideboard and pulled a two-liter bottle of soda from the fridge. Tracey poured the soda into glasses while she lit white candles perched in crystal holders.

"The privacy of the hills creates the perfect sanctuary for me after working with those legal alligators all day," Harianne continued. "I can nestle in bed with the down pillows and my comforter…once I'm in, I never want to get up. This place is very special to me."

"No doubt."

"So what do we have here? Chicken broccoli, garlic shrimp, garlic vegetables—a ton of garlic!"

Tracey put his hand on her arm. She smiled, swept up by his warmth and gentleness.

"Any favorites?" he asked.

"No, I don't have one," she responded.

Tracey spooned a little of everything onto her plate, then helped himself to some very generous servings. He took his seat at the table and fixed his gaze on Harianne.

"Your friend Jasmine was very close to the truth," he said, chewing.

Harianne kept eating and listened carefully.

"I can't pinpoint the vital facts that led to her death," he said. "In fact, I don't know who killed her yet."

"I hired Jasmine to investigate Matthew Daytona before I took on his representation," Harianne told him. "I thought it was odd for him to hire me since he didn't really like African Americans."

"What do you mean?"

"When he was dean of UCLA's law school, he denied entry to many African-American students, including me."

Tracey gagged on his shrimp. "Daytona barred you from law school?"

Harianne nodded. "That's why I didn't go to UCLA. I didn't understand his reasoning, so I asked Jasmine to do some digging for me."

"Jasmine had no idea how deep she was digging, did she?"

"No, she had no idea," Harianne said as tears slid down her face.

"I'm sorry, Harianne."

Tracey chewed the last bit of his food, and folded his white cloth napkin on his plate.

"Dessert?" Harianne asked. "I've got pound cake with vanilla yogurt. It's the best."

"Yeah, sure. Sounds good. And then we've got a lot of ground to cover."

"You want to review the case? It's Friday night."

"You're right, but it's worth it."

Harianne glanced over at the coffee table piled high with books, pencils, highlighters, legal pads and her laptop computer. She knew it was the beginning of a long night. She was still distracted with worry about her MRI test, but recognized that she couldn't obsess over it.

"Well, you only live once," she murmured softly.

"What?" Tracey asked.

"Nothing," Harianne replied brightly. "I'll make some coffee and bring it into the living room."

Tracey retrieved his laptop from his car while Harianne carried dessert and a hot thermos of coffee into the living room. Tracey seated himself opposite her in the burgundy velvet wing chair near the open window. They arranged their papers and laptops on the bay window seat. The music of Tony Bennett and Frank Sinatra played on the stereo in the background as they worked on their notes.

In preparation for trial, Tracey read all of his homicide reports and notes on the murders of Shana Bernstein, Hillary McDunn and Jasmine Thomas. While he reviewed the conclusive findings from the medical examiner, Harianne prepared trial subpoenas of DNA experts, Amy Kanter, Erin Peters, Maggie Weiner and Lara Smith. She poured the last of the coffee, dividing it evenly between their two cups.

"Do you really think Amy Kanter saw Matthew?" she asked.

"Shana Bernstein's neighbor? Well, when Zack and I questioned her she stated she was playing the piano and didn't see or hear a thing."

"But…?"

"But she's very nosy, according to the local merchants in Malibu." Tracey shrugged.

"Any other witnesses?"

"No."

"Do you really think Matthew was capable of committing a crime like that?"

"I'm not sure," Tracey admitted.

Melissa barked and began to trot in circles near the door.

"Oh, I have to walk Melissa," Harianne said. "Do you mind?"

"No," Tracey responded, rising from his chair. "I'll come with you."

They exited through the front door and sauntered down the winding driveway to the front of Harianne's property. They walked around her neighborhood for a long while.

"What was Jasmine like?" Tracey asked.

"She was one of the driving forces in my life," Harianne recalled fondly. "I say 'one' because my mother was the other one. Jasmine was born to an alcoholic teenage mother and then lived in a plethora of foster homes most of her life. As soon as she turned eighteen she got out of the system and landed a job as an assistant to a private investigator."

"How sad! How old was her mother?"

"Fourteen or fifteen years of age."

"Wow! Where was her first foster home?"

"In Los Angeles, in the Mid-Wilshire district. After that, it was mostly downhill. The most horrible thing that happened to Jasmine was her skin color."

"How's that?" Tracey inquired.

"Jasmine's complexion was dark-blue black. People made fun of her and nobody wanted to adopt her. If your skin was light—light brown or almost white—you had a good chance of being adopted."

"Racism," Tracey said with a snort. "It'll never go away."

"You're right. It's been a hot topic for decades and it'll never die."

"My very first job, I was in college, 18 years old and working as a store clerk," Tracey confided. "My car was in the shop and my father, an African American, picked me up from work. When I went to work the next day, the owner told me he had 'fallen on hard times' and couldn't keep me on payroll any longer. One month later, I saw one of my white friends working there." He paused and swallowed. "He told me that I really got fired because my father was African American. The owner had assumed I was white because my skin's so fair." He shook his head with disgust. "Mixed heritage can be an advantage or disadvantage."

"Oh, my God!" Harianne exclaimed. "That's awful. I don't think I could bear that."

"Sure you could." Tracey smiled, looking her straight in the eye. "You're a strong woman."

"I guess we'll always be mistaken as white people."

"That's true." He paused thoughtfully. "It sounds like your friend Jasmine had it a lot tougher than we did."

"She did have a really tough time," Harianne agreed. "Neither African-American nor white families would adopt her. People viewed her as a public embarrassment. It was sad and I felt bad for her. In my eyes, she was like my sister."

"Man, that's incredibly sad. You seem to know a lot about adoptions."

"Well, when my parents were killed in a plane crash off of Tahiti, good friends of theirs adopted me. I was so lucky—they even hired my nanny, Austria. She's known me since I was a baby. She lives in the rear cottage now, behind my house."

"Sounds cozy. How did you and Jasmine meet?"

"In grade school. We've been like sisters ever since."

"Ah. That explains a lot."

"Mmm. So enough about me. Tell me more about your family."

"Well," Tracey hesitated. "I told you about Marina."

"Your wife?"

"Yes. She died on the job. She was a very brave cop."

"I feel for you," Harianne said. She impulsively gave his arm a sympathetic squeeze.

"Thank you. You know…you kind of remind me of her."

"How so?"

"She was beautiful, knowledgeable, a great police officer and very methodical; she always planned ahead. She was also a good cook, a great listener and extremely giving. She was my rock."

"Sounds like a wonderful lady."

"I thought I'd never get over her death," he admitted, clearing his throat. "It all happened so fast."

"What happened?" Harianne asked gently.

"Marina was used as a decoy to catch a possible suspect in a murder-rape case. I'll never forget the date: February 20. One o'clock in the morning. She fought so hard. She punched him, kicked him in the groin, yanked his scrotum, scratched his face and eyes…but she lost the battle. No one could reach her in time. He raped her, and then he strangled her to death. So instead of catching the killer, the PD got another murder to write up."

"He raped her?" Harianne repeated quietly.

Tracey nodded his head. He felt a large pit in his stomach as he explained. "They found her on the bedroom floor, with a long knife left in her back. The killer cut her down the center of her body, turned her over, sliced her nipples and placed them on her eyes." He swallowed hard, trying to fight back his memories and the sudden urge to throw up.

Harianne stopped and touched his arm. "Are you all right?"

"Yes. No. Excuse me." He leaned over a nearby bush while Harianne knelt to pet Melissa. Tracey rejoined them a few minutes later.

"Are you sure you're OK?" Harianne asked. "We don't have to talk anymore, if you don't want."

"No, it's OK," Tracey said. "This is probably good for me. Moving to L.A. was supposed to be a cure—you know, erase the memories, the good and the bad. But I miss New York, some of my family and friends."

"You have Zack."

"I know. But when I'm asleep, I have flashbacks of Marina's death. I'm in so much pain. Life has been hard without her." He pulled a handkerchief from his pocket and wiped a tear from his face.

"Really? Are you on medication for the flashbacks?"

"No," Tracey said firmly. "I'll live with it."

"Well…you have to start somewhere, Tracey."

"This was the place to start over again," he said, gesturing around him. "L.A. Meet new people and move my life forward."

Harianne slipped her hand into his and smiled. "I know a little of how you feel," she said. "I miss Jasmine all the time."

"This case is personal for me," Tracey told her. "I will get the killer! I've been haunted by the murders of Jasmine and Shana…they remind me of Marina."

"I can understand that, Tracey, but try to relax. Take some time out for yourself."

He dropped his head. "I never thought I'd be a widower this young."

"Losing family and someone you love so much can be unbearable. But we have to go on with life."

"Yeah. I miss her. But you're right. It's been a long time. I have to keep going forward."

"Speaking of which…we'd better get to work."

Back at the house, Tracey and Harianne worked into the early morning hours, until their eyes were covered with sleep. Tracey leaned back, locked his hands behind his head and yawned.

"Why don't we stop for now?" he suggested. "I'm getting tired."

Harianne moved her neck in a circular motion. "I know. I'm tired, too."

He gently took her hand. "Well, what time tomorrow?" he asked.

"Why tomorrow?"

Tracey smiled. "Are you asking me to stay?"

Harianne turned her head slightly and met his eyes as she answered: "Yes."

He tenderly rubbed his hands through her hair and she responded by running her hands through his. Tracey wrapped his arms around her, kissed her soft olive-toned skin and moved straight to her lips.

"What's the name of that song?" he inquired.

"'The Shadow of Your Smile' from the movie The Sandpiper."

"That was a beautiful old movie. Very romantic. Did he get the girl in the end?"

"I can't remember…"

Tracey lifted Harianne to her feet and carried her toward the stairs; as they passed the living room light switch, Harianne flipped it off. Upstairs, she kicked the creaky bedroom door lightly with her foot. Tracey eased her onto the bed and they removed their clothing slowly, piece by piece.

Harianne pulled the sheets back and Tracey fell on her slender body. He brushed her hair off her face, stroked her firm breasts with his masculine hands and gently kissed her. Her skin was soft, like velvet, and the color was even.

"You have cute, petite ears," Tracey whispered. "They're so soft…like cotton."

"Tracey! You know I like the way you kiss me. I've never been kissed like that before."

"No? Well, there's more."

He kissed each nipple with his wet lips and sucked them until they stood up straight to a point. She moved his hands to her thighs, motioning to him to push her legs apart, and took his penis and slowly put it inside of her. He went deep inside of her then pulled out briefly and put his fingers inside of her. She moaned and yelled his name for a long time.

"Tracey! Tracey! Don't stop!"

"I won't. Hold me, Harianne!"

The wetness on his mouth and fingers was soothing. She responded with a vocal outburst, yearning for more. He kissed her forehead and face with little short kisses. While she received the kisses, she threw her arms tightly around Tracey and squeezed him. He made love in slow motion, gazing into Harianne's light green eyes. He slowly ran his fingers over her body and brought her to tears.

Tracey built up his pace until the thrust of his motions was so powerful that Harianne reached orgasm. Suddenly there was a knock at the door.

"Did you hear that?" she gasped, frightened.

"No." The knocking persisted and began to get louder.

"Do you hear it now?"

"Let me get my gun."

He put on his shorts and proceeded down the stairs. Harianne watched from the top of the staircase.

"Who's there?" Tracey called out.

No one answered. Gun in hand, Tracey unlocked the hard deadbolt lock with one flick of the hand and aimed his gun straight out, ready for anything. No one was there. A breeze swept fallen leaves into a small whirlwind funnel on the circular drive. Tracey closed the antique door and returned to bed.

"Who was it?" Harianne asked.

"It's OK, everything is fine. Let's go to sleep."

"How odd? But I'm sure I heard—"

"I heard it, too. But no one was there."

Harianne woke from a fitful sleep; the silver clock on the nightstand read four o'clock. The case was once again foremost on her mind, but it was too early to begin the legal process.

She turned and Tracey felt her movement. He pulled her close to him and embraced her.

"Are you OK?" he asked.

"Yeah. I can't sleep."

"Stay close to me. Put your head on my shoulder."

"I'm going downstairs for some herbal tea," she whispered. "I'll be right back."

The hardwood floor hallway leading to the kitchen was glowing with white moonlight streaming through the large skylight above. Harianne looked up to take in the view of the moon—and screamed when she saw a red silk scarf attached to one of the hinges, hanging like a breezy red flag. Tracey came bolting down the stairs like an alley cat, gun in hand.

"Harianne! What happened, honey?"

"Look up there!"

Tracey saw the red scarf and knew. They immediately phoned the sheriff.

Tracey and Zack arrived at the crime scene, both wearing black trench coats against the chilly weather as they trudged through the front doors of the all-too-familiar building housing Jasmine Thomas' office. A police officer led them down the long hall corridor to an Art Deco-style bathroom within the office.

"What's this about?" Zack asked as he looked over his shoulder while walking.

"I'm afraid to ask," Tracey replied.

The officer opened the paint-flaked door to the bathroom. Drops of blood painted the stall. Zack heard water running from the faucet of the large porcelain washbasin. He moved to turn it off but found that it was already off, just broken.

"Shit."

"Maybe our killer likes clean hands," Tracey suggested.

The fragile, light brown-skinned body of a young woman was perched on the toilet seat, leaning to one side of the tile wall; her arms hung loosely beside her. Her body was stripped naked like potato shavings from a russet potato. The room wreaked of death as blood streamed down her entire body. The infamous red silk scarf was wrapped around her neck with a printed note stapled to it: "Got Ya Get With It!"

The forensic team and crime scene technicians arrived and started swabbing blood from the floor, tile walls, toilet and countertops in the bathroom. They combed surfaces for hair and clothing fibers and did the usual rape kit.

"How long has she been dead?" Tracey inquired.

"About twelve hours, probably."

"Anything else?"

"Not sure, but we think it's like the others: rape and a possible overdose of cocaine. All the signs fit."

There were a few tenants in the building at the time. Zack visited a part-time locksmith tenant who had only been there for a month.

"Did you see anything last night?" he asked. "Anything unusual?"

"No."

The next tenant, an artist who lived there full-time, said she'd been home all night, working. She'd heard noises early in the evening, but ignored them.

Zack and Tracey searched for clues behind the building, but nothing was evident. When they returned to the bathroom, the crime scene technician approached them.

"Detective Sanders! I found a wallet on the floor near the doorway."

# CHAPTER 18

As usual, everyone entering the Los Angeles Criminal Courts Building waited in long lines for security clearance. On the third floor of the building, loud sounds of Sheriff's Department and L.A.P.D. officers with keys could be heard down the hall.

Matthew Daytona entered the courtroom for his preliminary hearing dressed in a black designer-knockoff suit, complemented by a crisp white shirt. He looked business-like but was visibly distraught; the wrinkles on his cheeks were like lines on a road map. He kept his head face down to the ground except to make occasional, worried eye contact with Harianne and MacKenzie. Harianne responded with confident, encouraging smiles.

Everyone stood as Judge Arthur W. Ringwald entered the courtroom. Almost seventy, with graying blond hair, Ringwald was known to be a man of his word, and fair. He welcomed bottom-line colloquies in his courtroom; he hated dealing with lawyers who danced around issues.

"Counsel, state appearances."

"Gaston Reeves for the People of the State of California."

"Harianne DeCanter, counsel for Defendant Matthew Daytona."

"The matter is here for preliminary hearing. We are on the record. People v. Daytona. Defendant Matthew Daytona is charged with violation of Health & Safety Code Sections 11350, 11351, 11351.5 and 11352. Would the People like to call their first witness?" the judge inquired.

"Yes," Reeves replied. "Your Honor, the People would like to introduce evidence by stipulation. We'd like to stipulate to the chemist report. Diane Church tested the chemicals."

"I'm sorry counsel, but I can't hear you. Oops! I forgot my hearing aid. I'll be right back."

Counsel and the entire courtroom chuckled. Judge Ringwald returned and, again, slowly approached the bench.

"OK. We're still on the record, People v. Daytona."

Gaston Reeves presented his case to the court: that Matthew Daytona had visited Shana Bernstein's home on the evening of her death; that he was the last person to see her alive; that DNA analysis fingered him as the murderer.

"People will introduce evidence by stipulation," Reeves declared. "People will stipulate to DNA profile as evidence. Nick Carlyle, forensic pathologist, profiled the DNA."

"Excuse me Mr. Reeves," Judge Ringwald interrupted. He sounded cranky. "Let's just get to the point. We don't have all day! Is there probable cause? Was there probable cause at the time the crime was committed? Is there probable cause to believe that the person in this courtroom today is the one who committed the crime?"

"Yes."

The usual court formalities of motions to dismiss were conducted and both People and Defense rested.

"Does counsel waive further arraignment?"

"Yes, Your Honor," Harianne and Reeves replied simultaneously.

Judge Ringwald announced the courtroom in which Matthew would be held to answer, and decreed, "Defendant to remain in custody. No bail set. This court is adjourned."

Tired and frazzled, Harianne and MacKenzie exited the hearing and hurried down the dimly lit court hall corridor to the escalators that led to the basement garage. As Harianne unlocked her car door, MacKenzie called out to her.

"Want to get lunch?"

"Sure. Where?"

"You decide, Harianne."

"OK. Follow me—I know a great little French restaurant in Westwood."

Heavy rain pounded the streets; the trip to Westwood seemed like a long journey. Harianne mentally catalogued the subpoenas, background checks and medical experts she would have to coordinate when she returned to the office; it helped keep her mind off Tracey.

At the restaurant, Harianne and MacKenzie both ordered starter salads, fish entrees and white wine. Then they sat there, hands wrapped around their wine goblets, each hesitant to speak first. Finally, MacKenzie pushed up the sleeves of her cashmere sweater dress and looked at Harianne.

"We haven't had a chance to talk. I thought this might be a good time."

Harianne sipped her wine.

"Yes," she agreed. "We've both been swamped and trying to stay afloat. But we really should get to know one another."

"Where are you from?" MacKenzie asked.

"Here—I grew up in the Windsor Hills district. And you?"

"New York."

"Manhattan?"

"Where else?"

As the conversation gradually began to flow more easily, their questions overlapped.

"Are your parents alive?"

"That's funny. You first, Harianne."

Harianne paused for a moment.

"My parents were killed in a plane accident. I was very young at the time."

"Really? My parents were killed also. We're both orphans, I guess."

"But I was adopted by good friends of my parents, so I can't really claim to be an orphan," Harianne elaborated. "I've been very blessed."

MacKenzie continued to eat and drink. As the conversation progressed, she turned her head toward the window while Harianne talked.

"How do you know Matthew?"

"You know that story, Harianne. We were once an item and worked together some time ago. My role in the office was important, but I didn't know everything."

"Were you a partner?"

"Yeah. I was the director of administration, but I left before becoming managing partner. A partner is a partner."

"But why would you leave before taking the managing partner position?" Harianne asked.

MacKenzie hesitated before responding. "I had been spending a lot of time in Japan," she said. "I left for personal reasons."

Harianne smiled, took another sip of wine and gestured to MacKenzie to tell her more. She was genuinely interested in MacKenzie's background.

Her eyes widened with intrigue. "Matthew tells me that you got his uncle off murder charges in Japan."

MacKenzie took a bite of her food. "Well—yes. It was a delicate case."

"Delicate?" Harianne repeated, sitting erect in her seat. "How's that?"

"Let's just leave it at that," MacKenzie replied firmly. She chewed her food slowly.

Harianne clenched her napkin and leaned against the leather backrest of their booth. She realized that MacKenzie was not telling her the truth—and wasn't going to, no matter how many questions were asked of her.

"Well. You knew about the Japanese drug-and-prostitution ring, didn't you?"

"Kind of. I went to Japan on business for Matthew, but I never really knew all of the aspects of the business in Japan. We didn't have an accounting manager at the time. I had access to the accounting books. You know, the usual."

"What does that mean—'the usual'?"

"Are you doubting me, Harianne?"

"No, but I'm curious. Did you handle his personal accounts?"

"Sometimes. He did his own. I was still kept apprised of things."

"That's a lot of responsibility."

"Our focus should be on the shipments from Japan."

"Do you know who the distributor was?"

"No."

"That's odd."

"I want Matthew to get out of this mess."

"I feel the same way. OK?"

Harianne's cellphone rang. It was Tracey.

"Excuse me, MacKenzie. I need to take this call."

She walked outside the restaurant to the sidewalk. "Tracey?"

"Hi, Harianne. I'm sorry to have to tell you this, but we just found Raquel, Jasmine's assistant. She's dead."

# CHAPTER 19

Stunned by the news, Harianne dried her tears and left the restaurant. Depression set in as her headaches returned with a vengeance. The thought of Jasmine's death had made her sick. Now Raquel had been murdered too? What had she been doing? Harianne struggled to understand Raquel's motive for being in Jasmine's office.

A few days later Harianne attended Raquel's memorial service, wearing dark glasses. She spotted Tracey and Zack and waved; they returned the gesture and walked toward where she was sitting in the last row. While waiting for them, she grabbed a tissue from her purse and remained in a quiescent state.

Several conversations took place around her. One in particular piqued her curiosity—an intense exchange between two officers in police uniform.

"She was killed the same way."

"Yeah. But one thing was different."

"The red silk scarf was immersed in blood?"

"You're missing it."

"What? Everything was identical to the other murders."

"Everything except the finger."

"The finger?"

"The middle finger on her right hand was cut off and placed on the bathroom counter with a note next to it."

"A note?"

"The note read, 'Yakuza.'"

"Women aren't allowed to be members of the Yakuza."

"Maybe, but the murderer's connected to the Yakuza."

"Was that in the police report?"

"I don't know."

As the memorial service got under way, Tracey placed his arm around Harianne in a show of support.

"I'm here for you," he whispered in her ear.

"I know you are," she whispered back. "I miss you."

The next morning, Austria was in the kitchen cooking poached eggs and her famous Swedish pancakes, when she heard voices at the kitchen door from the dining room. She quickly pulled the apron from her waist and moved toward the door, when it abruptly opened.

"Oh! I almost hit you, Austria! Are you OK?" Harianne hugged her.

"I'm fine, dear," Austria answered with a smile.

"Austria, this is Tracey Sanders," Harianne said, gesturing toward Tracey with her hand.

"Detective?" Austria beamed with delight.

"That's right," Tracey said. "Detective Tracey Sanders. So you're Austria!" He chuckled in amazement.

"Nice to meet you, Detective—"

"You can call me Tracey." He took hold of her hand and put his over hers in reassurance and smiled.

Harianne put her arm around Austria. "This is my angel and my rock. She was my trustworthy nanny, but now she's family."

Austria looked at Harianne and returned to the stove.

Harianne and Tracey spent every night and as many days as they could together, capturing every possible moment to better know one another.

One morning, after Austria's usual breakfast and a long walk in the park with Melissa, they hurried out of the house to see the latest exhibition at the Museum of Contemporary Art in Los Angeles. When they arrived, they found people were already lined up. They waited in line for half an hour, shifting their body weight so their hips and legs wouldn't tire out.

Tracey noticed a man of European descent standing off to the side, with dark glasses, black hair, tan pants and a black T-shirt. He thought nothing of him until the man pulled out a camera and held it off to the side. Tracey pulled Harianne close to him, wrapped his arms around her, hugged her tight and whispered in her ear.

"Listen, honey, very carefully. There's a man standing to the right of me near the ticket office. I don't want to worry you, but I think he's a paparazzo. Stay close to me right now and don't look over there."

She reciprocated with a tight hug and held onto him. "How did they find us?"

"We were followed. I didn't even think about it because we've been pretty relaxed lately. I'm having too much fun spending time with you and watching DVDs with you and Austria."

She hugged him tighter. "Me, too, Tracey. I'll wait for your cue."

He kissed her on her cheek. "Good. I'm sorry we're going to miss the exhibition."

"Don't be," she whispered.

"I'll make it up to you," he promised. "Now listen: the parking lot is behind us. He hasn't spotted us yet. Let's quietly fall out of line and walk slowly back to the car. Don't run."

"OK."

The paparazzo turned his head and looked toward the side of the building in the opposite direction.

"Right…now!" Tracey whispered loudly in Harianne's ear.

They ducked out of line and slowly retreated to the car. As they drove past the parking attendant booth, Tracey turned his head around and saw the paparazzo standing by the ticket booth line, gazing out at the parking lot.

The day before Matthew was due back in court, China greeted Harianne at her office with a stack of papers in one hand and migraine medicine in the other. MacKenzie joined them shortly thereafter.

While China prepared subpoenas and witness lists, copied curriculum vitae of medical experts and other necessary papers, Harianne and McKenzie consumed two pots of coffee as they reviewed pages of notes. Harianne went over Matthew's whereabouts the night of Shana Bernstein's murder again and again, while MacKenzie analyzed medical reports and DNA results. Nothing was strange; everything was concise and accurate. They had to win the case.

The Criminal Courts Building on Temple Street was gray and foreboding. Built in the 1970s of concrete and steel, it had been renamed the Clara Shortridge Foltz Criminal Justice Center in 2002, in honor of California's first female lawyer. It had been filmed for many motion pictures and television shows over the years. Harianne had not set foot in it for ten years, but when she took the elevator to the third floor and proceeded to Division 3, her internal radar told her exactly where to go.

Fifty to sixty people were crowded into the hallway. Some lashed out at one another, cursing, while others just yelled to be heard over the argumentative conversations that formed a continuous background hum. Harianne suddenly remembered the lies people often told to get themselves off. Elegantly dressed in a black coatdress, she felt eyes trained upon her as she passed people sitting on the wood benches that lined the stained, beige-colored walls.

"They look like caged animals at the zoo," she thought to herself.

This time she had the big tuna, not a guppy—a case that would make the history books and the pages of *California Lawyer*.

Harianne greeted MacKenzie with a wave from the defense table as MacKenzie, dressed in a dark-gray suit, made her way toward the front of the courtroom. Harianne's papers were laid out neatly on the table, with the chronology of events on top. She was ready. MacKenzie smiled and followed her lead by organizing her papers accordingly. The trial was still half an hour away.

Harianne felt her cellphone buzzing in her pocket and discreetly pulled it out to see if it was China. But it was a text message from Tracey: "I miss you." She quickly snapped the phone shut and slipped it into her purse.

An array of people entered the courtroom. Harianne recognized Matthew's office staff, including Lara Smith, with dark glasses, who sat in the last row on the defense side. Dr. Jonathan Hooks, DNA expert for the defense, sat in the second row behind Harianne and MacKenzie. He nodded his head to acknowledge their presence and Harianne returned the gesture. Soon Zack and Tracey entered and sat on the prosecutor's side, in the second row. Harianne studiously avoided looking at Tracey.

Gaston Reeves entered the courtroom in a black suit that complemented his salt-and-pepper hair and swarthy complexion. The prosecutor's smooth demeanor masked an astute, deadly serious mind. His track record spoke for itself: eighty convictions—including three death penalties—and two mistrials. He specialized in prosecuting white-collar criminals.

Harianne nudged MacKenzie with her arm and spoke softly.

"MacKenzie! That's Gaston Reeves, our illustrious prosecutor—otherwise known as 'Dancing Gaston.'"

"Hmm. Nice suit."

"It's Armani. Quite the fashion statement for a prosecutor."

"What's his record like?"

"He doesn't need a resume. Just give him some hard evidence and DNA samples and you've got a permanent change of address along with a death sentence—a proper farewell. Jurors are dazzled by his stories. He acts out the murders."

"Doesn't that turn off judges?"

"Frequently, but juries love him. Defense lawyers hate him."

"Are you ready for him?"

"You bet. Bring it on!"

The bailiff stood and called the court to order as Judge Chester Hamlin entered the courtroom and approached the bench. Harianne and Gaston Reeves were called to approach the bench. After a brief, off-the-record discussion, Judge Hamlin proceeded.

"We are on the record, People v. Daytona, Case No. 55-111-5555. Counsel is present. We will proceed with jury selection."

Judge Hamlin informed the jury pool how the voir dire jury selection process worked and explained the change in seating arrangement in the jury box. After three hours of numerous peremptory challenges, a jury was chosen. It consisted of seven women and five men: eight whites, two blacks, one Hispanic and one Asian American. Their occupations reflected L.A.'s diverse culture: MTA bus driver, graphic artist, legal assistant, singer, human resources consultant, real estate broker, nurse, certified public accountant, television writer, actress, veterinarian and dental hygienist.

Judge Hamlin called a brief recess before proceeding with the trial. Reeves was called upon to present his opening statement. As usual, he used his hands as directives when he addressed the jury.

"Ladies and gentlemen of the jury," he began. "Do you know why we're called here today? I'll tell you, it's not the *Price is Right*—but the price can be right. Our man, Matthew Daytona, is not a decent man. He's famous as a big-time entertainment lawyer, but now he's known to everyone as the most famous serial killer in the country. This is not a normal person. He's a menace to society. Matthew Daytona loves to entice women; he relishes the intimacy and closeness with them. He raped and strangled Shana Bernstein, leaving her naked body in a blood bath around the toilet. He had intent to kill. And he had motive.

"Who will be the next victim? Will you? Will your mother? Will it be your grandmother? Who will it be? Sure, he'll tell you he didn't do it, and he'll try to change your mind. But the evidence and testimony will convince you otherwise."

Reeves went on for another half-hour before giving his final statement: "If you want to live in Los Angeles peacefully, you will find that the defendant, Matthew Daytona, intentionally committed murder in the first degree. Otherwise, you're the next victim on the toilet in a red blood bath."

Harianne quietly walked across the floor and placed both hands on the wood ledge in front of the jury.

"The everyday life of an individual is unknown. But here are a few known facts about Matthew Daytona: he's a lawyer working in the judicial system; a son; an uncle; a colleague; and a friend. He is a good man—a man of substance, understanding, credibility and wisdom. He built his firm from scratch and personally established a team of stellar lawyers. He wanted to give his clients his undivided attention and satisfaction.

"He himself always wants the best in his life. Don't we all? That little piece of heaven in our life is an essential element. It is like air; we cannot breathe if we do not have it. Small things such as drinking a cup of coffee, taking a shower, reading, eating a cookie—they're just a few of the little things in life that we take for granted. Why would Matthew Daytona risk all that? Why would he jeopardize his career and his life? And how could this decent man, in such good standing in the legal community, commit a premeditated murder? You tell me, ladies and gentlemen. I'm pleading with you to examine all the facts that will be set before you. There is no turning back. Matthew Daytona is sensitive. He's not a killer. He's a man loved by many friends—and these women were his friends. He had no motive to kill them. Based on the evidence that you will hear, you will find that he is innocent."

Gaston Reeves called his first witness to the stand: Lara Smith. She peered around the courtroom before she approached the stand. She looked fragile and nervous in her dark blue suit as the court clerk swore her in.

"Do you solemnly swear to tell the truth, the whole truth, so help you God?"

"I do."

"Please spell your name for the record, please."

"Lara Smith. L-A-R-A S-M-I-T-H."

"Ms. Smith, how long have you known the defendant?" Reeves asked.

"Just a year."

"What is your current position at the firm?"

"I'm a second-year associate."

"Did you know Shana Bernstein?"

"Yes. She conducted the second job interview for the associate position."

"Did you ever socialize with her?"

"No."

"Did Matthew Daytona interview you?"

"Yes. He was first."

"What did you think of him?"

"Think of him?"

"What were your immediate thoughts of him?"

"He seemed nice and I really wanted to be an entertainment lawyer. I attended several seminars and conferences he gave and he just kind of grew on me. He had style, and I liked it."

"Did you see him on the evening of the murder of Shana Bernstein?"

"Yes. He worked late, but then left. I was still there."

"Did you ever see him socially?"

"No."

"Did you ever see him with anyone—like a girlfriend of some sort?"

"Not really. I'm so busy with my work. I hadn't paid attention."

"Have you ever seen him angry?"

"One time."

"With whom?"

"Shana Bernstein."

"When was this?"

"About a month ago, in her office."

"Do you know what they were arguing about?"

"No. There was a lot of yelling for about five minutes and then they shut the door."

"No further questions, Your Honor."

"Thank you, Ms. Smith," Judge Hamlin said. "Please call your next witness, counselor."

"The People call Detective Tracey Sanders."

After Tracey was sworn in, Gaston Reeves continued with his queries.

"Please state your name and spell your last name for the record."

"Detective Tracey Sanders, Los Angeles County Sheriff's Department, Homicide Division. T-R-A-C-E-Y S-A-N-D-E-R-S."

"What did you find when you arrived on the scene?"

"A woman in her thirties, leaning on the toilet to one side, with blood dripping from her vaginal area with a red silk scarf tied around her neck."

"What were your thoughts?"

"Rape."

"What were some of your other findings?"

"There were traces of cocaine in her system. A possible overdose was in the workings."

"Was that the cause of death?"

"Well, she was raped and savagely beaten. But according to forensics her bloodstreams contained substantial doses of cocaine."

"Where did you first see the defendant?"

"In his office."

"Did the defendant seem remorseful?"

"I'm not sure if he was remorseful. He was disturbed."

"What did you say to him?"

"He was wearing a red silk scarf with his suit. I asked him about his red silk scarf and his whereabouts the evening of Shana Bernstein's murder. He told me that the scarf was imported from Japan."

"Was there any conclusive evidence that pointed to Matthew Daytona?"

"Yes. The DNA profile."

"No further questions, Your Honor."

Harianne and MacKenzie listened patiently to crime-scene technicians Parker Benjamin and Larry Smalwitz, forensic pathologist Nick Carlyle and various other witnesses. Their testimony dragged on until the lunch break. The two women walked to the cafeteria on the second floor and grabbed a table in the corner. Neither was hungry, but they each ordered half a sandwich and coffee.

"In three days, it's our turn," Harianne said. "I subpoenaed Taka Sousushi."

"You didn't tell me!" MacKenzie exclaimed. "When?"

"Yesterday. He's in Japan, but he's due to arrive in the United States today. I made arrangements for him at the New Otanni Hotel."

"I don't believe you."

"What's the problem?"

"You should have consulted me first."

Harianne looked up at MacKenzie. "You're right. It's procedure. Sorry about that."

"Don't let it happen again. I don't like that."

"OK! Don't get upset."

"What time is he arriving?"

"This evening. We need him. Matthew and he worked together." She paused. "Look, I know what you're thinking."

"Well, we agreed to work together and keep each other in the loop," MacKenzie reminded her.

"I'm sorry," Harianne repeated. "But we need him. He's a key witness."

Day one of the trial ended at five o'clock. MacKenzie ran out immediately and Harianne ran after her.

"Hey, wait up! Are you OK?"

"I'm fine. Sorry if I frightened you."

"We really should work tonight."

"I agree, but I have to go home first. I'll meet you at your office at, let's say, nine o'clock?"

"Any earlier?"

"I can't, but don't worry," MacKenzie said firmly. "I won't be late."

Harianne arrived home and parked her Mercedes in the garage. Inside, she tossed her coat and briefcase on the foyer bench. She entered the living room and found Austria admiring a dozen red roses in a white basket on the coffee table.

"Harianne, my darling, are these from your favorite guy, Tracey?" Austria inquired.

"Oh! I don't really know. Is there a card?"

"Yes. You already know, though."

"I don't think so," Harianne said, puzzled. "I mean, we just started dating."

She read the card: *"Just wanted to say hello. T."*

"And?"

"You're right," Harianne admitted. "It's Tracey. How sweet is this?"

"I'd say that he's a strong candidate, my dear."

"Who knows…"

She gave Austria a big hug and kiss on the cheek before heading into the kitchen. She fed Melissa, tossed a frozen dinner in the microwave and turned on the TV in the kitchen. While pouring water into the coffee maker, she saw a news bulletin flash across the screen: *Breaking News: Japanese tycoon Taka Sousushi killed in head-on collision. All passengers in limo killed on impact.*

The glass coffee carafe slipped from Harianne's fingers; tiny slivers of glass covered the sink and floor.

Austria heard the crash and ran into the kitchen. She grabbed a broom and dustpan and gently moved Harianne to the side.

"Are you all right, Harianne?"

"Yes, I'm fine. I got distracted." Harianne sighed.

"Distracted by what?"

"The news about this case."

"The case you're working on?"

"Yes. It's on the news. A key witness was just killed in an automobile accident."

"Oh, no. I'm sorry. This changes things for you, doesn't it?"

"It changes the entire scope of the case!" Harianne exclaimed, disgusted.

Austria tossed the glass in the trash and brewed some tea. Harianne tried Tracey at the precinct and on his cell, but he didn't answer either phone.

Harianne dashed out to make her meeting with MacKenzie on time. She parked her Mercedes in front of her office just as MacKenzie strolled across the courtyard.

"Where were you?" Harianne called out, slamming her car door.

"What?" MacKenzie asked.

Harianne looked at her, annoyed. Why wasn't MacKenzie focusing? "You don't know, do you?"

"Know what?"

"Taka Sousushi was killed tonight. It was on the news. There goes our witness."

"Was he really going to be a key witness for us?"

"I thought so. Didn't you?"

MacKenzie shrugged. "Possibly. It's all relative."

# CHAPTER 20

Court was called to order at eight-thirty on the second morning of the trial. Harianne, MacKenzie and Matthew engaged in a whispered consultation while awaiting the judge's entry into the courtroom; Harianne made visible hand gestures to Matthew.

Shortly thereafter, the twelve jurors entered the jury box.

"All rise," the clerk called out. "The Honorable Chester Hamlin, Judge Presiding."

The crowded courtroom, filled to capacity, stood as Judge Hamlin entered and approached his bench.

"Please be seated," the clerk advised the crowd. Judge Hamlin silently read through the court documentation.

"People vs. Matthew Daytona," he began. "We're still on the record. I want to welcome the jury back. Would People call its first witness?"

Gaston Reeves rose and addressed the judge. "Your Honor, the People call Dr. Todd Silverman."

A tall man of slender build took the witness stand. He sported a dark tan and streaks of gray in his blond hair.

MacKenzie leaned over and muttered in Harianne's ear, "He's known as 'the Silver Spirit.'"

"Seems like I read something about that," Harianne replied. "I can't remember the details."

"He's the most highly recognized DNA expert in the state of California," MacKenzie whispered.

"Yes, that much I do know," Harianne whispered back. "He's testified at many trials, mostly for the prosecution. Defendants in those cases are usually found guilty."

"Dr. Silverman," Reeves began, "would you please state and spell your name for the record and state your occupation for the record, please."

"Dr. Todd Silverman, S-I-L-V-E-R-M-A-N," he replied in a sonorous voice. "I am a professor of pathology and have a joint appointment in the Department of Molecular Biology at the University of San Francisco. I teach and do research at the university. On occasion, I testify as a DNA expert."

"Are you familiar with the record and the circumstances surrounding the indictment of the defendant, Matthew Daytona?"

"Yes."

"Were you asked to investigate the DNA from the defendant and obtain a profile?"

"Yes."

"Were you asked to investigate and analyze DNA from the defendant and compare that with the DNA obtained from the victims?"

"Yes."

"Would you please explain that process?"

"I will explain the process of analysis as simply as I can. DNA obtained from the sample identified as coming from peripheral blood of the defendant was compared to that obtained from swabs taken from the vaginal secretions found in the victims. The DNA was extracted, amplified by the PCR method and digested with specific endonucleases.

"DNA analysis is a powerful tool because certain regions within it are unique to each individual. We identified these regions from the defendant's DNA and amplified them, and compared those with similar regions from the DNA that we collected from the swabs. The procedure involves a determination of base sequences, which are associated with a sugar-phosphate chain to form a genetic blueprint of organisms that may extend from bacteria to Homo sapiens. Fragments of the DNA are located in specific regions of chromosomes and satellite regions that are known as VNTRs, or Variable Number of Tandem Repeats. These regions are unique to each individual and are studied by scientists in much the same way that a criminologist would study fingerprints."

"Were VNTRs used in this case?"

"Yes. But in this case, the sources of DNA were vaginal fluids sampled using swabs on the victim, Shana Bernstein. In this particular case, we extracted the DNA using a chemical process and broke it into fragments using restriction endonucleases. These fragments, which are in solution, are then sorted by length using a technique known as electrophoresis, in which an electrical charge is placed on gel in fragments, separated and spread apart by size. The fragments as separated are then transferred onto a nitrocellulose sheet."

"What is the next procedure used?"

"In the next step, probes selected from the subjects are used to determine which sequences may be in common. These probes are added in solution and when hybridization is complete, nitrocellulose filters are then sheeted to fix and dry them. Since the probes prepared by PCR technology are labeled with a radioactive chemical, 32P, complementary sequences can be detected using X-ray. VNTRs are highlighted and registered on a radiation-sensitive film. The film is developed using the common X-ray developer, and the final result is an autoradiograph, also known as an autorad. Let me emphasize that the technology can be difficult and at times the band patterns may be foggy and unclear. This may occur in part as a result of decomposition or degradation of the deoxyribonucleic acid, which occurs before extraction. The gel with the band that lights up resembles a bar code. Ms. Bernstein's autorad was compared to Mr. Daytona's autorad, and each was probed from persons unrelated to this case for the sake of comparison. Controls were also used. The comparison of the Southern blot patterns is shown on the screen."

"Please describe the semen comparison," Reeves directed.

Silverman nodded. "The comparison of semen taken directly from the defendant with that of the DNA found in the vaginal fluid of the deceased indicates distinctive differences when sequences taken from the DNA in the vaginal fluid are hybridized directly to that DNA taken from the semen of the defendant. Greater than eighty percent of the bands obtained on Southern blot analysis were these that compare directly with those of the defendant, Matthew Daytona. These were matched with his alleles, genes at a particular site, in 100 percent of these cases. The patterns are unmistakably similar."

"What about the remaining, unmatched bands?" Reeves asked. "Why don't they compare? Where could they come from?"

"We believe that these came from the cells of the victim herself," Silverman replied. "Her cells are mixed with the semen but in a much smaller proportion. Since the DNA from the victim's cells were more dilute, the amount and proportion was less on amplification."

Reeves scratched his head. "Could you prove this?"

"Yes. When we compared the restriction digested and DNA amplified from the victim, they matched the remaining bands. The nonmatching bands were from the victim.

"As an additional match," Silverman continued, "we employed a VNTR pattern obtained from the mother of Shana Bernstein against that of the defendant, as well as against her own daughter. As expected, it compared uniquely with DNA from her daughter. The nonmatching DNA is from the victim. This again proves that the defendant is likely to be the source of the DNA and the vaginal fluid. Based on this analysis, I would judge that the defendant had less than a one in five thousand chance of not being the rapist."

"Is there another test for DNA?"

"There is another test called Restriction Fragment Length Polymorphisms, better known as RFLP. This test depends upon the establishment of a close relationship between two parties with respect to certain sequences, and then determining where they may differ. This means that a certain number of reasons were compared with two known individuals and against the sample DNA. Basically, a map of an individual is established."

"Would the RFLP be a good test to utilize in this case?"

"No, since Mr. Daytona is the prime suspect and possibly connected with the murder in question. The technique, however, is less definitive in nonconsanguineous parties. Therefore, we chose to use the VNTRs and sample probes prepared by the preliminary chain reaction, or PCR method, in order to obtain a better fit."

"Cross-examination, Ms. DeCanter?" Judge Hamlin asked.

"Yes, Your Honor." Harianne rose and approached the witness stand. "Dr. Silverman, how can you be sure that these samples taken from the defendant were not contaminated or inappropriately labeled?"

"Using techniques recommended highly by the National Committee on Clinical Laboratory Studies which involve separate rooms for manufacture of PCR probes and probing process, the likelihood of amplicon formation is very unlikely. Amplicons, which are packages of amplified contaminants, are prevented in this way—by having them in two rooms. And we used a technique that monitors and detects the possible presence of amplicons. However, it is not impossible, and given our result, which shows that the comparison between the defendant and the DNA is so similar, the likelihood of amplicon contamination could not be completely eliminated."

"No further questions, Your Honor."

"Very well," Judge Hamlin stated. "The court will recess for lunch. Please return at two o'clock."

Gaston Reeves was terribly impressed by the jury's focus on the DNA testimony of Dr. Silverman. Harianne glanced at Reeves for a moment. She'd heard that he was the best, but she had never argued a case with him until now. He was quite a dancer when he was on the court stage. He grinned from ear to ear as he exited the courtroom with his legal team.

Two hours later, court was back in session. Judge Hamlin called the room to order and addressed Harianne.

"Would the defense please call your next witness?"

"Defense calls Dr. Jonathan Hooks."

A large man—sloppy, obese, with unruly black hair and a ruddy face—stood and approached the bench. He wore a dark polyester blend suit.

"Would you please state your name," Harianne asked him after he was sworn in, "and spell your last name and state your occupation for the record, please."

"Dr. Jonathan Hooks, H-O-O-K-S," he replied. "Forensic DNA analysis expert employed at Stonemark Laboratories in Oakland, California, and I have a clinical appointment in the department of biology at UC Davis. I'm also a partner in a small laboratory in Van Nuys which specializes in forensic work, including paternity testing."

"Would you please tell the court the results of your investigation into similarities, or lack thereof, between the DNA which was found in the victim's vaginal fluid and that of the defendant, Matthew Daytona?"

"We used a number of probes in contradistinction to Dr. Silverman," Hooks explained. "We prepared probes from a slightly different region of the DNA, although some forty to eighty probes were used. What kept appearing on a consistent basis was that the semen found in the victim had about a ninety-five percent comparison. Although this difference may sound minor in genetics, given the frequency of overlap among sequences among individuals, this is considered a significant difference. Stringency of DNA is the most important variable to control. In this case, I not only did eighty probes, I conducted the hybridization under high stringency conditions in my analysis. Given the results of my studies, the defendant had less than a one in twenty possibility of not being the individual involved. This conflicts with the one-in-five-thousand figure mentioned earlier. The DNA profiles are similar to those of Dr. Silverman, but with these exceptions I believe that it does not absolutely establish the defendant as the criminal. Some of the exceptions did not match the victim's blood. Since there was no other source of contamination found in specimens collected, the chances that the mismatched bands are coming from anyone other than the rapist are virtually nil."

"Please clarify that for the jury," Harianne said.

"One in twenty sounds a lot like saying that the findings argue that the DNA is from the defendant. This is less compelling when you consider that any one of the next twenty people or forty men could have the same DNA profile. While we were able to determine that some of the mismatched sequences in the minisatellite regions were from the victim, there were other sequences that matched neither the defendant nor the victim.

"In addition," he continued, "we kept the specimens under chain-of-custody conditions which prevented any possibility of intermixing. The conditions in which we performed the hybridizations are highly sterile and not given to the possibility of a contaminant. In Mr. Daytona's case, one can still be uncertain as to whether or not this is a clear-cut DNA match. There are a great number of sequences in testing DNA. So to answer the question, I am not convinced that this DNA match is matched closely with the defendant, Matthew Daytona. A more thorough DNA analysis could take up to nine months, perhaps longer, with no assurance of resolutions of the differences in the analysis. Using the nested sequence means testing the reliability of the probes."

"Cross-examination, Mr. Reeves?"

"No, Your Honor."

"Very well. We will return tomorrow morning."

On the morning of the sixth day of Matthew's trial, Harianne motioned to MacKenzie to meet her outside the courtroom. MacKenzie followed her down the hall to a corner where Harianne was standing with her cell phone.

"China just phoned," Harianne said. "We've got a surprise witness who wants to help Matthew."

"Who?" MacKenzie asked.

"Amanda Weddington."

"Never heard of her."

"Me neither."

"Let's speak to her then."

"We don't have time."

"Why?"

"She's on her way here to testify."

Harianne turned to put some papers in her Bottega Venetta briefcase, already packed with yellow legal tablets, when she noticed Austria taking a seat in the back row. Very quietly, she had been entering the courtroom every day to see Harianne's court performance.

"Let's continue," Judge Hamlin announced as he gaveled the court back into session. "We're still on the record, People v. Daytona." He smiled at the jury. "Let me remind the jury that you are still under oath."

Judge Hamlin read through and rearranged the papers before him. "Mr. Reeves, please call your next witness."

Reeves stood proudly. "The People call Detective Tracey Sanders." After Tracey was sworn in, Reeves said, "Would you state your full name, spelling your last name for the record, and state your occupation for the record, please."

"Detective Tracey Sanders, S-A-N-D-E-R-S. Los Angeles County Sheriff's Department, Homicide Division."

"What time did you arrive at the Shana Bernstein residence?"

"The next morning, maybe seven-thirty or eight o'clock."

Gaston paced the courtroom. "Do you have a partner or did you go alone?"

"I went with my partner, Detective Zack Grimes."

"What did you see when you first arrived at the scene?"

"A woman, completely naked."

"What was your first thought?"

"That she had been brutally raped and murdered. Her body was ripped to shreds, even her personal parts."

"Any signs of forced entry?"

Tracey cleared his throat. "No."

"Was the house ransacked?"

"No."

"Did you find anything else of significance?"

"Oh, yes! A red silk scarf wrapped around the victim's neck."

"What is that known as?"

"A signature killing."

"Any witnesses?"

"No."

"Where did you first encounter the defendant?"

"In his office, when we went to ask questions about Shana Bernstein."

"Is the defendant in this courtroom today?"

"Yes."

"Can you point to him?"

"Yes. The gentleman seated at the table on the left at the far right."

"What is his name?"

"Matthew Daytona."

"That's all, Your Honor."

"Ms. DeCanter, cross examination?"

"No, Your Honor."

"Would the defense call its first witness?"

"Your Honor, the defense calls Maggie Weiner."

Maggie Weiner rose from the crowded back row of the courtroom and approached the bench. She was wearing a beautifully tailored black tweed tuxedo suit, and had pulled back her hair with a gold clasp.

"Please state your full name, spelling your last name for the record, and state your occupation for the record, please," Harianne directed her.

"Maggie Weiner, W-E-I-N-E-R. I'm Mr. Daytona's legal assistant and client relations director for the law firm of Daytona, Bernstein & McDunn." She looked over at Matthew and smiled.

"How long have you worked at the firm?"

"Twelve years."

"Did you always work in this capacity?"

"No. When I first started, I was a receptionist. Later I became an assistant for both Shana and Matthew. I worked my way up the ladder," she added proudly.

"How long have you worked for Mr. Daytona?"

"Six years."

"Are you aware of his day-to-day business affairs?"

"Yes. I keep track of his calendar and bill my time on cases."

"Have you noticed anything unusual about Mr. Daytona in the last six months?"

"No. He's always been the same: very quiet and to the task. He's extremely work-oriented."

"Do you handle his accounting ledgers?"

"Sometimes. When I do, it's for personal items only."

"Can you give me an example of a personal item?"

"Taking his clothes to the cleaners, his shoes to the repair shop—things like that."

Harianne turned to Judge Hamlin. "Your Honor, may I introduce Defense Exhibit 1: a red silk scarf." Maggie sat up straighter in her chair.

Harianne retrieved the red silk scarf from the defense table, positioned herself in front of Maggie and held it up high, like a banner. "Have you seen this red silk scarf before?"

"Many times." Maggie stared at Harianne.

"Does he wear them every day?'

"Mr. Daytona wore them every day with his suits, except in the summer."

"Where are they from? What company distributes them?"

She paused in thought. "I don't know."

"Thank you. That's all, Your Honor."

"Cross, Mr. Reeves?" Judge Hamlin inquired.

"No, Your Honor."

Courtroom chatter escalated midmorning when Darci Daytona entered the chamber wearing dark glasses and a black suit and hat. Matthew turned around and caught a glimpse of her as she took a seat in the first row behind the defense.

"What is she doing here!" he exclaimed in a tense whisper.

"She's our witness," Harianne told him, organizing papers. "I told you that. You're not paying attention, Matthew."

After the twenty-minute testimony of the prosecution's witness, Judge Hamlin turned to Harianne.

"Ms. DeCanter, please call your next witness."

"Yes., Your Honor. The defense calls Darci Daytona."

Darci was sworn in, and Harianne directed her to state her name and occupation for the record.

"Darci Daytona, D-A-Y-T-O-N-A. I'm an attorney, but I don't practice by trade."

"Do you recognize the defendant in this courtroom today?" Harianne asked.

"Yes."

"Can you point him out?"

"Yes." She pointed to Matthew.

"When was the last time you saw the defendant?"

"Oh, it's been years."

"Can you tell the court how you know the defendant?"

"He was my husband."

"How long were you married?"

"We were married for six years, but we were together for longer than that. We met in law school."

"Did the defendant ever harm you?"

Darci hesitated, and struggled for words. "Well. Not really."

Harianne moved closer to her. "What does 'not really' mean?"

"He hit me, but he didn't mean to. It was an accident."

"What was an accident?"

Darci pulled down her dark glasses. "I have only one eye."

The courtroom erupted with chatter. Judge Hamlin banged his gavel down.

"Order in the court!"

Harianne paused for a moment before continuing her questions.

"How did it happen?"

"He was angry over a case he lost and hit our glass French doors to the sun porch. I was standing in the middle of the room when the glass shattered and particles flew in my face. I lost my right eye."

"Was Matthew attentive to you?"

"Oh, yes. He was great. He got me the finest surgeons and specialists that money could buy. I was lucky; I could have lost both eyes. He paid all the medical bills and costs relating to plastic surgery up front and out of pocket." She slipped her glasses back on.

"Why did you never opt for a glass eye?"

Darci swallowed. "The damage was so severe that they couldn't use a glass eye."

"Is Matthew Daytona a killer?"

"No. He's not a killer. He wouldn't hurt anyone."

"That's all. Thank you."

"Mr. Reeves, cross?"

"Nothing, Your Honor."

Darci Daytona stepped down from the witness stand and promptly left the courtroom. She was followed by Amy Kanter, whose testimony lasted for thirty minutes.

"Very well," Judge Hamlin declared when she was done. "We will take a short recess of fifteen minutes." He struck his gavel and stepped down from his bench.

After recess, Judge Hamlin again called the court to order.

"Is the prosecution prepared to close?" he asked.

"Yes," Reeves replied.

Harianne spoke up. "Your Honor, may counsel approach the bench?"

"Yes, Ms. Decanter."

Harianne and Reeves approached the bench and leaned toward Judge Hamlin.

"I've just been informed that I have a surprise witness en route to the court as we speak," Harianne informed them. "I want her to testify."

"Ms. DeCanter, Mr. Reeves is ready to make his closing statement."

"I know, Your Honor, but this is critical to my client's defense."

"Well, this adds drama to the case!" Reeves exclaimed. "Who is it?"

"Amanda Weddington. She's key to this case, Reeves."

"I don't see how, but I'll allow it, your Honor," Reeves stated.

"Very well," Judge Hamlin said. "Proceed."

Harianne returned to her table as a petite woman walked down the aisle toward her.

"Hello, I'm Harianne DeCanter. You're…?"

"Amanda Weddington."

Matthew turned and raised his eyebrows in surprise. Harianne quietly noted his startled response.

"I do remember you now," she said to Amanda. "I subpoenaed you a while back, but you never responded. Why are you here now?"

"Because he's innocent."

"Do you have proof?"

"Yes. He was once a very close friend of mine. He wouldn't cause harm to anyone. Especially murders of such a brutal nature."

"Ms. Weddington, that may speak to my client's character, but the court demands proof regarding his actions. What kind of information do you have to offer?"

Amanda gave Matthew a meaningful look before answering. "I know more than just his character, Ms. DeCanter. I know his secret."

"What?" Harianne looked at Matthew. He closed his eyes and nodded. Harianne leaned over his shoulder and hissed into his ear. "Matthew! What is she talking about? What are you hiding from me now?"

Before Matthew could respond, Judge Hamlin interrupted. "Counsel?"

Harianne hurried to the bench again. "Yes, Your Honor. We're ready. She's here."

Harianne returned to Amanda. "Why are two women dead who were closely connected to Matthew and his firm?" she demanded.

"I'll answer it on the stand if you'll allow me."

"This better be good," Harianne warned in a low voice.

"Trust me," Amanda promised. "They'll see Matthew in an entirely new light."

Harianne turned and addressed the judge. "The defense calls Amanda Weddington."

Matthew turned his head and locked eyes with Amanda as she was sworn in. He gave her a grim half-smile.

The court clerk stood and read the oath to Amanda: "Do you solemnly swear that the testimony you will give before this court will be the truth, the whole truth, and nothing but the truth, so help you God?"

"I do."

"Please state and spell your full name for the record, please," Harianne began.

"Amanda Weddington, W-E-D-D-I-N-G-T-O-N."

"Ms. Weddington, please state your occupation."

"I'm an architect for a small firm in Santa Monica."

"Ms. Weddington, how long have you known the defendant?"

"Four years or more."

"When was the last time you saw him?"

"Six months ago."

"Where?"

"In Shana's office."

"Were you with Ms. Bernstein the night she was murdered?"

"Yes—much earlier in the evening, though. She was meeting Matthew later at the house for a working dinner. They did lots of working dinners. Matthew didn't murder her. And he couldn't have raped her."

"Why is that, Ms. Weddington?"

"Because Matthew Daytona is gay. So am I. Shana Bernstein was my lover."

# CHAPTER 21

Judge Hamlin gaveled the courtroom to order after Amanda Weddington's explosive testimony.

"Order in the court!" he bellowed. "Court is adjourned until ten o'clock tomorrow morning!" He rose and left the bench.

After speaking with Gaston Reeves, Tracey waved to Zack, who was seated in the first row, directly behind the prosecution. As they walked out the courtroom, Tracey motioned to Harianne with his hand to his ear, miming "Call me." She responded with a nod.

Outside, Tracey and Zack headed toward their car.

"You know, I'm hungry for some steak," Tracey said.

Zack eagerly seconded the suggestion: "Me, too!"

They drove to Morton's in downtown L.A. on Figueroa and parked in the 7th Street Mall parking lot. The place was packed with after-work crowds of people who piled in, beelined for a seat at the bar and drank their hard day at work away. Tracey and Zack took a seat at the bar and ordered cocktails and food from the bartender, who was a friend of theirs.

Four flat-screen televisions broadcast the daily news from different locations around the restaurant. Two screens offered local news while the other two were tuned into CNN, which was running constant coverage of Matthew Daytona's entire trial.

Tracey spotted footage of Darci Daytona from that morning's court session on the monitor above him and Zack. He nudged his partner in the ribs and nodded toward the television screen.

"There they go, the news media frenzy! It's footage from this morning."

"Hey!" Zack called over to the bartender and pointed at the TV. "Turn that up, will ya?"

The bartender quietly complied. Zack and Tracey watched as a local newswoman delivered a live report from the front of the courthouse steps:

"There was an enormous surprise today in the murder trial of celebrity lawyer Matthew Daytona. The defense brought forth Matthew Daytona's ex-wife Darci Daytona, whose dramatic arrival provoked considerable buzz in the courtroom. Dressed entirely in black, Ms. Daytona made a bombshell appearance. She swore to the jury that her ex-husband is not a killer."

"She looks worried and worn," Zack observed, taking a bite of his salad.

Tracey patted him on the back, chewing his food. "Her testimony is probably the most dramatic and surprising of all."

"That's for sure!" Zack poured steak sauce over his meat and smothered his baked potato with dollops of butter. "Why do you think she's so protective of him?"

Tracey cut into his steak, took the first bite and smiled with pure enjoyment. "I think he still controls her. Of course, that's just my opinion."

Footage of Darci Daytona and the DNA expert testimony was ongoing. Tracey and Zack left the restaurant as soon as they finished eating and headed home.

Amanda Weddington's testimony had been powerful, but Gaston Reeves ignored it completely in his closing statement the next day. He stuck faithfully to his original depiction of Matthew as a dangerous killer. Harianne prepared for her own closing statement while she listened.

Reeves approached the jury slowly, looking at each juror before he started to speak.

"Shana Bernstein enjoyed her own personal space, a sense of comfort and a sense of security," he began. "The defendant violated Shana Bernstein's comfort zone and killed her. He took advantage of her and won her confidence. He shared her thoughts, concerns and needs. She made herself vulnerable to him. She had freedom, the right and the will to live—just like any other human being.

"Matthew Daytona robbed her of all of that. We'll never see her again. It's sad and not fair. Fairness is what I want—a fair verdict of guilty. You've seen a series of witnesses and heard the testimony. Beyond a reasonable doubt, Matthew Daytona is guilty. Give me a verdict of guilty. You won't be sorry."

He sat in a chair, with his legs far apart. "Just imagine your body propped up on a toilet, legs apart, with gashes in your head. Imagine an instrument cutting away your personal body parts."

Reeves screamed and yelled as if he was one of the murder victims.

In astonishment, the jurors' eyes widened, as they quickly turned their heads and moved to the edge of their seats, their attention riveted by Reeves' antics. A few shook their heads in disbelief.

"The prosecution rests, Your Honor."

Reeves sighed in relief, returned to the defense table, and crossed his fingers in the pocket of his suit.

Next it was Harianne's turn to pique the interest of the jurors and reel them into her psyche.

She walked over to the jury box with an ivory-handled magnifying glass. She spoke very slowly and accurately as she addressed the jury. She raised the cold magnifying glass to her nose, looked at the jury and spoke of special thoughts, peace and love throughout the world.

"When you look through this from a distance, writings and objects are out of focus. You can't read or see anything. Isn't that funny? Each and every one of you could look through this magnifying glass and see nothing.

"Well, ladies and gentlemen of the jury, this case is completely out of focus when you're far away from the facts. But when you pull the magnifying glass closer to your eyes, this case comes into focus.

"Similar murders have occurred in recent years, and since Matthew Daytona's incarceration. But our focus is the murder of Shana Bernstein. Matthew Daytona is not the killer. I stress the word 'not.' His reputation in the entertainment community has been well established. Words won't touch it. His clients employ him for his genuineness and caring attention to their needs; he's known for loving everyone. The public views him as an entertainment attorney idol. Until this trial, his personal life was envied. His business colleagues respected him. His friends were devoted. He isn't a killer.

"I'm asking you to keep an open mind, a willing heart and give me a verdict of 'not guilty.' Not because you have to, but because you want to. I'm not asking for compassion, but I do want you to remember his compassion for people."

Both the prosecution and defense rested.

The judge instructed the jury. "Ladies and gentlemen of the jury: At this point in the trial, I am required to inform you as to the law governing this case to guide you in your deliberations. This statement by the judge as to the law of the case is known as a charge, or instructions. It is my duty to preside over the trial and to determine what testimony and evidence is relevant under the law for your consideration. It is also my duty at the end of the trial to instruct you on the law applicable to the case. You, as jurors, are to decide the facts. But in determining what actually happened in this case—that is, in reaching your decision as to the facts—it is your sworn duty to follow the law that I am now in the process of defining for you.

"You must not change the law or apply your own idea of what you think the law should be. Both you and I are bound by the law as stated in this charge. You are not to single out one instruction alone as stating the law, but must consider the instructions as a whole. Neither are you to be concerned with the wisdom of any rule of law stated by me. Regardless of any opinion you may have as to what the law is or ought to be, it would be a violation of your sworn duty to base a verdict upon any view of the law other than that given in the instructions to the court, just as it would be a violation of your sworn duty, as finders of the facts, to base a verdict upon anything other than the evidence in the case.

"You are permitted to draw such reasonable inferences from the testimony and exhibits as you feel are justified in the light of common experience. In other words, you may make deductions and reach conclusions that reason and common sense lead you to draw from the facts that have been established by the testimony and evidence in the case. The law makes no distinction between the weight to be given to direct and circumstantial evidence. It requires only that you weigh all of the evidence and be convinced of the defendant's guilt beyond a reasonable doubt before he can be convicted. You should carefully consider the testimony of each and every witness and not overlook any testimony or any evidence. This does not mean, however, that you must accept all the testimony as true or accurate."

Judge Hamlin went on for at least another half-hour. Finally, he slammed his gavel down on the nicked wooden bench.

"Court is adjourned."

Later that evening, Harianne caught up on back paperwork at the office. Her shoes were off, her blouse unbuttoned halfway and she had kicked off her shoes to walk around in her stocking feet. She pulled open the top drawer of China's desk and read through a pile of take-out menus. There wasn't much available to satisfy her health regimen, but she settled on a Cobb salad and splurged on garlic bread. A half-hour wait for the food necessitated a rest on the beige-and-pink brocade chaise lounge in her office. The buzzer to the courtyard gate and the phone rang at the same time.

"Just a minute, I'll be right down," she yelled into the intercom as she picked up the phone.

"Hello?"

"Hi! It's me, Tracey."

"Hold on."

She ran downstairs to the courtyard gate, grabbed the white plastic bag without looking inside and paid the deliveryman. She dashed back up to her office and retrieved the phone.

"I'm back," she said. "Do you mind if I eat? My stomach is growling."

"No, go ahead," Tracey replied.

"Damn!"

"What is it?"

"They forgot my garlic bread. Oh, well. It isn't worth calling them back to redeliver." She dug into her salad. "So what are you doing?"

"Well…I'm still not convinced."

"Convinced about what?"

"Amanda Weddington's testimony. I think there's more information in Jasmine's office."

"What makes you think so?"

"Jasmine was onto something before she got murdered. It could be drugs, or…anything. I'm not quite sure yet. I want to go to the office tonight."

"Tonight? Oh,Tracey, it's—"

"Too late? Too bad. We've got to do it now. You wanted me to work with you. Time was never a factor."

"I know. But there shouldn't be anything left there that hasn't already been checked out—no clues, no evidence, and no history. What will we find?"

"Handwritten notes or documents."

"Do you think Amanda Weddington's the killer?"

"I don't know. That's what we need to find out."

"OK. What time?"

"Nine o'clock. I'll call you on the cell before coming up the driveway."

Harianne polished off her salad, changed her clothes and glanced through the day's mail. Tracey phoned promptly at nine o'clock.

"Zack and I are a mile and a half from your house."

"I'll meet you at the gate."

They arrived at the old brick building that housed Jasmine's office in a particularly rundown section of downtown L.A. The broken steps to the entrance looked like a construction project. The office directory was written in pencil on a stained piece of beige paper inside a rusted metal box that hung by the front steel doors. Smoke from outside funnels, vents on top of buildings and the sound of a freight train in the distance were reminiscent of a scene from an old gangster movie. Harianne didn't like returning there one bit; it was no place she wanted to be late at night.

Upon entering the dirt parking lot, they turned off the headlights, drove to the back of Jasmine's office and parked alongside the wrought-iron fence on a bed of wet leaves. Zack exited the vehicle first, with Tracey and Harianne following suit. Tracey walked in front of Zack and motioned for Harianne to grab his hand.

They entered through a delivery entrance and encountered an old metal door. Harianne pulled out the key Jasmine had given her and unlocked the door. The door hinges squeaked when they opened it.

Tracey pointed toward a gray metal file cabinet in the corner of Jasmine's office. "Let's start there," he said, pulling open the top drawer. "These aren't marked, but they're alphabetized. Here. Check out every single piece of paper you find."

He handed ten files each to Harianne and Zack, then settled in with a stack of his own. He read the travel file until he found a manila envelope labeled "M. Daytona." He pulled the papers folded in half from the envelope and unfolded them.

They were notes handwritten on rose petal rice paper. He couldn't read the small handwriting.

"Harianne, come here. Can you read this?"

Harianne put down her files and read the note over Tracey's shoulder:

~

*Dear Matthew,*

*I know you made the decision to break up, but I have a choice in the matter, too. I love you. I thought you loved me. We had everything. All I want is you. Why do*

> *you have to go to Japan still? You never take me. Why can't I go? We can be together. I'll never give you up. I'll always be near you until I get you.*
>
> *Love,*
>
> *Mac*

"Who's Mac?" Tracey asked. "MacKenzie?"

Harianne took the remaining papers from Tracey's hand and searched inside the manila envelope for other documents. Finally, she came across a rose petal rice paper envelope bearing a return address.

"MacKenzie McShay," she agreed.

"And?"

"There's nothing else. A dead end."

"I'm going to keep reading."

"Whatever. I think it's a waste of time."

Zack pulled a file entitled "Japan." He found another manila envelope inside with more rose petal rice paper stationery and envelopes. He unfolded another letter from a post office box and read it line by line.

> Took care of five women. Gave them all yellow scarves to wear. Wire $5,000,000 to Tokyo Bank. Twenty keys for MD.
>
> *Sincerely,*
>
> *JD*

He scanned the letter for a date; there wasn't one. The postmark had been chemically erased from the envelope. Only the year was discernible; it had been written when Matthew was in Japan—two years earlier.

Suddenly the office door flew open and a stream of bullets flooded the room. The shooter entered the room in dark clothing with fully covered head gear, moved to the middle of the room and fired in a circular motion. Zack was thrown to the side near an antique roll top desk and slid to the floor. Tracey exchanged fire and kept shooting.

Harianne scrambled into the other room, hid underneath the desk and called 911 on her cell phone. She prayed Tracey and Zack were OK as the gunfire continued.

Finally, the gunfire stopped. It was silent except for the sound of sirens from police cars approaching the property. Harianne carefully lifted herself up and tip-toed through the glass chips and debris on the hardwood floors. She saw nobody.

"Tracey?" she called out. "Zack?"

Silence.

"Tracey?"

Harianne heard a moan in the darkness, but couldn't tell where it was coming from. The creaky closet door on the other side of the office swung open and closed again; she cringed when she heard it squeak.

Carefully, quietly, she inched toward the jumbled pile of chairs and sofas in the corner of the room. She kept hearing moans, but still couldn't see Tracey or Zack in the dark. She looked toward the other side of the room; the front door was wide open. She turned and almost tripped over a dead body in front of the closet.

Suddenly the sofa began to move. Harianne scurried back to the corner and tipped it over and found Tracey, holding his arm. She gasped.

"Are you all right?" she asked.

"Yes," he grunted.

"Were you under there the whole time?"

"I'm afraid so. Where's Zack?"

"I haven't found him yet."

"Get the files that we pulled—this just turned into a murder scene. Anything the cops find becomes the property of the sheriff's office. Zack? Zack!"

They upended furniture until they found Zack slumped on the floor behind the chairs and love seat, unconscious. Tracey pried a sheet of crumbled paper from his clenched fists and handed it to Harianne. She read it in disbelief and put it in her hip pocket, then tried to calm Tracey.

"Zack! Zack! No!"

An ambulance arrived along with the police motorcade. Tracey hovered as they carefully hooked up Zack to tubes, IVs and monitors, and lifted him into the ambulance. His shirt was soaked in blood from a large hole in the side of his plump stomach. Harianne stood off to the side.

"I'm riding with him," Tracey announced.

The first officer on the scene approached Harianne. "Good evening. What happened here?"

"Officer, first of all—"

Tracey spotted Harianne speaking with the officer and ran toward them. He knew the routine; deflection of the issues at hand was important. Nothing could get out. He didn't want to enter the bullring of questions.

"I'm Detective Sanders," he said, interrupting. "I was in the middle of an investigation. We really don't know what happened. Here's my card if you have any questions." Tracey stepped back and pulled Harianne closer to him. "The assailant's body is right over there. Her name is Amanda Weddington. You'll find everything you need on her."

He and Harianne climbed into the ambulance behind Zack and left.

# CHAPTER 22

❀

Austria greeted Tracey when he arrived through the back door. She had just brewed a fresh pot of coffee.

"Good morning, Tracey! Come on in. I'll let Harianne know you're here."

"Thanks, Austria." He stood there and soaked up the warmth and coziness of the room.

"Before I go upstairs to get her, I want to tell you something."

Tracey smiled. "What's that?"

She placed her hand on the counter. "I'm concerned about my girl. She's been working so hard and she's taking a beating from this trial. She's restless and I just—"

Tracey placed his hands on her shoulders. "Austria, stop! She'll be fine. Really, she's all right. I'm keeping close tabs on her."

She smiled and spoke softly. "Thank you. You're good for her."

After Harianne joined Tracey in the living room, they danced around the topic of MacKenzie McShay.

"How's Zack?" Harianne asked.

"Better, but he's still in critical condition," Tracey said.

"How long will he be in the hospital?"

"A week or more." He paused. "Got any coffee?"

"It's almost ready."

Neither of them wanted to talk about MacKenzie. Stalling, they settled into the plush sofas.

"What next?" Harianne inquired.

"I was hoping we could forget this case," Tracey said. He lifted Harianne's soft chin and pulled her toward him for a kiss.

"Forget? Huh? This thing is hot! We've got to read the rest of those files."

Tracey looked at her lovingly.

"Give me a minute. I know we do. It's easy; the Japanese drug cartel killed them. We need more evidence about the cocaine."

"Pour me a cup of coffee, would you?"

Harianne retrieved files from her office at the other side of the house and brought them to the coffee table. Tracey met her there with two cups of hot coffee. They sat side by side on the floor.

"Which one?" he asked.

"The M. Daytona medical file."

"Where was that one? I didn't see that."

"Under 'M.' C'mon, you've got to be quick, Tracey."

"I see that. Let's get started."

Two pots of coffee later, Harianne found a subfile on AIDS. She read aloud: "After a series of tests, patient is determined to be HIV negative. Patient has expressed a strong desire to have a child."

Harianne took another sip of her coffee. Tracey waited patiently and moved his sock feet in a circular motion while she read.

"A child! Is that what you said?"

"Yes.

"But he's gay."

"Yes."

"A gay man wants a child?"

"Yes."

"We didn't know he wanted a kid. What's the name of the donation center or clinic?"

"I can't read it because of the coffee stains blocking the name."

"Great!"

Tracey took the paper and picked up the magnifying glass nearby on top of a pile of books. It reminded Harianne of her closing statement. "A gay man wants a child" and "serial killer" did not add up in their minds. Some critical information was still missing from this case.

"Why are you looking at me like that?" Tracey asked.

"Oh, nothing. Just thinking. Can you read it?"

"No. It's impossible."

"I'm going to speak with her about this."

"No, you're not. Just wait, Harianne."

She laughed. "Why?"

"You don't really know MacKenzie McShay, do you?"

"Not exactly."

"Then wait until I give you the signal."

"Maybe."

MacKenzie arrived early in the morning at Harianne's office with her laptop and BlackBerry. Harianne greeted her with a cup of coffee in hand and they dove into work. Periodically China entered to give Harianne letters attached to files for signature and checks requiring endorsement for deposit at the bank.

Two hours passed with everyone working uniformly and quietly. MacKenzie used the restroom and got a glass of water. She returned and sighed as she sat in the big chair in Harianne's office.

"I'm tired."

"I know what you mean. So am I."

"Last night, your phone rang and rang until the answering machine picked up. Where were you?"

Harianne didn't want to respond, but MacKenzie pressed.

"I went out with a friend," Harianne finally said.

"Where?"

"Just out."

"But where did you spend the evening?"

Harianne swallowed before speaking. She knew she was making a mistake by answering, but she was curious to know what was going through MacKenzie's mind.

"If you must know, I went to Jasmine Thomas' office."

"Why Jasmine's? Wasn't that your friend?"

"Yes. We were like sisters. I miss her."

"Isn't that case closed? I read something about that in the newspaper."

"No. It's still pending. They might link her death to the women that have been killed in Matthew's case."

"That wouldn't be good for Matthew."

MacKenzie remained reserved, but restless. A half-hour later, she started pacing the floor between her office, the law library, the kitchen and Harianne's office. Harianne tried to infer from her actions what was going on with her. They continued working.

Finally, an hour later, MacKenzie closed the law books and put her head down on the desk.

"All finished for the day?" Harianne asked.

"Yes, for now," MacKenzie said, lifting her head. "I wanted to talk to you."

"About what?"

"Matthew's case."

"And?"

"If Matthew is found guilty, will we appeal?"

"Of course. Why? You know that's standard procedure."

Little balls of sweat rolled across MacKenzie's forehead while she spoke. She pulled back her hair with both of her hands and clipped it in back.

"I know, but we've done a lot for him and covered all the bases."

Harianne's suspicions were raised. She couldn't believe what she heard and wanted, so badly, to ask about the kilos of cocaine and the murders, but she wouldn't betray Tracey. He would hate her if she did that.

"Are you telling me that you think he killed those women?" she asked.

"No," MacKenzie said. "I just can't work with you on the appeal."

"There's still more work and if we lose, we're appealing. Don't back out now!"

"Fine. I've got one problem in terms of my calendar."

"What?"

"I've got another commitment on a case."

"That's OK. I can handle it and understand the issues. But I thought when Matthew hired you, you were totally committed to him for the trial."

"I was, but something came up."

"Interesting," Harianne said with disgust.

"What are you getting at?"

MacKenzie reached for her purse and briefcase and proceeded toward the door. Frustrated, Harianne grabbed her arm. MacKenzie threw her hands off.

"What's wrong with you?" she demanded angrily.

"I'm sorry, MacKenzie. It's just—"

Harianne gasped when she caught sight of MacKenzie's arm; it was covered with black, blue and red marks.

"Did I do that?"

"No. That was there. It's nothing."

"Nothing?"

"It's just a scar from a needle."

"A needle?" Harianne echoed.

"Really, Harianne! I've got to go."

"Wait a minute! It looks really bad."

"I'm diabetic," MacKenzie explained impatiently.

"How did—"

"I inherited it from my mother." MacKenzie pulled her things together and opened the door. "I'll call you later."

Supremely irritated, Harianne turned back toward her office, only to find China standing there.

"Tracey's on the phone, Harianne. He sounds disturbed."

"What?" Harianne hurried to her desk and picked up the phone. "Tracey, what's going on?"

"I wish I knew," he told her. "The medical examiner just called with the results of Amanda Weddington's autopsy. She didn't die of any bullet wounds, Harianne. She was already dead from a drug overdose."

# CHAPTER 23

At Cedars-Sinai Hospital, Zack prepared to check out. Tracey picked him up from the hospital and drove him home, where a Polish convalescent nurse greeted him at the door. Tracey helped him inside the house and retrieved his belongings from the car while Zack settled into his favorite armchair. A fluffy white Himalayan jumped up and sniffed his bandage.

"Hey, there, Lilly, how ya doin', girl?"

Tracey did a double take. "Is that…?"

"Yeah," Zack admitted sheepishly. He shifted in his seat as he scratched the cat's ears. "So when can I return to work?"

"Oh, maybe two weeks. At least that's what I was told. Don't quote me."

"I won't. I'll call tomorrow."

"You've got to relax and stay healthy. Maybe this little setback will help you get some rest."

Harianne and Austria took a walk in the canyon with Melissa that evening. Austria took Melissa's leash for a while, relieving Harianne from a hard day.

"I received a phone call from England about my brother today," she said.

"Really?"

Austria stopped walking and linked arms with Harianne. She paused. "He's very ill with Hodgkin's disease."

"I'm so sorry, Austria." Harianne hugged her with a tight grasp.

"I am, too," Austria said tearfully. "He's a good man."

"Are you going to visit him in England?"

Austria wiped her eyes with a wrinkled pink-and-white handkerchief she clenched tightly in her hand.

"Maybe. I might have to handle his financial affairs." She sniffed and wiped her eyes again.

When they returned home from their walk, Austria busied herself in the kitchen. Twenty minutes later, she emerged with a wicker tray laden with white porcelain cups brimming with hot chocolate and marshmallows mounted high, and placed it on the coffee table. Harianne joined her on the sofa.

"This is delicious," she said, sipping slowly.

"I need to talk to you," Austria said seriously. "This won't be easy and it'll take a while."

"Don't be silly, Austria. What is it?"

"I love you so much, Harianne, and only want the best for you. When you told me you weren't feeling well and the headaches were persistent, I got worried. Maybe I shouldn't."

"Just tell me!"

"OK. The time is right."

"The time is right for what?"

"Your mother—Marissa."

"My mother is dead. Remember, Austria? They were both killed in a plane crash. You're not losing your memory, are you?"

"No, Harianne. I'm not *that* old—not yet! Listen to me, honey. This is very painful. Your mother is alive. I don't know where she is, but she's alive."

"Alive! What?"

"Yes. Her name is Gretchen Duet."

"My parents' name is Duet, yes, but my mother's name was Marissa."

"No, Harianne. Marissa wasn't your mother. She was your grandmother."

"What?!"

Startled by the news, Harianne grabbed some tissues and paced the floor. She was angered and hurt.

"Where's my mother?"

"Gretchen was presented as your sister and her mother, Marissa, adopted you as her own," Austria quietly explained. "Marissa loved you so much. She was a wonderful lady."

"How old was my mother?"

"Gretchen was—is—eighteen years older than you."

"Who's my father?"

"I don't know his name, but as I remember, he was a nice-looking man—light skin, great features, very robust. A handsome man. But Marissa and Andres were appalled because he was African American. They were very concerned about their reputation in the community. Back then, as you know, interracial relationships were extremely controversial."

"So where is my mother today?"

"I don't know. Mrs. Duet really wanted her to have an abortion so that she could continue her studies, but the doctors ruled against it because she had had several already. She was rather wild. The best thing for Gretchen, at the time, was to have you. After you were born she started her first year in law school. She moved out of her parents' house into an apartment of her own, and the Duets legally adopted you. You lived with them from that point onward."

"And the plane crash?"

"It happened while they were flying to a summer vacation in Tahiti. Gretchen completely vanished and never returned." Austria paused and placed her hand on Harianne's lap. "The DeCanters were very good friends of your parents. They vowed to me they would never tell you about Gretchen. They knew how much the Duets loved and cared for you; you were their little angel."

"Did you ever hear from her, Austria?"

"Twice. Your mother tracked me down somehow and wrote to me after she married a wealthy Beverly Hills businessman. She wrote me again after he died—of some sort of liver disease, I believe. But I haven't actually seen her since she was eighteen."

"What was her married name?"

"She never took his name, dear. As far as I know she always kept her own."

Harianne sat down, ran her hands through her curly hair, then jumped up and started pacing again.

"I wanted to tell you about your mother a long time ago, dear, but…I didn't feel it was my place," Austria said. "But now I don't have a choice."

"Why? What do you mean?"

"Harianne, Marissa and Gretchen were both diabetics. In fact, while in high school, Gretchen gave Mrs. Duet her insulin shots and then gave herself a shot. Gretchen was bedridden when she was carrying you. After you were born, she was housebound for weeks with severe migraine headaches."

"That must have been the woman whose face I couldn't make out in my dreams," Harianne said softly.

"When you got sick, I felt it was important to finally tell you the truth, in case your doctor needs the information," Austria continued. "Your parents—the DeCanters—always took great care to monitor your health and took you for checkups every year to make sure you showed no signs of developing diabetes. After you got out of college and still seemed thoroughly healthy, they finally started to relax. But I'm worried. I love you too much."

"Don't worry, Austria. I'm fine."

"Are you sure?"

"Yes. Don't worry, OK?"

"Are you still having headaches?"

"Yes. Not all the time. Don't worry about me. What happened to my mother?"

"I don't know. I haven't heard from her in almost twenty years."

Harianne sighed. "Thank you for sharing this with me, Austria. I love you."

"I love you too. You're special to me, Harianne."

"So are you."

Austria could tell Harianne was having difficulty processing all the information, and her shock.

"I know this is a lot to take in, dear, but it's important that you know. I'm sorry I had to tell you this. We can talk again later, if you like. I have a gift from your mother to you, but I'm not going to give it to you until you've had time to digest all of this."

Austria returned to her cottage and Harianne went upstairs to her room. She stretched across the bed with Melissa at her feet and tried to dismiss the thoughts swirling through her head. No luck.

Her mother's name was Gretchen? And she was alive? Where was she? What was she like?

She needed to talk with someone, but with whom? Tracey? No…he was busy helping Zack.

It was at times like these that she missed Jasmine most. Jasmine would have comforted her and told her to be strong.

"Jasmine had no parents," Harianne thought, "and here I have parents that I don't even know."

# CHAPTER 24

On his first day back on the job, Zack phoned Tracey on his cellphone in the morning and picked him up from Harianne's. They proceeded to the offices of Daytona, Bernstein & McDunn.

When they stepped off of the elevator, they were greeted by ringing telephones and mail runners bustling between the law firm's occupied conference rooms. Zack smiled at the receptionist as they approached her desk.

"Hello, Erin," Zack said. "We're here to see Lara Smith."

Lara promptly joined them in the reception area. Conservatively and professionally dressed in a white wool suit and crisp white shirt with the collar slightly tilted up, she escorted Tracey and Zack to a small conference room. They seated themselves in black leather chairs around a long mahogany table.

"Coffee? Water?" Lara politely inquired, gesturing toward an armoire cabinet by the door displaying a tray of Evian water bottles and a white china coffee service.

"No, thanks," Tracey said, motioning to Zack to remain silent. "Who's the distributor of those scarves?"

"It's a small company just outside of Tokyo," Lara said. "It's in Shibuya. If I knew more, I would tell you."

"I'm sick and tired of this goddamn shit, Lara!" Tracey exclaimed.

He slammed his large hands on the table so hard that it shook and rattled the glasses on the glass tray at the other end of the conference table. Lara jumped, startled.

"Why are you yelling at me?"

"Because you know who it is!"

Lara stood up as if to leave. She turned and regarded Tracey with a deadlocked gaze.

"No! No! No! I don't know."

"I don't fuckin' believe you, Lara."

Zack placed a firm hand on Tracey's shoulder and pushed him into a chair by the window.

"Calm down, buddy. Now, Lara. I'm sorry for the outburst, but we're running on limited time here. Are you familiar with the initials 'GDMS'?"

"That's the distributor."

"Is it a corporation or an individual?"

"It could be either."

"What do the initials stand for?"

"I haven't a clue," Lara said firmly. She sounded angry and humiliated.

"That's all then," Zack said, frustrated. "Thank you for your time."

He helped Tracey up from his chair and the two departed. Behind the closed elevator doors, he turned on his partner.

"Yo, Tracey! When did you turn into such a cranky-assed fuck-up? What, did you roll outta Harianne's bed this morning and decide you must be God or something?"

"What're you talking about?" Tracey fumed.

"What the hell was all that about back there—threatening Lara Smith?! What's wrong with you? You know better. That's unacceptable."

"Someone is withholding information from us!"

"I don't think so. You didn't give her a chance. Give it time."

"I shouldn't have yelled at her," Tracey admitted.

"No shit, Sherlock. You owe her an apology."

By the time Zack and Tracey returned to their precinct office that afternoon, both men were feeling the worse for wear. Tracey rubbed his bloodshot eyes and scratched his prickly five o'clock shadow with irritation before tossing a wrinkled jacket over his desk chair. Zack pulled a ham sandwich from the refrigerator. He'd taken only a few bites from it when the phone rang.

Zack reached for the phone; no one was there but the dial tone. Just as he sat on the sofa, the phone rang again. He punched the speaker button and let the machine answer.

"This is Troy Garland. Please call me on my cell at (310) 555-1010. I really need to speak with you."

"Troy Garland?" Zack mouthed. "Who's that?"

Tracey shrugged.

Several hours later, Tracey answered a call from Dispatch.

"Got another homicide."

"What's the location?" Tracey asked.

"Daytona, Bernstein & McDunn."

"We were just there this morning!"

"Aw, Tracey," Zack said, "you don't think it's—"

"Lara Smith?"

They drove ninety miles an hour and met the first officer in the Daytona, Bernstein & McDunn lobby.

"Who is it?" Tracey asked. "Lara Smith?"

"Marci Catlin. She's an associate and hasn't been working here that long."

"Can we see her?"

"Follow me. She's in the bathroom down the hall inside Matthew Daytona's office."

When they arrived, the fragile, naked body of a twentysomething woman with long, black curly hair was hanging from the chrome shower head. Blood dripped from her neck down into the drain hole. A red silk scarf was tightly tied around her neck, which bore black and blue marks. The bruises triggered painful memories of Marina.

Tracey took a deep breath and turned away.

"She's young," he commented. "This is a different one."

"How's that?" the first officer asked.

"The killer is angry. We're on to him. All of the other murders, the victims were on the toilet."

"I read that in the report, but it's still the same person, don't you think?"

"Oh, yeah," Tracey and Zack replied simultaneously. "We're with you on that."

"Where's Lara Smith?" Zack asked.

"No one else was here," the officer said. "Just Marci Catlin."

"That's odd," Tracey said.

"Why is that?"

"Lara Smith always works late. Did anybody see anyone or hear anything?"

"No, sir."

"Did the guard downstairs see anyone or did anyone sign in for this floor?" Tracey asked.

"No, sir."

"Fine."

Tracey and Zack sealed off the law firm so that no one was allowed to enter.

"Hey, Zack, let's get out of here and let forensics do their job," Tracey said. "We can wait in the lobby downstairs."

"Yeah," Zack agreed. "It's going to be a while."

"Where the hell is Lara Smith?" Tracey wondered.

"If she's smart, halfway to Borneo," Zack wisecracked. "She's the only lawyer in this joint who hasn't been offed yet."

"Funny."

Tracey called over the first officer and gave him terse instructions: "Put out an APB on Lara Smith. We need to find her immediately."

Tracey pulled out his cellphone.

"Who ya calling?" Zack asked.

"Harianne."

Zack smirked, then pulled out his cellphone.

"What're you doing?" Tracey asked.

"Whaddya think? Checking messages. I've got a life too, ya know. Hey, that Troy Garland phoned again. Sounds important."

"Oh, yeah? Let him take a number and stand in line."

"He really wants to talk to us."

"He can wait!"

The next morning, Tracey phoned FBI Agent Michael Diggs.

"Agent Michael Diggs, please."

"Agent Diggs."

"This is Detective Tracey Sanders, L.A. County Sheriff's Department Homicide Bureau. I've got a dangerous serial killer in L.A. who's out of control."

"How can I help?"

"I thought we had our man. He's in jail pending a verdict. But I think we have a copycat. All the victims were lawyers in the same firm, and the same MO was used each time."

"Sure, we can be of assistance. Understand, we'll call the shots, but I'll consult and keep you close to the vest."

"I'll still want to be on top of the case."

"That's not possible if the FBI takes over. You know that."

"I want to be kept in the loop."

"I'll see what I can do."

"There's something else: a Japanese drug-and-prostitution ring may play a key role in the murders. I'm concerned about that."

"You'll have to brief us on the Japan information. The killer is smart. He's right under your nose."

"He is?" Tracey asked, puzzled.

"You're not seeing clearly."

Four black Hummers lined up single-file in front of the L.A. County Sheriff's Homicide Bureau. Agent Diggs and sixteen other FBI representatives met Tracey and Zack in the conference room, which was set up with coffee and pastries for a full briefing on the gruesome murder case.

The agents listened closely as Tracey described the murder victims' naked bodies, their bruises, how they were beaten, how their legs were spread apart, and the murderer's trademark: the infamous red silk scarf wrapped around their necks. The details of Taka Sousushi and the mysterious distributor GDMS caught everyone's attention.

"Who's Taka Sousushi?" one agent asked.

"He's Matthew Daytona's former business partner in Japan, also his uncle," Tracey explained. "I think he's a major player in this case. But he was killed before he could testify."

Harry walked in, whispered in Tracey's ear and handed him a red folder. Tracey opened it and found a receipt and computer printout from the New Ottani Hotel—signed by Taka Sousushi before he died. The guest section read "GDMS." Tracey glanced at his watch and smiled. The meeting lasted most of the day.

"I'm sorry for taking so much of your time. We appreciate the FBI coming in today to help catch this killer. GDMS is a problem. I don't know who it is."

Agent Diggs approached Tracey and Zack afterward.

"I think you've done a fine job, but it's out of your hands now," he said. "This is pretty serious. Does that folder pertain to this case?"

"No," Tracey lied. "It's something else."

He and Zack looked at each other. Unbeknownst to Agent Diggs, they weren't about to get out of the case. They were sticking close by.

Tracey and Zack returned to their office and Zack shut the door behind them. Tracey pulled the computer printout from the folder.

"What's that, Tracey?"

"A printout that reflects monies received by Taka Sousushi from the Japanese distributor for the shipment of red silk scarves."

"What!"

"Yeah." Tracey grinned with assurance.

Zack cleared his throat. "You should have turned everything over to the FBI. Why didn't you give them that?"

"Hell, no! The FBI will eventually get a copy from records and figure it out. For now, they have enough to go on."

"Ah, hell." Zack pointed to his stomach.

"What's wrong?" Tracey asked.

"My stomach. It's calling for—"

"Oh, Zack! I thought you gave food up?"

"No, Tracey," Zack said, exasperated. "Richard Simmons did not visit me in the hospital."

"I wish he did," Tracey retorted. "He might have helped rewire your thought patterns so you'd stop thinking about food all the time."

"C'mon. Let's grab some dinner."

Zack grabbed Tracey's coat along with his own and closed the door behind them. Outside, he stopped to look for the car.

"Where'd you park, Tracey?"

"On the street."

They started crossing the street but ducked behind some bushes when a black Range Rover came barreling their way, headed for Tracey's parked car at a high rate of speed. It exploded on impact, igniting an orange and red ball of fire that lit up the sky.

"Tracey!" Zack grabbed his partner. "You OK?"

"Yeah, yeah."

"Call the fire department."

"They're already coming. Don't you hear the sirens?"

The fire department responded immediately. Tracey's vehicle was burnt to a crisp.

"You guys are lucky as hell," the lead fireman told them.

"What the hell was that?" Zack asked.

"A timed vehicle."

"What the—"

"No one was in the car."

"My God!" Tracey yelled. "Glad we weren't in there!"

"Someone doesn't like us," Zack agreed.

"No shit!"

"I guess we're not going to eat."

"Give it a rest, Zack!"

Zack flipped open his buzzing cellphone just as Tracey's cell began to ring.

"What!" Zack yelled. He heard heavy breathing, then a strange voice speaking.

"Lara Smith was murdered. See ya 'round." Zack pulled the phone away from the loud dial tone ringing in his ear. He looked over at Tracey.

"Dispatch says that Troy Garland guy left another urgent message," Tracey said, snapping his phone shut. "What's up?"

# CHAPTER 25

❦

Tracey phoned Harianne from his cellphone while he and Zack made their way across town in a loaner from the precinct garage. She picked up on the fourth ring.

"I was beginning to think you weren't there," Tracey said.

"No, I'm just watching TV and drinking hot chocolate. Can't sleep."

"Well, I hate to interrupt, but you really can't sleep now," Tracey told her. "Another person was killed tonight."

"Where?"

"1303 Canyon Bay Drive, Malibu. Our buddy at the precinct just called. He's keeping us in the loop even though the FBI's on the case now."

"The FBI?"

"Later. Call MacKenzie and tell her another person was murdered, but don't give her any details. I need to speak with both of you. Zack and I will pick you up in ten minutes. Have you heard from the jury?"

"No. They're still out."

"Good. We've got a serious problem. The FBI will be there when we arrive. We'll have to stay in the background and let them do their work. You'll stay in the car at all times, OK?"

"Fine with me. Who is it?"

"I don't know yet, but the murder occurred at Lara Smith's home."

Harianne yawned and moved her neck from side to side to loosen the muscles. She put on pants, a big sweater and tennis shoes.

This would be the first time that she had phoned MacKenzie late in the evening. She hesitated at first, picked up the phone, and then put it down. Then she picked it up and dialed the number.

"Hello?" MacKenzie answered in a lethargic voice.

"It's Harianne. There's been another murder this evening."

"That's the second one in two days. This is ridiculous. It's a copycat."

"I know. The detectives wanted you to know since we're representing Matthew."

"Thanks for calling me. What are we going to do?"

"I don't know yet. I'll call you later."

When Tracey, Zack and Harianne arrived at Lara Smith's home, FBI agents in dark jumpsuits were covering the grounds like a black blanket. Harianne stayed in the car while Tracey and Zack sought out Agent Diggs. Thunderous helicopters hovered above the house and covered a one-mile radius of the property.

"Tracey!" Agent Diggs yelled. "We're dealing with a real psycho. I can't believe what he did to her!"

Tracey and Zack responded in unison. "We can."

"What do you mean?"

"Is she naked on the toilet seat?" Tracey asked.

"Yes. But wait'll you see the rest. You'll have to hurry. Don't forget, I'm calling the shots now."

Diggs guided them to the bathroom in the house. There they found Lara Smith's naked body completely immersed in blood, placed on the toilet. Each leg was cut in half, causing red blood to gush across the cold, white-tiled floor. The pedestal sink cradled her decapitated head; a red silk scarf was tied around her forehead.

Tracey took a handkerchief from his pocket and buried his face in it. Zack hurried out the front door toward a large gardenia bush to the right of the house, where he promptly threw up. After several belches, he uttered a sigh of relief, and wiped tears from the corners of his eyes and beads of water from his forehead. He ran back to the car and jumped inside.

"What's wrong, Zack?" Harianne asked.

"Oh, Harianne," he groaned, his head between his knees. "It's Lara Smith!"

"What happened? Why her house? I thought the murders were only happening in offices."

"Killers know where you are at all times."

"Where's Tracey?"

"He's still in there."

Harianne was scared and concerned. This situation was out of hand. She sat quietly, waiting for Tracey to return.

Zack's cellphone rang. He reached in his pocket and answered it, out of breath.

"Zack here."

"Sorry to bother you," said the Dispatch messenger. "We've got a white male dead on the toilet."

"Heart attack?"

"Not sure. It's the Truman Medical Supply Company downtown, near the Garment District. We're not releasing this to the FBI. It's unrelated."

"I'll tell Tracey. He's not back yet."

"Who's that?" Harianne asked.

"The precinct. Another murder victim."

"A woman?"

"No. As a matter of fact, it's a man."

Twenty minutes later, Tracey returned to the car.

"Did you phone MacKenzie, Harianne?"

"Yes. She didn't say anything other than we've got a copycat killer on our hands. She's waiting to hear from me."

"OK. This is a really bad one. It's so bad, I'm not giving you the details this time."

"That bad! What's the big deal?"

"I've seen everything, but this…this hit home with me," Tracey said softly. "I don't feel good."

"Me, neither," Zack said.

"Oh, guys!"

Zack tucked his shirt in and took a box of Altoids from his inside coat pocket. "Tracey, we've got to go to Truman Medical Supply," he said firmly.

"When did that come in?" Tracey asked.

"A few minutes ago. They said it's unrelated, but…I'm skeptical."

They drove directly to a dead end in a rundown area of the Garment District. A night guard answered their knock on a door of the dingy gray building.

"Did you phone the sheriff?" Tracey asked.

"Yes, sir. Come in."

"Who's the vic?" Zack asked.

"Niles Cortland Brock," the guard answered. "He's the owner of the supply house."

They swiftly crossed the old, stained Italian-tile floors to a long, narrow hall that took them to a bathroom at the rear of the building, where they were greeted by a janitor. The smells of urine, mildew and death hung heavy in the air. Tracey stopped at the doorway.

"Harianne, why don't you wait here." The look on his face made clear it was an order, not a question.

Inside a bathroom stall, Tracey and Zack examined the victim: white, male, early thirties, dark hair. He was naked on the toilet seat with a red silk scarf tightly wrapped around his neck.

"What's happened here?"

"I don't know, Zack, but I've got a funny feeling we'll know soon."

They met Harianne outside. She stood there, nervously looking at them. They returned her look with a nod of their heads, confirming another murder by the serial killer.

They waited for the forensic team, then took Harianne home and returned to their office to write up their report. Tracey thought about Marina every time he saw the murdered women in his mind.

The phone rang three times before Tracey picked it up.

"Tracey!" It was Dr. Todd Silverman. "I've just completed the probe process. The DNA is the same."

"Wait a minute, Doc. Zack is motioning to me. I'll put you on speaker."

"Is everyone there?"

"Yes, go ahead," Tracey replied.

Zack leaned forward in his chair, listening intently, while Tracey sat erect in his chair, tapping a tablet with his pencil.

"The probes read one out of million."

"So he's our guy?" Zack asked.

"Not necessarily—hold on," Silverman cautioned. "This could be a copycat killer."

"Especially since Matthew Daytona is in jail," Tracey drawled.

"Shit!" Zack swore angrily. "Could Daytona have solicited someone to kill those people?"

"One out of a million is a narrow margin," Silverman said. "The probe process points to one person."

Tracey stood up from his chair, placed his hands on his hips and walked to the window.

"A copycat...I'll be damned!"

In frustration, Zack sighed and placed his hands on his forehead.

"This case has got to come to a close," he said. "People keep getting murdered and no one sees anything."

"With all the media attention and Matthew Daytona's wealth," Tracey mused, "he could be getting framed by...anyone."

# CHAPTER 26

It was ten the next morning by the time Tracey made it home, exhausted. Before retiring, he went to the kitchen and cooked breakfast: toast, scrambled eggs, and orange juice. Pictures of Marina in heart-shaped magnet frames lined the refrigerator door.

He moved into the living room and saw more pictures of Marina on the piano and sofa end tables. It was appropriate to soak in memories of Marina; today would have been her birthday and their eighth wedding anniversary.

Tracey sat down at the piano and stroked a key. He hadn't played in weeks. It used to be that he played every night before heading to bed, but lately, his bed was a couch at the precinct. Or Harianne's.

The sheet music for "The Way You Look Tonight" sat on the piano. He hit a few bars, started playing and began to sing:

*Some day, when I'm awfully low,*
*When the world is cold,*
*I will feel a glow just thinking of you*
*And the way you look tonight.*

He played it over and over, sobbing and wiping away his tears. Finally, he went upstairs; he fell face first into the plush pillows on his bed and fell asleep almost instantly.

He was awakened later that morning when he rolled over and hit something hard on the other side of the bed. It was a string of red silk scarves tied in knots under the sheets. Startled, he jumped up, looked around the room, checked underneath the bed, ran to the adjoining bathroom and found no one. He ran downstairs and perused the entire area until he saw the back door wide open and felt a cool breeze blowing through the house.

MacKenzie phoned Harianne from the office at noon.

"Are you awake yet?"

Harianne yawned. "Yeah. Did you hear anything from the court?"

"No."

"I didn't check my voicemail. I got in so late."

"Why?"

"I met Tracey after he called last night. Two people were murdered: a man at Truman Medical Supply downtown, and Lara Smith, from the law firm."

"Lara Smith? Is she a partner?"

"She's an associate. I'm shocked. She was murdered at her home."

"How was she murdered?"

"The murders were the same as the other victims. Well, there was something different, but Tracey and Zack wouldn't tell me any details."

"Hmm. Well, I still need more information from you, Harianne. Are we getting together today to discuss the case?"

"I'm afraid not. I have an appointment this afternoon. Keep researching the case law. See if you can find cases on point pertaining to an appeal. We need to be prepared for a guilty verdict."

Harianne arrived at Dr. Zenfried's office promptly at two o'clock. The doctor entered the room with a serious look on his face.

"Please have a seat, Ms. DeCanter."

"Thank you."

Dr. Zenfried stood with his arms crossed, embracing Harianne's file. "Well, it's a microadenoma, just as I suspected. It's really nothing."

"Nothing?"

"Nothing. These are very common. That's why I wanted to do an MRI. We'll dissolve it with medication."

"Dissolve it? Why not surgery?"

"Surgery is risky and it could ruin your sense of smell. It is a very delicate operation. There are some superior surgeons out there who claim they're the best in the county at this, but I'm skeptical. We'll dissolve it."

"Will I be OK in the future?" Harianne inquired nervously.

"You'll be fine now and in the future. It's a tiny microadenoma."

"What's the medication? Does it have side effects?"

"Just Dostinex. As you already know, it causes some side effects in some people. You'll take half a pill once a week at bedtime for the rest of your life. Trust me on this."

"OK."

"How are your headaches?"

"The medicine's helping."

"Good. Then I'll write a new prescription. Relax, Harianne."

Later that afternoon, Tracey met Zack at the office. He made up his mind not to mention the scarves; he didn't want Zack to worry about him. He'd had enough stress already with the shooting. He and Zack sat in their office and struggled to focus on paperwork while they awaited the results of one more DNA probe. Nothing was more important or interesting to them than the Matthew Daytona case.

Tracey was logging names of murder victims into the computer database when the phone rang. He punched the speakerphone button and, after a brief silence, heard a James Cagney-type voice speaking.

"Is this Detective Sanders?" the voice whispered.

"Yes," Tracey answered. "Who's this?"

"I can't say. I've got to meet with you."

"Who are you?"

"I have information on your serial killer. It involves the woman lawyer. I'll tell you when I see you. Meet me in Marina Del Rey at Pier 31, Slip 20 on the yacht My Gracious Lady. I'll stand up so you can see me when you enter the dock gate."

"The woman lawyer?" Tracey repeated slowly. "OK then. I'll see you in thirty minutes."

Tracey slid in his socks across the wood floor to Zack's desk.

"Get your coat, now! I'll put on my shoes."

"An informant?"

"Sounds like. Let's go!"

They took the freeway to Marina Del Rey, drove down Main Street to Pier Canal, turned right and headed straight ahead into the parking lot. Tracey turned off the ignition and headlights, and slowly coasted to a parking spot in front of Pier 31. He and Zack exited the car and walked down the wood-plank pier. It was dark except for one light at the entrance gates. Suddenly, they saw a flash of light from a yacht; a man in dark clothing stood with a searchlight in his hand, flashing it on and off continuously.

"That's him," Tracey said.

"How do you know?" Zack asked. "It's too dark to see who it is."

"Stop worrying—just follow my lead," Tracey said, looking directly at Zack.

"The last time I followed your lead, we almost got killed," Zack muttered.

"OK, you're right," Tracey agreed. "You're the authority."

"Listen up!" Zack commanded. "Stay close. Don't try to be a hero. We don't know what we're dealing with yet. *Capish?*"

"You got it!"

The light continued to flash on and off. Tracey and Zack pulled out their .38 revolvers and cautiously approached. As they got closer, the light was beamed on the yacht's name, lettered across its back end: My Gracious Lady.

A thin Caucasian man with a manicured brown goatee greeted them beside the yacht. "Hello, I'm Troy Garland."

"I remember your name—you left me several messages. I'm Detective Tracey Sanders."

"Detective Sanders. You never returned the calls. What a naughty boy!"

"This is my partner, Detective Zack Grimes."

"I forgot you guys travel in pairs. Please come in."

Garland escorted them into the cockpit. Zack let out an appreciative whistle as they surveyed the plush leather furnishings, beige pillows and teakwood fixtures.

"Nice digs, mister."

"Thank you."

Down below, the galley gleamed with cherrywood cabinetry and granite countertops that spoke to Garland's wealth and taste. Assessing him in the light, Tracey and Zack judged him to be in his fifties.

"What kind of boat is this?" Zack asked, admiring its beauty.

"Carver 44 Cockpit motor yacht."

Tracey rubbed his hand on the countertops of the bar and along the side of the interior. "I really like the wood."

Garland sat in a leather chair and faced them. "It's breathtaking, isn't it? Teak wood is the finest."

He pulled out a pipe. "I'm glad you were able to respond so quickly. Do you mind if I smoke my pipe? It's vanilla tobacco, my favorite."

"No, that's fine, Mr. Garland," Tracey replied. "I apologize for not—"

"Never mind! I've got information and you wouldn't even respond until I disguised my voice!"

"I was wrong for not returning your calls, Mr. Garland," Tracey admitted. "But we are interested in the information you have."

"Very well then. First of all, I must warn you that you can't relinquish my identity to anyone. The information and statements you hear tonight can't go any further than the people in this room. I want total immunity. Understood?"

"That can be arranged through the district attorney," Zack said. "We don't have the authority. I don't think it will be a problem, but we'll have to check that out."

"Please sit down then," Garland said. "Can I get you anything?"

"No, we're fine," Tracey said. "Why don't you just tell us who you are and what this is about?"

"I'm the CEO and president of Vista Del Mar Sperm Bank in Agoura Hills."

"A sperm bank?" Zack echoed.

"Yes," Garland said. "After inheriting it from my uncle, I moved out here from Chicago and opened banks in other areas of California. They're doing quite well, too. Of course, I didn't invite you here this evening to dwell on my prosperity."

"Why did you call us?" Tracey asked.

"Because of Matthew Daytona's murder trial. Are either of you familiar with a woman named MacKenzie McShay?"

"We know of her," Tracey replied. He exchanged a surprised look with Zack, who was restlessly shifting his weight from one leg to the other and chomping on his gum.

"What's the connection between you and MacKenzie?" Tracey asked.

"She's a business acquaintance."

"OK. Proceed."

"Matthew Daytona came to see me about six years ago," Garland continued. "He donated his sperm in the hopes of being a father. He's a very confused man. After numerous conversations, Matthew started to trust me. He told me that Ms. McShay was very much in love with him, but he felt differently. He informed me that he's gay and wanted to move on with his life. He wanted very much to be a father, but with another man. This was the main reason he broke up with her, but Ms. McShay didn't know he was gay."

"She does now," Zack snorted.

"Zack," Tracey warned.

"Ms. McShay continued to work at his office for a while, but eventually left the firm."

"Could you please get to the point, Mr. Garland," Tracey interrupted. "How exactly is your sperm bank connected to our case?"

"A year ago, I received a telephone call from Ms. McShay, inquiring about Matthew's sperm donations," Garland explained. "Since the invoices were sent to the office, she had knowledge of his sperm donations. With one exception, they were marked 'Personal and Confidential,' but she opened them."

"Don't you need approval from Matthew Daytona to discuss his sperm?" Zack asked.

"Yes. But Ms. McShay was…persuasive. And Matthew's signature was present on the request form. Obviously, he requested the withdrawal of the sperm."

"What withdrawal?" Tracey asked. "When?"

Garland turned his head away to puff on his pipe. The story was burdensome to the detectives, but he had their attention. Tracey cleared his throat, encouraging him to continue with his story.

"According to Ms. McShay, Matthew had hired several women lawyers and dated them. She was angry. She didn't agree with their breakup. I, of course, didn't reveal the information he had given me in confidence.

"Then, late one afternoon, she abruptly entered my office and demanded access to his bank. She handed me a signed release with Matthew Daytona's signature."

"Did it look like his signature?" Tracey asked.

"Yes. Ms. McShay paid me $300,000, in cash, for each purchase of frozen intercervical vials and $20,000 in cash for each additional donation made by Matthew. Matthew made donations continuously. She told me that they had agreed to have children through this method. I was quite surprised, since I knew Matthew's, uh, preference."

"So she paid you off to look the other way and not tell Matthew Daytona that she was buying his sperm."

"Essentially, yes."

"Didn't that alert you? Why didn't you phone Matthew?"

"I had his signature on the form. It raised my suspicions, though, so I hired a private investigator. I found out that she had had abortions and other medical problems that led to a hysterectomy. A portion of her gynecological records was crossed out in thick black ink, but it's clear she's unable to have children. She's a bitter woman."

"Why didn't you inform Mr. Daytona immediately, or call the police?" Tracey asked.

"The large amount of cash was a factor," Garland admitted. "Besides, I thought he had changed his mind.

"Then, of course, he went and got himself arrested by you fellows. According to your investigative reports and the news media, the DNA found on the victims at the murder scenes was Matthew Daytona's. But then the murders continued after he was arrested. And I found it strange for him to be involved."

"That may be, Mr. Garland, but you still accepted the cash," Tracey pointed out angrily.

"Seminal fluid doesn't kill you," Garland said, tad defensively.

"Go on," Tracey said.

"Not long ago, Ms. McShay paid me a visit. She was in a rage. She closed the door and locked the double bolt and said, 'I will pay you $500,000 per vial to permanently shut up or I'll kill you.' That's why I asked both of you here."

"Where did she get that type of money?" Zack asked.

Garland shrugged. "She's wealthy."

"There is one other thing," Garland said. "You may have heard about the medical supplier who was murdered in the Garment District?"

"We know all about it," Tracey said.

"Really?" Garland puffed on his pipe and smiled. "Did you know Ms. McShay paid off the Truman Medical Supply House so that she could obtain medical supplies?"

"What kind of supplies?" Zack asked.

"Cotton swabs, vials, syringes, a black medical bag—that sort of thing. She's a doctor."

"I thought she was a lawyer," Zack said.

"She's both."

"So she's a doctor," Tracey mused. "Doctors order medical supplies. So what are you getting at, Mr. Garland?"

"Niles Cortland Brock called me out of concern," Garland explained. "He could not locate her medical practice. We compared notes. I never heard from him again."

Tracey and Zack sat back, digesting Garland's information. Zack finally broke the silence.

"Whaddya think, Tracey?"

"Nothing."

"What?"

"Let's do absolutely nothing."

"OK, then," Zack said. "Thank you, Mr. Garland. We'll phone headquarters and request a round-the-clock guard for you, starting immediately. We'll be in touch."

Tracey and Zack waited on the pier until a guard showed up, then headed toward their car in the parking lot.

"Strange lady," Tracey mused with a puzzled look.

"McShay? No shit."

Tracey gave Zack a puzzled look and asked what they both were thinking: "How could she not know that her lover was gay?"

# CHAPTER 27

Half asleep and unable to see anything clearly the next morning, Tracey wiped the sleep from his eyes as he flipped open the cellphone ringing on his nightstand.

"Hello?"

"Rise 'n' shine, sleeping beauty."

"Zack?"

"The one and only. I just bumped into our pal down at the precinct and picked up a little tidbit that might interest you."

"Shoot."

"Seems someone broke into the Vista Del Mar Sperm Bank last night and made off with biometric machines, medical supplies and specimens."

"Specimens, huh?"

"That's the word."

"Shit." Tracey swung his legs over the side of the bed and stretched. "Any news about Troy Garland?"

"No. Nothing yet from the D.A. Have you heard from Harianne?"

"No. I'm worried about her."

"The jury's been deliberating for a long time. It doesn't look good for Daytona."

"I agree."

"You should just drive over and see if she's at MacKenzie's," Zack suggested.

"I'm not sure if she's there or not."

"Did you call her?"

"Several times. Where the hell is she? Something's wrong."

"Go get her!" Zack yelled.

Tracey hung up with Zack and phoned Harianne's house again. No answer. He tried the cellphone. No answer. The office was the last option. China answered.

"Hello, China, this is Detective Sanders. Is Harianne there?"

"She's on her way downtown. We just got the call that the jury's reached a verdict. Court's in session in half an hour."

Tracey phoned Zack and told him to meet him at the courthouse.

By the time Tracey arrived at the courthouse, the front steps were milling with hordes of people. He scanned the huge crowd for Harianne or MacKenzie, but it was virtually impossible to locate them amidst the sea of dark suits, briefcases and news cameras. He turned at a sudden tap on his shoulder and found himself staring straight into the eyes of Gaston Reeves, elegantly dressed, as usual, in Armani.

"We've won!" Reeves exclaimed. "I'm sure of it."

"Let's just wait and see," Tracey cautioned. He spotted Zack at the courthouse entrance and waved. He looked around for Agent Diggs but he was nowhere to be seen.

Inside, everyone piled into Department 14 of the Los Angeles Superior Court, Criminal Division. Tracey and Zack sat behind the prosecutor. Tracey looked across the aisle and saw Harianne and MacKenzie at the defense table, both sporting black suits and briefcases. Matthew Daytona, handsomely attired in a dark suit, was being escorted to his seat next to them by the bailiff; his hands were red from chafing at tight metal shackles.

"Everyone please rise," the bailiff called out. "The Honorable Chester Hamlin, Judge Presiding. Please be seated."

Judge Hamlin took his seat and addressed the jury.

"Has the jury reached a verdict?"

The jury foreman, a portly, sixtysomething African-American bus driver named Sanford Williams, rose and addressed the courtroom.

The jury foreman stood up. "Yes, Your Honor."

"May I see it, please."

He handed the verdict to the bailiff, who gave it to the judge. Judge Hamlin returned it to the bailiff, who gave it to the court clerk.

"Very well," he said. "Please read it to the court."

"We, the jury, find the defendant, Matthew Daytona, guilty of murder in the first degree."

The courtroom immediately burst into excited conversation; the chamber buzzed with noise. Matthew sat in his chair in stunned silence.

"Order in the court!" Judge Hamlin bellowed.

The court clerk continued reading.

"On Count One of the indictment, we, the jury, find the defendant, Matthew Daytona, guilty. On Count Two of the indictment, we, the jury, find the defendant, Matthew Daytona, guilty."

"Defendant is remanded into custody until sentencing in one week," Judge Hamlin decreed. "The jury is dismissed. Court is adjourned."

Trial observers pushed, shoved and generally forced their way to the exit doors. Paparazzi flew into a frenzy to photograph Matthew's distraught and bewildered face. Reporters from five local television stations in L.A. were present along with reporters from *L.A. Business Journal*, *Variety*, *The Hollywood Reporter* and the *Los Angeles Times*. Some ran to news vans outside for editing while others hovered close to the courtroom, trying to dig up more information. All five television reporters kept their cameramen close by at all times.

Harianne's stomach churned with nausea and dismay over the verdict. Disappointment was plainly visible on her face. She shook her head in disgust as she reached out to Matthew.

"I'm so angry with that jury," he whispered. "I can't believe it."

"Me neither," Harianne assured him. "We presented a good case, it just wasn't enough for the jury."

"We did everything right, Harianne. Everything. At least I thought so." He cleared his throat.

Harianne hugged Matthew and whispered in his ear. "We'll appeal this. Don't worry. You don't deserve this."

MacKenzie walked over to Matthew and placed her hand on his shoulder.

"That's right, Matthew. Don't worry. You'll get what you deserve."

"How's that?"

"You're innocent," MacKenzie said. She smiled. "We'll set the record straight."

"I still can't believe it," Matthew said. "This is all so surreal." He leaned back in his chair and waited for the bailiff.

Harianne and MacKenzie packed their briefcases, left the courtroom and made their way down the long, crowded hall. Harianne heard someone say "life without parole" as she passed by.

"I feel responsible for Matthew," she murmured. "He's innocent."

"Don't," MacKenzie chided her. "That's not good enough. Shit happens, Harianne. Justice was served!"

Harianne was taken aback by her callousness, but held her tongue.

"Do you still plan to appeal?" MacKenzie asked.

Harianne turned to answer and found a microphone thrust into her face. It was a reporter from a downtown TV station.

"Ms. DeCanter," he asked, "are you surprised by the verdict?"

"Yes, I am."

"You've had a great track record for so many years," he remarked.

"You win some and you lose some," Harianne said calmly. "We gave it our best shot. We presented a very solid case."

"Are you going to appeal?"

"By all means, yes! Now if you'll please excuse us, we have a lot of work to do."

Harianne pressed on down the long corridor and was accosted by more reporters. She threw up her hands to hold them at bay.

"No more!" she cried.

Harianne didn't want any publicity, but knew it was on the horizon. Dodging reporters, she shoved her way through the packed corridor until she reached the front entry. She paused briefly to hear a press conference on the courthouse steps.

A horde of reporters and photographers clustered around Sanford Williams. Cameras and microphones were thrust into the jury foreman's face as he explained the jury's verdict.

"We didn't know what to believe," he said. "But we stuck with the facts to make our decision. The DNA evidence was the most interesting and overwhelming. DNA doesn't lie.

"Regardless of conflicting testimony, the jury was ultimately convinced by the circumstantial evidence and corroborating DNA. You know that old term: 'Wrong place, wrong time.'"

Tracey and Zack emerged from the courthouse corridor to find Gaston Reeves engaged in deep conversation with a reporter on the front steps. He was basking in the glory of victory.

"Hey, Gaston, nice win!" Zack called out.

"Yes! Yes! I got a big one! The DNA clinched it."

"You presented a great case," Tracey congratulated him.

"Dick Wolf of *Law and Order* phoned about using this case as—"

"Ah, let me talk to you later, Gaston," Tracey interrupted. "I just saw someone I need to talk to."

Tracey hurried over to Agent Diggs, who was standing on the other side of the courthouse steps.

"Agent Diggs!" Tracey yelled.

"Hi, there!" Diggs replied. "What's going on?"

"Listen, I know this is officially your case now, but we've got an informant. His name is Troy Garland. He revealed the killer."

"And it isn't Matthew Daytona."

"You got it."

"Who is it?"

"Mackenzie McShay."

"What! Isn't she one of the lawyers that was trying this case?"

"Yes. It's complicated."

Tracey's cellphone rang; it was Harianne.

"'Scuse me, Diggs."

By the time Tracey answered, the screen on his phone read "NO SERVICE." He speedily text-messaged Harianne; there was no response.

"Shit! Look, Diggs, everything points to her. MacKenzie McShay is deadly."

Agent Diggs regarded Tracey intently. "Sanders, are you telling me this woman has Matthew Daytona's semen?"

"Yes. She paid off a sperm bank. Somehow she used his semen as evidence, pointing the finger at Daytona."

"Why would she set up her own client?"

"That's what we don't know yet."

Diggs shook his head. "Are you sure?" he asked.

"I know the case is over," Tracey said excitedly, "but we have real evidence. McShay paid monies to a medical supply house in downtown L.A. She threatened to kill Garland. And there are other corroborating facts."

"You're supposed to be off this case, but I know it's personal."

"Thanks for understanding. I'll get the search warrant for MacKenzie's residence."

"Where's McShay now?"

"She just left the courthouse," Zack said, jerking a thumb over his shoulder. "Maybe she's in the parking lot?"

"OK, gentlemen," Diggs said, pulling out his cellphone. "Let's move."

Tracey's cellphone rang again as he and Zack hurried back to the precinct. It was Harianne.

"Harianne!"

"Tracey, I've been trying to reach you. My battery's low—"

"Harianne, are you OK?"

"Yes, I'm headed back to the office."

"Where's MacKenzie?"

"She's on her way—" Harianne's voice cut out for a moment.

"Harianne? Harianne! What's wrong?"

"I lost." Her voice sounded muffled.

"You're lost? Where are you?"

"No, *I* lost. The case. Did our relationship get in the way?"

"What? No, that wouldn't affect the case. Harianne, I love you! And we need to talk, now!"

"I love you, too, but maybe this was a bad idea. I don't know—" Her voice cut out again.

"Harianne, are you there? Listen! Harianne? Harianne!"

"What?"

"We need to talk! You're dealing with a real—"

Tracey's cellphone beeped and went dead.

# CHAPTER 28

In all of his years working homicide, Tracey had never seen anything of this magnitude. Bullet holes, dead people, blood, faces of grieving family members, heartache—all that he'd seen, and known. But this was entirely different. MacKenzie McShay was not only a menacing and cruel murderer, she was a highly intelligent, innovative and creative woman with an untraceable modus operandi.

As far as he was concerned, all the evidence needed to arrest her was intact. Troy Garland would break the case wide open, ending the hunt for the notorious serial killer.

But first, they had to track her down. Tracey prayed that Harianne was nowhere near her.

Dejected and more than a little angry about losing Matthew's case, Harianne threw her briefcase onto her living room sofa and kicked off her shoes. Austria surprised her with a steaming cup of tea.

"I heard the news on the radio, dear," she said sympathetically. "I'm so sorry. Here, have some tea. It'll soothe your nerves."

"Thanks, Austria. Can you believe that jury? It's so obvious he's innocent! I've got to start work on his appeal right away. The pressure's really on now."

The sound of Harianne's cellphone buzzing in its charger interrupted their conversation. Harianne looked at the screen and saw Tracey's name. She turned off the volume.

"What's going on?" Austria asked. "You know he's left several messages for you on the house line already. The poor man sounds positively frantic."

Harianne shook her head. "I don't want to talk to him right now."

"Why not?"

"Maybe we made a mistake getting involved…maybe that's why I lost…maybe I lost my focus on my client. I don't know. I just need to think things through." The house line rang and she waved it off. "Ignore that. It's probably him."

"Harianne!" Austria exclaimed. She sounded irritated.

"What?"

"Excuse me, my dear, but I think what you've lost is your senses."

"What's that supposed to mean?" Harianne asked heatedly.

"It means it's time for me to give you something to place everything in perspective. Enough of this. I'll be right back."

Perplexed, Harianne fixed herself another cup of tea while she waited. Austria returned in short order bearing a large box wrapped in brown paper and a heavy gold rope. She lowered it onto the dining table as if she were laying a baby in a cradle.

"This is for you," she told Harianne. "I've been saving this in my room. I should have given it to you years ago but I didn't know how you would react."

Harianne raised her eyebrows quizzically. "React?"

"It belonged to your biological mother, Harianne."

She removed the paper and the rope. Inside was a beautiful cherrywood box with red velvet trim. The initials "HD" were carved in gold letters on the top. The underside of the lid was engraved with a message: "*My Daughter: Your Past, Present and Future. I Will Love You Forever.*" Reading it, Harianne started to cry. Austria slipped her a white handkerchief.

"I made a pact with your mother," she explained, "that if I never heard from her again, that I would release this box to you."

"Why did you wait so long?"

Austria sighed. "Somehow I always believed she would return. Obviously, she never did."

Two stacks of beige letters were tied with white ribbon inside the box. A white envelope was standing up in the middle of the stack. Harianne gingerly opened it.

*My child,*

*If you're reading this letter, then I never returned to see you. But I didn't want to give you up. I loved you so much. You are my heart and my lifeline. I won't be there for your first tooth, your first birthday, graduations or, most importantly, your wedding. But I am a good person and a good mother.*

*Your GRANDPARENTS, my PARENTS, demanded that I leave and never return home. You were born out of wedlock to an African-American man and me. My parents hated your father. They considered him to be trash. In this box, you'll find words of love from me. I wrote you a letter every year for 21 years. Hang on to these letters. That's all I have to give you. I'll always love you. I'll never forget you.*

*Love Always,*

*Mom Gretchen*

Harianne's eyes welled with water and her lower lip quivered.

"So she—Gretchen—sent you a letter every year?"

Austria nodded. "Yes. And I kept them filed away in here for you."

"She—she remembered me every year?" Harianne asked in a small voice.

"Yes, Harianne," Austria said softly. "Every year. On your birthday. She loved you too much to forget you." She paused. "You should know that she has a box identical to yours, but with her initials carved on top of the box. Wherever she is, I imagine it holds the letters I wrote to her every year until you were twenty-one. I also sent her one of your first baby shoes, a silver spoon and fork, a number of pictures and a cassette tape. You might say the boxes tell a story."

Harianne gently ran her fingers along the edges of the letters.

The house phone rang again.

"Do you want me to answer that?" Austria asked.

"No," Harianne said, sniffling. "No, that's OK, I'll deal with it."

Harianne picked up the kitchen phone expecting Tracey. She was surprised to hear MacKenzie's voice on the other end.

"Hi, Harianne!"

"MacKenzie? Uh, hi. What's up?"

"Am I working on the Remittitur?"

"We both are. But remember we might not need it. How's the research coming along?"

"I've been online most of the afternoon. I need to compare my research with yours. Why don't you come meet me at my house?"

"Well…" Harianne hesitated.

"Oh, come on, Harianne. Aren't you curious? You've never even seen my place. How 'bout it? I'll make dinner."

Forty minutes later, MacKenzie greeted Harianne at the front door of her Zuma Beach house wearing a leopard-print sweater and a pair of black slacks.

"Come on in!" she said cheerily.

"You look comfortable," Harianne remarked.

"You look beat," MacKenzie responded. "Let me fix you a drink. What'll you have? Wine? Brandy? Gin?"

"White wine, please."

"Good. I'll have red. Let's set up in the dining room."

She gestured toward an elegant mahogany table surrounded by eight chairs bearing purple slipcovers and beige pillows. The living room beyond looked out over a balcony and the Pacific Ocean. It was a scene fit for a photo spread in *House Beautiful.*

"It's lovely in here," Harianne said admiringly.

"Thank you. Are you hungry? I fixed us a little something to eat."

"You didn't have to do that, MacKenzie." Harianne looked at MacKenzie and for the first time saw that she was a deeply lonely woman. Despite her misgivings, she felt herself softening toward her.

"It's a veritable feast!" Harianne exclaimed. "It smells wonderful. What is it?"

MacKenzie shrugged. "Chicken salad on a bed of lettuce greens, portobello-mushroom-and-Gruyere-cheese casserole, and, for dessert, sliced peaches with drizzled Kaluha liqueur on top. I've got vanilla ice cream in the freezer too, if you want."

"Mmm, sounds delicious," Harianne said. "I need to wash my hands first. May I use your bathroom?"

"Sure. It's down the hall at the end, opposite my office on the right."

Harianne admired a sizable collection of Dali artworks adorning the walls as she made her way to the bathroom. When she reached the end of the long hallway, she peeked into MacKenzie's office, which commanded an impressive ocean view. With books neatly ordered by subject matter and loose papers tossed in a deep wicker basket alongside the desk, it looked very much like a judge's chambers—except for the plethora of pictures. Photographs were displayed in small, medium and large frames all across the red wall, and in tiny frames on the desk. Harianne's eyes fell on an antique frame around an old picture of a woman holding a baby, but she couldn't make out the face.

She pulled herself away long enough to duck into the bathroom to wash her hands. When she emerged, she yelled down the hall: "I'll be right there, MacKenzie!"

From the hallway she could see a large box sitting on an antique Queen Anne table in MacKenzie's office that resembled the box Austria had just given her. Moving closer, Harianne made out the initials "GD" on the box lid. She tried to open it, but it was locked. Was it possible…?

Her thoughts running wild, she looked around and spotted another box sitting on an empty bookshelf. She gently removed the lid and gasped. Inside were six syringes, two pairs of latex gloves, ten vials of cocaine, six bottles of saline, ten bottles of Anectine, and ten empty vials labeled "ICI." A plastic jar was stuffed with cotton balls.

Harianne quickly scanned the room for evidence of Gretchen Duet. There was nothing. She turned to leave and found MacKenzie in the doorway, furiously eyeballing her.

'That was certainly a long trip to the bathroom. Why are you in my office?"

"It looked so inviting," Harianne stammered, trying her best to be charming. She decided not to mention the box. "I'm sorry, MacKenzie. I just had to stop and admire your pictures. I'm sorry for being nosy."

"Well," MacKenzie relented. "OK. Let's eat. We've got a lot of research to do."

After dinner MacKenzie made a fresh pot of hot coffee and they worked for hours, researching case law online and reviewing a multitude of videotapes of the trial. Harianne fell asleep on the sofa around three in the morning. But vivid memories of the boxes disturbed her rest. She woke and saw MacKenzie standing between the French doors on the balcony, gazing out at the slowly disappearing moon.

MacKenzie heard Harianne stirring and moved inside, sensing her uneasiness. "Harianne? What's wrong?"

"Matthew."

"You've got to stop beating yourself up. It's over. We'll appeal."

"I know. It's a hard case." Harianne paused. She wanted to confront MacKenzie about the boxes in her office, but refrained. Instead, she asked about the picture.

"That picture in your office—the one in the antique frame?"

"Yes?"

"Is that your mother holding you as a baby?"

"No." MacKenzie paused before continuing. "I never knew her."

"Your mother?"

"No. My daughter."

Harianne's heart beat a little faster. "How many children do you have?"

"Just one daughter. I can't have children. I had abortions."

Guarded yet fascinated by MacKenzie's answers, Harianne sat up and poured a cup of lukewarm coffee.

"Where is she?" she asked.

"I don't know," MacKenzie admitted. "It troubles me that I have not seen her in years. I wrote letters to her every day until she turned twenty-one."

"How old is she?" Harianne asked carefully.

"She's older now," MacKenzie said evasively. "I was forced to leave after she was born. My parents agreed to raise her but then they were killed in a plane crash."

Harianne spilled coffee on her lap.

"Is there anything wrong, Harianne?"

"No! No. Please, continue."

"Her new adopted parents moved away and I never saw her again. She's a mixed-race child: African American and French. My nanny sent me that picture of her. Otherwise I'd have nothing. I don't even know what name they gave her. She wasn't really old enough at the time to understand let alone know me."

Harianne discreetly reached into her briefcase and turned on the tape recorder she stored there.

"What's your nanny's name?" she asked.

"Austria. I haven't heard from her in so many years she's probably dead too."

"No!" Harianne blurted. She jumped up and stood there, shivering, staring at MacKenzie. "I'm your daughter!" she cried.

MacKenzie regarded Harianne numbly for several moments before impulsively reaching out and hugging her. The two women clung to each other tearfully.

"Harianne! You're my daughter? How could this be?"

"It's true. Everything adds up. Austria told me that my mother was a diabetic. I saw the box in your office. She just gave me my box with all your letters this afternoon."

"Oh, my baby!" MacKenzie wrapped her hands around Harianne's head and kissed her forehead, then pulled her tight. "I just can't believe this. My daughter!"

"But wait…" Harianne backed away and looked at MacKenzie with a puzzled expression. "Austria said your name is Gretchen Duet." She saw MacKenzie stiffen.

"It's MacKenzie McShay."

"Oh, my God…" Harianne grabbed her cellphone from her purse and started text-messaging Tracey. She saw that he had left her a string of messages.

"What—Harianne, what are you doing? Who are you calling?"

"You lied to me," Harianne accused her, wiping tears from her cheeks.

"No! No, when—"

"You misrepresented yourself! Your name is Gretchen Duet. That explains 'GDMS.' You cheated us! You made Matthew suffer for your actions."

"He won't suffer." She gave Harianne an odd, vaguely threatening smile. "He's the problem."

# CHAPTER 29

Tracey was crashed on the couch of his office when he was awakened by the sound of his cellphone ringing in his shirt pocket. He pulled it out and saw Harianne's cellphone number on his caller ID screen with a text message: "Help! MacKenzie's!"

"Dammit!" Tracey yelled. He punched up Zack's number while he pulled on his jacket. "Zack! She's at MacKenzie's. Time to move!"

Tracey zoomed up the freeways until he hit the early morning traffic on PCH.

"Shit!" he exclaimed. He phoned Dispatch. "This is Sanders from Homicide. I need choppers to meet me at the home of MacKenzie McShay in Zuma Beach."

"What's going on, Sanders?"

"I have reason to believe McShay is holding a hostage: Matthew Daytona's lawyer, Harianne DeCanter. Suspect is armed and deadly. Tell them not to go in until I get there."

"Got it. Stand by."

Tracey text-messaged Harianne several times, but there was no response.

"Fucking cellphones!" he hollered. He switched on the siren and prayed he reached Harianne in time as he zipped between cars and sped down the narrow shoulder of the road. Dispatch came back on the line.

"Are they there yet?" Tracey asked.

"They're holding," Dispatch replied. "They've verified there are two women in the house."

"Stay on them, but stay out of sight. I don't know what McShay will do."

"Got it. Ten-four."

Harianne and MacKenzie heard what sounded like loud thunder explode, and within seconds a cluster of helicopters was hovering over the property. MacKenzie grabbed Harianne by the arm and pulled a gun from behind the bar.

"MacKenzie!"

"Shut up! I don't want to lose my temper and have to shoot you."

"You'd shoot your own daughter?" Harianne cried with horrified disbelief. "How could you?"

They heard a helicopter whirring overhead and a voice booming out of a loudspeaker.

"This is the Los Angeles Sheriff. MacKenzie McShay! Come out of the house! We will not hurt you. Repeat, MacKenzie McShay, come out of your house now!"

MacKenzie darted to the stairwell window, dragging Harianne with her. They saw a black sedan parked behind the entrance gate, but no other cars or people. Another loudspeaker crackled outside, and a new voice spoke. Harianne gasped when she heard it.

"MacKenzie McShay! This is Detective Tracey Sanders, L.A. County Sheriff's Department, Homicide Bureau. I need to talk to you right now. Call me on my cellphone at (213) 555-5555. Let's make an arrangement."

"That's your detective hero," MacKenzie snarled. "He wants to make a deal. Ha!"

"MacKenzie, please," Harianne pleaded.

MacKenzie lifted her hand, ready to hit Harianne in the face. Harianne saw that her eyes were glassy.

"MacKenzie, calm down!"

"Just shut up!"

Outside, Tracey found a small, open window on the side of the house and silently climbed in. No one saw him.

MacKenzie pushed Harianne away and rapidly paced the floor, gulping down wine. She gripped the loaded gun tightly with her right hand. The wine seemed to fuel her anxiety, as she alternately cried and raged at Harianne in a monstrous voice.

"MacKenzie," Harianne pleaded, struggling to remain calm. "Listen to me. I can help you. Tell me about the syringes."

"How do you know about the syringes?"

"I saw them in your office."

"You're a busybody!" MacKenzie yelled.

"Talk to me about them," Harianne coaxed. "What did you do with them?"

"I killed those damn attorneys with the syringes." MacKenzie fell onto the sofa. The gun was still in her hand.

"How did you do that?" Harianne asked, eyeing the gun warily.

"I'm the best doctor! I had access to all the drugs, syringes, and vials."

"What about the cocaine?"

"Haven't you figured that out yet?" MacKenzie grinned. "I'm the Japanese distributor."

"So Tracey was right about you!" Harianne shook her head. "I can't believe you're my mother."

MacKenzie pointed the gun at her, glaring. Unflinching, Harianne held her gaze.

"So as a practicing doctor you knew the procedure for injections, and you injected the cocaine into all those women."

"Hell, yes! I practiced on an orange."

"But why?"

"Because Matthew belonged to *me*!" MacKenzie roared. "*I'm* his true love, not them! He saw those women every night…he's crazy about women. So I devised a master plan to make him pay for breaking up with me." She laughed. "And it worked. He's mine. I love him. No one else can have him!"

"Except now the truth is out," Harianne declared. "It's over, MacKenzie. Talk to Detective Sanders!"

"Shut up!"

MacKenzie grabbed Harianne's arm and pinned her to the wall. Harianne saw that her eyes were glassier than before, and she was repelled by the strong, sour smells of wine and coffee on her breath. She tried to keep her face expressionless when she spotted Tracey darting from the kitchen into the hallway closet, but she cried out in fear when MacKenzie locked her in a neck hold and pulled a syringe from her pocket.

"MacKenzie, please stop it!" Harianne begged. "You're hurting me!"

"Ssh, quiet! Listen to Mother, Harianne. You're going to help me get past that bothersome detective of yours."

MacKenzie moved toward the breaker box in the kitchen and threw off all the circuit switches. The house was plunged into darkness, save for slivers of moonlight falling through the windows. MacKenzie groped for a flashlight in a drawer and pushed Harianne back toward the living room.

"Tell me one thing," Harianne demanded. "Did you kill Jasmine?"

"Yes. She got too close."

"How could you!" Harianne cried out.

"Don't make me hurt you!" MacKenzie warned. "You see, Harianne, I loved killing those women who wanted my man. He's mine! I finally had my own life, with my own man, a man I loved very much."

"But Jasmine had nothing to do with Matthew!" Harianne protested. MacKenzie snorted.

In a tired voice, MacKenzie stated. "I killed Amanda Weddington before you and Tracey arrived at Jasmine's office that evening."

Harianne surprised. "YOU killed her?"

"Yep!" MacKenzie smiled.

Harianne sighed. "Why? She did not harm you."

"She lied to us! She's not Shana's lover!" MacKenzie angrily responded.

Harianne shook her head in disgust. "I'm afraid she was."

"You don't know what it was like before you were born. My mother always held me accountable for her: giving her shots, feeding her, writing for her and physically doing everything for her. I was always at her call and by her side. I thought men, and you, would be my ticket to freedom—but then they took you away from me too. Your father disappeared, and none of the men I met until Matthew were worth anything more than their money. I'm tired. No more women!"

Harianne detected Tracey's shadow by the window and tried to stall for more time. "I guess I can understand your motive, MacKenzie, but I still don't understand how you killed them."

"It was beautiful!" MacKenzie crowed. "The technique was brilliant. I sat each body on the toilet seat perfectly and spread their legs apart. I prepared a mixture of saline, cocaine, sperm and Anectine together, using a syringe with a twenty-three-inch gauge needle and carefully injected it into their vagina. The vaginal wall of a woman's body contains the highest degree of blood. It killed them instantly. Anectine is untraceable. The detectives thought it was cocaine." She laughed harshly. "It was and it wasn't."

"They were all naked. Can you explain that?"

"Sometimes, I sedated their drinks. Otherwise, I just knocked them out and held a knife to their throat. I ripped off their clothes, injected them with the syringe, placed them on the toilet and wrapped the red silk scarf around their necks. The infamous 'rape.' I don't like to struggle."

MacKenzie took another swig of wine. Harianne twisted her head to the side just in time to see Tracey crawl behind the sofa.

"You're wicked, MacKenzie!"

"Not wicked, my dear, just smart. Just like you. Like mother, like daughter, eh?"

"That's revolting!" Harianne exclaimed. "If you're so damn smart, why didn't you know that Matthew's gay? Why did you continue to kill people even after that was admitted in court?"

MacKenzie released Harianne immediately. "Those women were sluts," she insisted. "They'd sleep with anything. Trust me: I've had to deal with women my entire life. They enjoyed Matthew's company too much. I wanted him to myself. Matthew respected me; he just didn't want me anymore. He only supported gay legal associations because it was the politically correct thing to do. He was having affairs."

"It was all in your head, MacKenzie. You're dead wrong!"

"I told you to shut up!" MacKenzie dug her fingers deep into Harianne's skin and dragged her toward the French doors fronting the balcony overlooking the ocean. Harianne looked out at the dark, rough waves and felt queasy. She spotted Tracey behind the sofa in the corner, but remained silent.

MacKenzie was growing weaker from wine consumption, but refused to relinquish her hold on Harianne. "Matthew and I were a great team," she cried. "He had no right to betray me. We enjoyed each other immensely!"

"MacKenzie, listen to me," Harianne demanded. "I will not let Matthew be sentenced to death for a murder he didn't commit!"

"We'll see about that!"

MacKenzie yanked up Harianne's sleeve and pointed the needle toward her arm; Harianne struggled to twist away. MacKenzie had just started to inject the syringe when Tracey slowly rose behind her. He aimed his gun directly at MacKenzie. She turned quickly but kept the syringe on Harianne.

"Well, well. It's the detective to the rescue. What will it be?"

"You're mine, McShay," he said angrily.

"Don't touch us!" MacKenzie screamed. Her eyes quickly circled the room as she backed Harianne against the balcony and tried to force her over the railing. Tracey immediately fired two shots out of his .44 Magnum through the French door, shattering glass; MacKenzie grabbed her stomach and fell to the floor.

Tracey ran to Harianne and wrapped his trench coat around her tightly. "Are you all right?"

"Is she dead?"

"I think so. Did you get her on tape?"

"Yes, we got everything. I think."

Tracey was helping Harianne up when she suddenly sensed MacKenzie's presence. She whirled about just in time to see MacKenzie raising her arm toward Tracey with a syringe in hand.

"Tracey! Look out!"

Tracey spun around and fired three more rounds into MacKenzie. She slumped down and sprawled out on her back; her eyes stared upward, open and vacant. Tracey dropped to his knees and felt her wrist; there was no pulse. He beat her on the chest.

"Tracey, stop it!" Harianne begged. "Stop it!"

"That's it," he said, breathing hard. "She's gone for sure."

They left MacKenzie's blood-soaked body on the balcony. Zack, Agent Diggs and numerous FBI and homicide detectives met them on the circular driveway.

"Tracey!" Zack called. "Are you guys all right?"

"We're fine," Tracey said. "Get the coroner. She's dead."

A few minutes later, Harianne and Tracey sat comfortably side by side in the squad car and rested their heads. The ocean breeze through the open window was cold and crisp. Tracey hugged Harianne.

"Matthew is a free man," he assured her. "Just before the verdict I learned about MacKenzie from an informant, but I had to follow procedure."

"You didn't believe me."

"None of us did," Tracey admitted, "but you were right. He's innocent. Sometimes you can't tell who is and who isn't these days."

Harianne began to cry. "I'm very happy for him."

"Are you OK?" Tracey asked.

"Not really. We killed my mother. She was very sick."

"I know. I heard you talking."

"All these years I've wondered who she was, and what she was about," Harianne said with real anguish. "Now I'll never know about her or myself."

Tracey pulled a box of Kleenex from underneath the accessory shelf in the seat as Harianne cried into his shoulder.

"Hey, hey," he said soothingly. "There's only so much another person can tell you about yourself," he said softly. He gently lifted her chin and gazed into her eyes. "Who you are is a lot more than who you came from."

Harianne snuffled into the Kleenex. Thoughts of her grandmother Marissa somehow eased her pain.

"Give yourself time to heal," Tracey urged her. "You've got a lot of soul searching to do."

"Yeah." Harianne looked at him. "Maybe we can get some wine and some rest?"

"Anything for you, Harianne. Anything!"

Filled with loss and mutual need, Harianne and Tracey returned to her house and made passionate love.

The next morning, while Tracey slept in, Harianne retrieved the newspaper from the driveway and nestled up into the kitchen window seat with a cup of hot coffee. She opened the newspaper to the banner headline: "*Tokyo's Yellow Silk Scarf Killer On the Run, Assailant Unknown.*"

978-0-595-37317-8
0-595-37317-8

Printed in the United States
96292LV00003B/220-228/A